THE PIONEERS

By Lawrence Gulley

L. E. Gulley

THE PIONEERS

Gulley, Lawrence
The Pioneers

ISBN: 978-1-7376772-9-1

Printed in USA

Contents

Prologue

It was a long, arduous trip, but Henry and James made the trip in seven days by horseback.

Henry Smith and his brother James made the trip from Duplin County, North Carolina to homestead land in south Alabama. The year was 1823. They found their biggest problem was crossing Goshen swamp back in Carolina. It had taken them an entire day to cut poles that would float them, their horses and their meager provisions across the wide swamp.

Henry was twenty-three, and James was twenty-one. Their father had died soon after James was born, so their mother Janie had raised them by herself until they reached maturity. When they reached twenty-one years of age, they received their inheritance, which was mostly land and slaves. Most of their land was given to their father by their grandfather, William Smith, Sr..

Their Grandfather Smith was a Revolutionary War veteran who was considered a man of wealth and lived about a half mile away in a big two-story house. His wife's name was Penelope. Including Henry and James' father, who was William Jr., the Smiths raised eleven children.

Henry and James knew very little about their maternal grandparents, as they lived in another county in North Carolina.

When they were growing up, they spent a good bit of time with their Grandfather Smith, listening to his war tales and about the hated British, especially. Both farms stayed

1

so busy, though, that as the boys grew older, they found they spent less time there and more time on their own place.

Both places had slaves, and someone had to make sure that things were done right. Henry and James' overseer saw that everything was tended to properly. However, their mother and their uncle Jesse made sure the boys did their part. By the time they reached their eighteenth birthdays, both boys reached six feet and two inches. In spite of their affluence, they didn't hang around taverns or bad company as did some young men in their position. The brothers had almost the same facial features, only different hair coloring. Henry had blond hair, while James' was chestnut brown. They wore their straight hair shoulder length but didn't wear it pinned back as some dandies did.

The thought had been in Henry and James' minds to settle somewhere else and start their lives. When their grandfather died and left them only one silver dollar each, and their mother remarried, that sealed the deal for them.

Really, they couldn't have hard feelings about their mother of grandfather. After all, when their father and mother married, their grandfather had given his son two hundred acres of land and farming implements to set up farming. William Sr. also did the same with his other sons, as they each married. With his daughters, he gave them a small amount of money and household goods.

When James turned twenty-one, he and Henry sold the sixty acres they had each inherited to their uncle Jesse, along with some of the slaves.

The man their mother married had two teenage daughters still at home, so naturally they came along with their father.

James soon fell in love with one of the girls, Mary. Her sister Faith sure chased Henry, but he had eyes only for Phoebe Harris, a girl he'd grown up with in the village.

The man their mother had married was likeable enough; his name was Edmond McMillian. He had sold his farm, which was about a mile away. He told Henry that he had no intentions of buying more land, and he felt he and their mother could live comfortable on their combined monies and the eighty acres.

Phoebe was only seventeen years old when Henry and James left for Alabama on a cold February morning. Phoebe had agreed to wait on Henry for a year, as did Mary with James.

Both the young men knew to be frugal with their money. After buying axes, saws, hatchets, and a shovel each, and stocking a small amount of other provisions, they took very little of their money with them. They buried their remaining cash in a barn, separately. They told only their mother where the money was hidden.

Chapter One

The young men crossed into Alabama from Columbus, Georgia, which at that time was just a small village of mostly tents. They had feared that one of their biggest problems would be crossing the rivers and streams. However, they discovered that most of the rivers had ferries and only charged a minimal amount for usage. They couldn't believe that most of their route was well traveled. It seemed that everyone was headed south to homestead land, looking for a brighter future. It sort of worried the two young men, for they hoped they could still find land to homestead.

Henry's steed was a white stallion named Buck, and James' horse was a large brown mare he called Daisy.

It took two days of hard riding to reach Wilcox County, Alabama. Once there, they found only one parcel of land that was available for homesteading and fit for farming. Since Henry was the oldest, he had first choice, but he told James that he could go to Carlton Bend and file homestead on it.

After making sure their horses were watered from a nearby creek, then fed, they built a campfire and ate a quickly prepared supper. They then rolled into their blankets and went to sleep with thoughts of their future in their heads.

When they awoke the next morning, they went back to the creek and washed the cooking utensils from the night before. They only gave the horses a small amount of grain, then tied the animals so they could eat the green foliage near the creek.

"Can you believe the warm weather down here? Things are already turning green," Henry said.

"Big difference from back home," James replied.

After drinking some weak coffee and eating a couple of flapjacks, the brothers embraced. Henry told James he was going to travel the beaten path that headed southwest. "Maybe I can find something suitable before the day is up."

"I wish you luck. I'm going to ask my nearest neighbor the way to Carlton; I intend to file claim today," James said.

"I'll be checking on you. I'll also let you if I find something; I pray it's nearby," Henry answered.

Henry rode until the middle of the afternoon before he found land with water. The land bordered Burnt Corn Creek, and was in Conecuh County, Alabama, about twenty-five miles from James.

Henry immediately rode Buck from post to post and removed the four signs that stated, "Land to homestead."

He had a crude map that he had drawn. He looked at the sun, then looked at his map. He knew he'd have to push Buck in order to reach Sparta, the county seat, in time to file his claim that day. He decided to take a closer look at the land and ride to Sparta the next morning.

Most of the land was wooded with pines, gums, and other assorted trees. Nearer the creek he found a meadow. He guessed the meadow was about ten acres, with ferns, small brush, and broom sage. Most of the trees weren't leafed, due to the season, but he was pretty sure he found a good stand of sassafras trees. He hoped it was, because sassafras made a delicious tea and was medicinal.

Along the edges of the creek were large magnolia trees, mixed with pines. The thing that interested Henry the most was the foot tracks that he saw along the spongy edges of the creek. He could plainly tell the prints were different sizes. Henry thought about the prints, then decided they must have been from people fishing along the banks of the creek.

Henry tethered Buck near the creek so the horse could drink water and eat the bamboo cane that grew near the creek. He then took Buck's saddle off, along with his own bedroll, the bag of assorted tools, cooking utensils, and the precious sack of grain. *"I sure hoped he could find more corn in Sparta,"* he thought. If he couldn't find grain, Buck would go hungry, feeding on just grass and foliage. If he was careful, Henry figured he had enough corn to last about two weeks.

After looking through his packed saddlebag, Henry found what he was after, the fishing line and a hook. He then overturned some rotten limbs and found two grub worms, after making a double knot in the hook, then tying a small pebble near the hook, to weight the line. He baited the hook and threw it about midway into the creek. Henry soon found the creek was abundant with bream fish. In fifteen minutes, he'd pulled five from the cold stream. The smoked fish were a welcome delight compared to the hardtack and dried beef jerky their mother had made for them.

Henry still got a whiff of smoke after extinguishing his campfire, so he walked out of the wooded area and saw a cloud of smoke to the north of him. Suspecting it was probably another homesteader clearing land, he didn't think much of it.

Although he didn't want to face the cold water from the stream the next morning, he shed himself of his clothes, and with a bar of homemade soap, he waded into the creek and took a bath. He wanted to look presentable the next day when he went into Sparta, to file for his land. *"Buck must have had the same thought, for he waded out into the cold stream, too,"* Henry thought.

After drying himself and putting on clean woolens, he broke small pine branches from the nearby trees and spread them into a pile. He then covered the sweet-smelling pine needles with a thick quilt, making his bed.

Henry threw a few pieces of wood on the fire and climbed into his bed, then covered himself with a woolen blanket. The fire made him feel more secure, and too, he might be in south Alabama but there was a chill in the air, so the fire's warmth was welcome. Quickly saying his prayers, he found that he missed James' company and wondered how he was making out. He wondered if he'd have time to go into Carlton to file for his land. After shifting in the pine branches to find a good position, Henry then thought of his fiancée Phoebe, his mother and kin back in North Carolina, and felt some comfort with his brother only a few miles away.

Of course, Henry wondered if they'd made the right decision about moving to Alabama. He had to admit that from what he'd seen so far, he liked it here. The weather was milder than back home, and the soil was rich and loamy. Clearing the land would be the biggest task, along with erecting a building to live in. He gave his situation some considerable thought. After filing on the land, he'd attempt to buy some supplies that he needed in Sparta. His next project would be to get started on his house, then when it was warm enough to plant, he'd start by burning some of the meadow. He had intentions of planting enough corn, squash, and peas to survive a season, and have enough dry seed to plant the next year. Cotton, the cash crop, would come after he had more land cleared, and better farming implements.

Henry was excited about his future, and he prayed that Phoebe would be too. He had to admit that people and towns were scarcer here than in North Carolina. He knew from the well packed roads and paths that it wouldn't last long before towns would be popping up everyplace, though. He just hoped he would have time to have a house for them to live in and land to farm when he brought her next year. He knew it would be scary for her, leaving her folks and all, but after all, that's what he was planning on doing.

Chapter Two

At first sight, Sparta was a big disappointment, but Henry decided to make the best of it. At the land registry office, answered all the necessary questions to file his claim. The official that asked all the questions and wrote down what Henry told him, introduced himself as John Salter, secretary to the judge.

Henry liked Mr. Salter, and in talking with him discovered that the secretary was from North Carolina too, but had a year's jump on Henry, having arrived a year earlier. Henry could detect from Mr. Salter's speech that he was an educated man, more so than himself. The little one-room school that James and he had attended only offered six grades, and they each only finished three of those. Their Uncle Jesse said that as long as they could read, write, and figure, that was good enough.

"You two know enough to keep people from beating you out of anything. Your penmanship is legible, and you can read well enough. It's experience on the farm, that's what's beneficial to you now," he had said. As usual, their mother had gone along with their uncle.

As the boys had matured, their backs had grown strong, and their bodies muscular. Their hands were tougher than those of most of the boys their age, due to the hard work. They might have had an overseer, but they worked as hard as, if not harder than the slaves. The main between them and the slaves was that the overseer didn't give them orders, their Uncle Jesse did. To begin with, the boys hated their uncle and constantly complained to their mother, but as they grew older, they began to love and revere him. As Henry stepped out of the log courthouse in Sparta that morning with the statement in his hands about his own land, he appreciated everything his uncle had taught him.

Henry also learned a few things from Mr. Salter that morning. For instance, various seeds, and a few household staples, could be bought at Mr. Casey's store, which was across the street from the courthouse. Mr. Salter warned Henry things would be expensive. "After all, he has to bring things in all the way from Pensacola, Florida, over rough terrain with mule and wagon, and there's always danger of Indian attacks. There's still a few Indians around, even though they have been defeated and a peace treaty has been signed," the man had said.

There were about four businesses in Sparta and one of them was an eatery, so Henry went inside to order lunch, and mull things over. He had been in such a hurry to leave that morning that he didn't eat breakfast. After looking at the menu, he ordered two fried eggs, a bowl of hominy grits, ham, two biscuits and a cup of coffee. He looked at the price of each item and saw that the meal would cost more than three dollars. *"My goodness,"* he thought. *"this same thing would cost about 75 cents in North Carolina!"* He was hungry, though, so he decided to pay the price.

While waiting on his food, he thought about some of the things that Mr. Salter had told him. His main concern was that his assigned property would need to be inspected for improvements the following year. The land officials had to see that he'd made improvements to the place to justify keeping the claim. The inspection requirement wasn't what concerned him most about the situation; it was the time frame. Phoebe had only given him a year's time in which to return for her, and he wondered if he could accomplish all these things and get back to North Carolina in the time he'd promised her.

After paying for his expensive breakfast, Henry felt better physically, but he hated to pay that much for such a simple meal. He knew laying in groceries was an essential step in his plan, so his next stop was the building that adjoined the eatery. Henry found that the building not only sold food staples, but also clothing, and a few farm implements. He bought a pound of hominy grits, and a pound of coffee beans. He didn't know how he'd bake the beans and then grind them, but he knew he'd figure out a way. The third and last thing he purchased was five pounds of corn meal. The three items cost seven dollars.

"Good heavens," he thought, *"at the rate I'm going the money I brought with me will be gone before I know it!"*

A real sweet lady, whose name was Juanita Carey, collected for Henry's purchases, then invited him back. His items weren't put in a sack or bag, she just handed them to him. On the way out of the door, he saw an empty wooden five-gallon barrel. He asked the woman the price of the barrel.

"Oh, just take it, it's free, and it's just in the way there," the kind lady said.

Henry was sure glad he asked about the barrel, for he could think of several things he could do with it. One of them was that he'd have a place to store the things he'd just bought.

He tied the empty barrel on the side of his saddle, then placed his precious items inside.

As he headed "home," he looked at the sun and guessed that it was about eleven o'clock. The day was gorgeous, and not a cloud could be seen. There was a cool breeze blowing from the northeast. *"That breeze will be just right for what's ahead of me,"* he thought, knowing he would soon warm up with the physical labor that awaited him. Knowing it would take him about an hour to get back to the land which was now officially his, he thought of all the things he had to do when he got there.

The first thing Henry did when he arrived at his destination was to scatter a layer of leaves on the ground about twenty feet from the creek. He then stored his newly bought items on top of the leaves and turned the barrel over top of them. The next thing was to throw sand around the barrel to keep the insects out.

After he unsaddled Buck and tied him to a tree near the creek, Henry walked up the small incline to find a place for his house. Knowing there would be times the creek would flood he knew it would be important to locate it on high ground. He soon found the very spot about sixty yards from the creek. The location didn't have many trees to cut down, and it wouldn't be far from the water.

Henry wanted his cabin to be thirty feet square, and he'd face it toward the west. Remembering the sweet gum trees he'd discovered on the property, he began cutting the tall trees down and hacking the limbs by two o'clock. He decided to cut down four trees each time, get them situated, then hack down four more.

Knowing the heart of the pine trees would eventually turn to lightwood, he decided to lay his foundation logs on top of pine blocks. Once he felled the trees, he'd saw down the pines, so they'd be straight and smooth. He wanted his cabin to be one foot off the ground, so he made sure the top of each pine stump was exactly that far from the ground. By four o'clock, he had his first layer of notched logs down. Henry didn't give himself time to pat himself on the back, for he knew he still had to catch some fish for supper. He went to the creek and baited his hook. Again, in less than fifteen minutes, he'd caught four big bream the size of his palm. After cleaning the fish and putting them on his homemade grill, he dipped into the creek for water and was soon boiling a small amount of hominy grits.

There were several iron rocks along the creek, so he picked a flat one and laid it in the fire. He set the small boiler of water on the flat rock. After the water came to a boil, he sprinkled a little of the salt into the water and added a measure of the dry grits in the boiling water. He also sprinkled a little salt on the smoking fish.

The sun was setting in the west by the time he finished his meal. He barely had time to wash his cooking utensils and take a bath in the creek before it began to turn dusk.

Henry pulled the thick woolen blanket off his homemade bed to check for snakes, and after a good search, he remade his bed. After finding things all right, he threw a few pieces of wood on the fire, covered himself and said his prayers.

He was tired, but several things ran through his mind as he watched the stars as they seem to twinkle, so many miles away. Naturally, he thought of Phoebe and things back in North Carolina. He wondered, as he had many times over the years, what his father looked like and what sort of man he was. His mother had simply told both James and him that he looked like them. "He was a hard worker, and was forever pulling pranks on me," she would say. She'd added. "He was your grandfather's baby son, so he and your grandmother, as well as his sisters, had done their best to spoil him rotten. If it hadn't been for your Uncle Jesse they

13

would have succeeded," she'd say. Their mother would always laugh when she'd say that.

"When your father died of that awful flu, for a while I thought your grandfather was going to die too," their mother said. "He was good to me and you boys, a good Christian man too," she'd told them.

Henry's mind next turned to his brother, James, wondering how he was coming along. He smiled, as he often did when he thought of his brother. Henry then turned on his side and went to sleep, feeling like he'd made pretty fair progress for his first day of work on his own land.

Chapter Three

Henry found the hardest task about building his cabin was the floor. Several more pillars had to be cut for the flooring to rest on, and they had to be square. He decided to make his flooring from pine. He'd chop all the pulp from the wood, leaving just the heart, which would eventually turn into lightwood, and it would last for centuries. After he'd finished with the flooring, he started back with the logs again, and was really doing well until the rains started. The only shelter Henry had was the small cave he'd hacked in a square hole in the bank of the limestone creek, for him to crawl into. He just prayed the creek wouldn't rise high enough to spoil his meager food supplies that were also stored in the limestone hole.

Not only had Henry been working, but so had Buck, for Henry had hitched the horse to every log so the animal could drag it back to the house. Henry dug two holes in the ground at each end of the cabin. He then tied a split log to the top of two more split logs, then slid the two logs in the ground and packed the dirt around them. The log at the top was used for Buck to pull the notched logs to the top so Henry could set them into place. The technique was quite simple; the hardest part was the back-breaking work of hacking all the limbs from the tree. Cutting or sawing the trees wasn't a picnic either, but Henry's big, callused hands sure helped with the situation.

Sitting idle in his shelter hole, watching it rain, was worse on Henry than the hard labor. After three days of constant rain, he decided to saddle Buck and visit his brother, James. He didn't mind working in the rain, but it was the slipping and sliding in the mud that was bad. Too, it was nigh impossible to see with the rain pelting him in the eyes.

Due to the weather, it took Henry about three hours to reach James' place.

When he arrived, Henry saw the beginnings of a building, and he had to admit he was impressed at his little brother's progress. At first there wasn't a sign of James, then Henry saw him run out of a thicket, with a wide grin on his face.

"Boy, when they say April showers brings May flowers, they mean it in Alabama!" James exclaimed, as Henry dismounted and the two brothers hugged, then patted each other on the back.

"What are you doing to stay out of this rain?" Henry asked.

"You're my brother, but if you ask a silly question, you're going to get a silly answer, my ass is staying wet, I imagine just like yours," replied James.

"Come on, follow me, let's at least get out of this mud," he said, as he led Henry behind the partially constructed cabin. Behind the cabin was a lean-to, constructed from pine branches and broom sage. The flooring was made from pine poles. The rain was dripping everywhere, but at least their feet were dry. The hastily built construction was about six feet square.

"So, you've been sleeping in here?" asked Henry.

"Yep, as you know, it stops raining after dark, so I put on some dry clothes and sleep the best I can," Janes replied.

"How do you keep your things dry?" asked Henry.

"Someone threw away an old trunk and a bunch of other stuff, mostly useless junk, but the trunk sure came in handy. I store my clothes and my small amount of food in it," James replied.

"Boy, you're lucky, I've been sleeping in a cave I dug out of the bank of a creek," Henry told him.

"Yeah, I've been thinking about you, brother, but as you can see, I've been busy," James said. "How about you…did you find a good piece of land?"

"Yeah, a beautiful place. The back end borders a creek, so I have plenty of good water, and fish to eat, but the food stuff in Sparta is ridiculously high," replied Henry. He then told James how much he'd had to pay for the few things he'd bought.

"Boy, that is high! I don't pay that much. Of course, I have to ride all the way to Fort Claiborne in Monroe County. It's a good ride, but at least I don't have to pay those prices," James said.

"Hmm, I'll sure check Fort Claiborne out, that's for sure," Henry told his brother.

"It would be a nice trip for you. It's situated on a high bluff overlooking the Alabama river. I wish we could have found land near there to homestead, but it was snapped up quickly. A steamship, the "Harriet," delivers goods there. I imagine by the time the store owners haul their goods all the way to Sparta, things would get expensive," James said.

"Okay, I'm convinced! Hell, let's change the subject. So, you're looking healthy, hard work looks good on your lazy self, little brother," Henry said.

"I wish I could say the same for you," James said, as the two laughed and slapped each other on the back.

"Boy, who would've ever thought we'd be living in such crude conditions, and all this back-breaking work? My God, it better be worth it," James told Henry.

"I know, and folks are homesteading all around me. I can hear them, but I guess they're like me, too busy to visit," Henry said.

"I know; it's the same here. I did walk across the woods and said a few words to my neighbor. He's already putting the shingles on his place, but we were too busy to get to know each other. He seemed likable enough. His last name is Allison," James replied.

"I haven't visited my neighbors yet. All I've seen is smoke. On the other side of me is the road that leads to Sparta. I don't reckon the land in front of me is available for homesteading, for I haven't seen any of the signs," Henry said.

"So, what do you think of my construction?" James asked.

"It's about like mine, except I'm using sweet gum trees. I see you're using pine."

"It's about all I had to use; if it wasn't pouring down rain, you could see for yourself," James said.

"Yeah, well, I have my flooring down and have three logs up on all four sides, then it started all this rain. I have hopes of planting a few vegetables, especially some corn and squash. It would sure change my diet of grits and fish," Henry laughed.

"There's one thing I have plenty of and that's rabbits. Shoot, I must eat three or four a week. I built two traps and use the figure 4 trigger, you know, Uncle Jesse showed us how to make the things," James said.

"I have plenty of rabbits on my place too. I've been tempted to shoot them, but I didn't want to blow them to pieces. What do you bait the traps with?" Henry asked.

"Sweet potatoes. I buy them when I go to Fort Claiborne. You can buy most anything there. I've been eating good. It's not like Mama's cooking, but I have rice, dried beans, peas, flour, as well as some smoked pork I use to season my vegetables with, and of course, tea, and coffee. It's just that my storage space is so limited," James described.

"Why you rascal, and here it is I've been worried about you!" Henry said.

"Nah, I've been doing just fine, just worked nigh slap to death," James laughed.

"One thing is for sure, we haven't been able to cook much in the last two or three days though," Henry remarked.

"Yeah, it's hard to cook with rain pouring into your pots and pans. I've managed though. Heck, all I've had for two days is raw sweet potatoes. I'm lucky; I might not have a creek on my property, but I do have an artesian well, right at the edge of my land at the rear. It sort of has a sulfur taste to it, but you get used to it," James said.

"Where does the water from the spring run to?" Henry asked.

"It's strange, I guess the Indians must have dug about a two-foot hole into the limestone to water their horses, then it meanders down a small hill and pours into another hole. It shoots out of the ground about four feet. It's a good place to take a bath. One day, if I ever get caught up, I thought I'd investigate it and see if I can find out where it goes. The water is clear as crystal. Daisy doesn't seem to have a problem with it," James said.

"So, not meaning to change subjects, but how do I get to your place from here?" James asked.

"It's simple enough, just go south down that wagon trace out yonder, and stay on it until you come to a crossroad. My place is on the left. I guess if you kept straight, you'd wound up in Florida. I imagine the road to the right will take you to Fort Claiborne, and of course, the one to the left goes into Sparta. Paying the high prices in Sparta is almost worth it; there's a pretty young thing there that runs an eatery. Her name is Juanita Carey. She's not only pretty to look at, but a good cook too," Henry told James.

"They have pretty girls at Fort Claiborne too, but I'm being true to Mary. She and Phoebe have 'forsaken all others' for a whole year for out sorry behinds, so I figure we should do the same for them," James said.

"Of course, little brother. Besides, we don't have the time, if we're going to have a roof over our wives' head," Henry laughed.

"I wonder if they know what they're getting into, leaving home with friends and family there, then starting off in a place like this," James mused.

"Shoot, with pretty land like this, I'd be willing to say there'll be houses and places of business everywhere, in a short while," Henry said.

All of a sudden, Henry hollered, "DAMN!" and dove out of the lean-to into the mud.

"Get outta there, there's a big cotton mouth moccasin coiled around a pole above your head!"

Not bothering to look, James bailed through the opening head-first, then ran for the hoe.

After returning with the sharp hoe, James asked, "Where is it?"

"Right there, it's a big old thing," Henry said, pointing toward the snake.

20

Staying as far from the opening as he could, James squatted until he saw the snake.

"I see that devil. It's flicking that tongue at me," he said, as he drew back the sharp hoe and chopped the snake. When he did so, James chopped the pole too, causing the roof to collapse.

When the lean-to collapsed, both brothers jumped back, expecting the snake to come after them.

"Why am I so fidgety? I chopped the thing in two. He's not coming after us," James told his brother sheepishly.

"Yeah, well, I jumped just like you. We're both already soaking wet; go ahead and take that hoe and rake the top away and see if you can find the thing, just to be sure," Henry said.

James did as he was asked until he found the snake's body.

"Good God, you weren't lying! It's chopped nearly in two and it looks like he's feasted on a rabbit, that's why he's so big around," Henry said. "Brother, if I were you, I wouldn't build this place back where it is, I'd move it someplace else. That snake might have laid eggs under the bottom of that thing."

"You know, you might be right," James agreed, as he began to rake away the poles that were used for the bottom of the lean-to. Even in the pouring rain they saw five leathery white eggs the moccasin had laid.

James smashed the snake eggs with the sharp hoe. He then picked up the withering snake with the hoe and chopped it across the head until there was no remaining doubt that it was dead.

"You know what?" he said.

"What?" replied Henry.

21

"To hell with all this mess. We can't work, due to the weather. Let's ride to Fort Claiborne and hole up in a boarding house They have two of them there. I know we didn't bring much money, but then we're not ducks either. We can buy a set of new clothes; they'll be dry too. They even serve meals in Mrs. Lambert's place. They have a livery stable there for old Buck and Daisy too," James said.

Henry didn't even have to mull the situation over.

"Saddle Daisy, I'm waiting on you. I've been wanting to see Fort Claiborne anyway," he said.

It didn't take James long at all to get ready; in fifteen minutes the horses were plodding through the mud and mire. It was a dark, cloudy day, with an occasional streak of lightning that popped too close for comfort.

"Once we get on the main wagon trail the dirt will the packed more, and it shouldn't be such a struggle for the horses. That way, we can put them in a trot, maybe," James said.

Henry couldn't look at the sun to gauge the time, but he estimated that the trip took about three hours. When they arrived in Fort Claiborne, he found that James was right about the place. He began to see houses and other structures about a mile before they reached the bustling town.

Their first stop was at the livery stable. Henry couldn't make out the man's name that ran the livery stable, as he had a foreign accent to his speech. He seemed to know James, though, and he told them it would cost two bits to stable each of their horses. "That includes fodder and grain," the man told them. They each pulled out a quarter and gave it to the fellow.

Their next stop was at a tailor's where they each were fitted with new work clothes. That stop cost them two dollars apiece. Putting on the new outfits, they rolled up their wet clothes and tied them tightly with string, making them easier to carry.

They both were well satisfied that the fronts of the buildings were covered with overhanging tops, so they didn't have to walk in the rain.

Surprisingly, Henry found that Mrs. Lambert's boarding house was built from wooden planks. He made a remark to his brother about the sawn planks. James said he had wondered about them too, and the owner lady had told him the boards had come in on a steamboat from Mobile.

Henry liked Mrs. Lambert from the get-go. She was a very friendly elderly lady, with graying brown hair and wide hips. He would find out later that she was widowed. She and her serving girls were steadily carrying platters, bowls, and trays of food through an open door.

"That's the dining room. Lord, I pray she has a room for us," James whispered to Henry, looking at the busy room.

"I know, just the aroma is making my mouth water," Henry whispered back.

They got Mrs. Lambert's attention when she came back through the open door, presumably to get more food.

"Yes, can I help you young men?" she asked.

"I know it's short notice, but we were wondering if you have an empty room?" James asked.

"Yes, I remember seeing you in town. You two have got to be brothers," she said.

"Yes, I'm James Smith and this is my brother, Henry," James said, as the two stood there with their hats in their hands.

"Well, you're in luck. I do have a tiny little room upstairs. It's the last one left; this place is packed. It only has one bed, but I guess with you two being brothers it won't matter. It wouldn't be Christian-like if I charged you boys more than a dollar a day for that little room. With two meals a day it will be two dollars a day for the both of you. We serve breakfast at seven in the morning and supper at seven in the evening. Come on, and I'll show you the room," she said, as she hoisted her skirt a small bit in order to climb the narrow stairs.

Mrs. Lambert wasn't lying about the room being small. Henry did notice a pitcher filled with water, sitting in a bowl, and a slop jar at the foot of the bed.

"Sorry, there's not a closet for your clothes or the slop jar. It looks like you boys are traveling light anyway," she said.

"It'll be fine," Henry remarked.

"Good; you can hang your clothes on the pegs up there," she said, as she pointed to a limb from a tree which was attached to one wall of the tiny space. The bark from the limb had been removed and the smaller twigs on it had been sawn off to where they were about four inches long.

Both Henry and James reached into their front pocket and gave the kind lady a dollar.

"The room will be fine; at least we're out of the rain," Henry told her.

Mrs. Lambert smiled, then told them supper would be on the table in about fifteen minutes.

"We'll be there," they both said in unison.

"Okay, then, let me lay down some rules. There's no cussing in my place, no drunkards, and no smoking at the table. Grace is said before each meal, and I would be

24

thrilled if one of you would honor my table tonight by blessing the food," she said.

"I would be honored," Henry agreed.

Mrs. Lambert then said, "Thank you. I could tell you boys were raised right. I'm a good judge of character. I have a young lady boarding here, who plays the spinet for my guests after supper each night. She only performs about thirty minutes; perhaps you two will enjoy the entertainment. Her name is Iris Mae, and her parents are on a business trip to Pensacola, so her stay here is only temporarily, unfortunately."

"I'm sure we will, we'll look forward to it," Henry told her.

"Wonderful. I'll see you in a few minutes," Mrs. Lambert said, then she nodded and left the room.

"What a sweet lady," Henry said. "I hope her cooking is as good as her manners!"

Chapter Four

It didn't take Henry and James but a jiffy to wash up and make their way downstairs. There were already six people sitting at the long table, waiting for Mrs. Lambert's appearance at the head of the table.

Henry walked to the front door and looked outside. "Well, just like usual, it's getting near dark, and sure enough, it's stopped raining," he said, as he and James made their way into the dining room.

They found two empty chairs that set side by side at the long table, so they pulled out the chairs and sat down. Everyone was waiting for Mrs. Lambert, and she couldn't get there soon enough as far as the brothers were concerned.

Henry recognized a pork roast, a huge platter of fried chicken, creamed potatoes with gravy, snap beans, butterbeans, cornbread, and biscuits. There was also an assortment of jellies on the table for those who had a sweet tooth. He counted heads at the table and there were ten, including him and James.

Mrs. Lambert soon entered with a very attractive young lady. She was dressed in an emerald-green dress that matched the color of her eyes. The young woman had coal-black hair and her skin looked as though sunlight had never shone on it. Henry noticed that Mrs. Lambert had changed dresses, as she was now wearing a nice gray dress with a white collar. He also noticed a pearl stick pin near the collar of her dress.

"One of our new guests will grace us by blessing the food tonight," Mrs. Lambert said, as she took a seat.

Henry blessed the food the same as he did back home, and as soon as he said amen, the food was passed around. An elderly man, who was dressed in a long topcoat, cut the pork roast and soon it was passed around the table also.

The two boys ate heartily, for they were starved, but they stopped short of being gluttonous. They did have a jellied biscuit after the main course, though. They needn't have worried whether the food would be any good; it turned out that Mrs. Lambert was an excellent cook.

Everyone soon finished, and began to make their way to their rooms, outside to smoke, or to the parlor. The serving girls began to clear away the table.

Henry and James followed Mrs. Lambert, Iris Mae, and a couple more people to the parlor. Everyone was soon seated in homemade, yet well cushioned benches or chairs. Iris Mae took a seat in front of the spinet and began to play.

Most of what she played they'd never heard. Her last selection was "Home
Sweet Home," and everyone in the parlor joined in with the song. Henry knew that everyone in the room was like them, from different places, and that they were all thinking of the homes they had left behind.

After the entertainment, most left the room after telling the young lady how talented she was. James attempted to strike up a conversation with Iris Mae, but she just replied with short, curt answers. She then got up and went upstairs, leaving Mrs. Lambert in the parlor with Henry and James.

After Mrs. Lambert knew the girl couldn't hear her, she apologized for Iris Mae's behavior.

"She's just worried about her folks; usually the poor dear is chipper as can be," the woman said.

"Aww, think nothing of it, I didn't. It's probably the way we're dressed, you see, we're working folks," James told Mrs. Lambert.

"I can tell from your big, callused hands, you young men have been working."

"Yes Ma'am, we're homesteaders," Henry replied.

"Well, I hope it's somewhere near here," Mrs. Lambert said.

"Actually, the properties are in two adjoining counties, Wilcox and Conecuh. We just couldn't work in all this rain, so we decided to take a hiatus, and go somewhere dry," Henry laughed.

"I see, but still, maybe you'll stop by often. A lot of folks do, coming to buy supplies and such. You never know, Fort Claiborne is on the boom. Several people find a trade and stay on with us," Mrs. Lambert replied.

"Yes Ma'am, but you see, we're farmers, and all the land even near here has already been asked for," James told her.

"That's what I'm told. Would you young men excuse me? I need to get with my servants. Lord, tomorrow will be here before you know it and I've got to start planning for another meal," she said.

"Sure, go ahead. It's stopped raining outside, so we might just walk around outside and stretch our legs," James said.

Mrs. Lambert stopped and turned around. "You are two good young men, I can tell. I'd advise you to stay away from that saloon down the street. They tell me they gamble in there and there's been several killings in that place."

"Well, it's dark outside, so we'll just sit for a spell on your porch then," James told her.

"That's fine, if you can find a place to sit out there. Several of the menfolks go out there to smoke or chew," she said, before she went on her way.

Surprisingly, there was only one person outside. He was sitting on a long bench. The boys could tell, even in the dim light, that the man didn't have a tooth in his mouth. Being toothless didn't hamper him from enjoying a big wad of tobacco, though. The boys watched as he periodically spat a long stream of tobacco juice onto the muddy ground.

"You boys local?" the old fellow asked.

"Not really, we're just here to get out of the rain. We live in the adjoining counties, though," Henry answered.

"It's a nice little river town. I'm a whiskey drummer. I come down the river about three times a year to take orders. My name is Luther Lee," he said, as he held out his hand to them.

The boys told him their names and shook hands with him.

"You two seem like good boys, I'd be willing to bet neither of you drink?" Mr. Lee asked.

"You're right, we're teetotalers," Henry replied.

"Good, keep it that way. I have yet to see a feller whip the bottle, but I've seen the bottle whip a lot of them. My daddy always said the stuff was meant to sell and not to drink, so I stick to that. I've sold lots of it too," Mr. Lee told them.

"Our father died very young, but his brother, Uncle Jesse, would have skinned us alive if we fooled with the stuff. Shoot, he kept us too busy working to even think about drinking," Henry said.

"Yep. He did give us time for courting the girls, but even that was at some kind of church function," James chimed in.

The toothless old man laughed, then spat another stream of tobacco juice into the darkness of the night.

"Well, it looks like we're in for it tonight," the old fellow said, as the sky lit up from lightning that lit up the south sky.

"Yep, it looks that way, but at least we'll stay dry tonight," Henry remarked, as the old man emptied his mouth of the wad of tobacco.

"Damn, that was good, but I'm going to my room, to hell with all this damnable rain. At least it keeps the mosquitoes away," Luther remarked, as he told them good night and walked back into the boarding house.

The boys stayed outside and talked for a while, speaking mostly of home, their soon-to-be wives, and their future.

"You know, I hardly ever remember hearing about Alabama until you came up with this homesteader's thing," James told Henry.

"Of course you didn't, because it was still Indian territory," Henry said.

"Well, it had better pay off. We've worked our asses off for three months and have very little to show for it. Why haven't we been seeing more people, if this is such a great place to live?" James asked.

"Well, if you'll take notice, we're running behind most of the other folks; they've already made improvements to their land. I bet they've gone back East to bring their families, or to sell it," Henry said.

"Yeah, I've noticed most of the places only have one corner of the cabin up, and not a soul around. Reckon what they intend on their family to live in while they finish their cabins?" James asked.

"I imagine they'll live in their covered wagons until they can put a dry roof over their heads," Henry told his brother.

"Yeah, I can just see Phoebe or Mary living in a covered wagon!" James laughed.

"I'll admit, I just wasn't thinking, or we would have at least brought Tricademus and Sol with us to help. I wasn't sure we'd get the land, though," Henry said.

"Well, we've just got to get it into our heads and backs to get it done," James said.

"That's right, little brother. We had it going too until all this rain started. I didn't really go over your land, but I think I've picked a good piece of dirt. It won't flood, for it has a gradual slope to it. All the excess rain simply runs into the creek," Henry said.

"My land is a good place for farming. I'll bet the topsoil is a foot deep. I can hardly wait until we start farming it," James said.

"Me either," answered Henry, then they too walked up the stairs to their little room, holding a lighted candle in front of them. It had been years since the two had slept in the same bed, but they didn't have a problem that night. After telling a few funny stories, they drifted off to sleep.

After breakfast the next morning, the two decided to tour Fort Claiborne. Henry was really surprised at the places of business, and homes in the town. He noticed there was a huge building being built on the high bluff over-looking the Alabama river. It was being built from sawn lumber too. After inquiring about the huge building, the two learned that the first floor was to be used for a courthouse and

31

meeting place. The second floor was to be used as a Masonic lodge.

"Wow, what a town! It's hard to believe that just a few years ago, Indians were occupying this place," Henry told James.

"I know; this river town is on fire. Shoot, it's even where the county seat is located," James said.

"They've got it going on for sure; they do have the river and all, but we're farmers. That's what we came here for. Who knows, maybe we'll be shipping our farm goods from this very place one day," Henry said.

"It's a far piece to come, but like I said, it's where I come to do my shopping. You can find almost anything you need here," James said.

"Lord, I'm going to miss Juanita in Sparta, but I believe I'll start coming here too. It's going to cost more than I was expecting to spend, but I'm going to see if I can find me something to store things in. I can buy all sorts of things here that I can't find in Sparta, and it's cheaper too. Maybe poor Buck can carry everything," Henry remarked.

That day was Tuesday, April 29th, and it didn't rain a drop. They spent that day shopping, just getting essentials. Henry couldn't find a trunk that was waterproof, so he wound up buying a twenty-gallon wooden barrel that sealed at the top. James just bought a small number of things, all foodstuffs, except for soap. Henry bought a small amount of flour, smoked pork, honey, dried beans and peas, more meal, corn hominy, soap, salt, and candles; his last purchase was corn for Buck.

James knew that he could just sling his items across Daisy's back, for everything was in two cloth sacks.

They rigged up a way to mount Henry's twenty-gallon barrel on the back of Buck's saddle. It meant that Henry had to sit forward in the saddle, but it was worth it to him.

That night after supper, they chose to sit outside and converse with Mr. Lee, instead of staying inside and listening to the snooty Iris Mae. They planned on leaving the next morning, right after breakfast. They learned from Mr. Lee that they'd be taking separate roads back to their places. James' route was almost due east. Henry would have to climb a steep hill that headed south, then veer off to the east to get to his place.

In bed that night, the two brothers talked of all manner of things. They agreed that their spirits had been lifted, just staying dry for a couple of days and eating regular food. Neither of them realized that just being around each other was actually the medicine they needed. James did mention the fact that he'd learned the location where his homestead was located was called Snow Hill.

The next morning, after loading their goods, they both went to the blacksmith's shop and each of them bought five pounds of ten-penny nails. They both laughed when the blacksmith handed them the nails.

"Well, we'll get there, eventually," Henry said, for both knew the nails would be for the shingles. "Whew, I don't know about you, but when I get home, or rather when I get to my place, I'm going to sit straddle of the artesian spring and take a bath," James said.

"I know what you mean, except I'll be jumping in the creek with a cake of my soap," Henry answered.

After hugging necks, and patting each other on the back, they went their separate ways.

Chapter Five

On the second day of May, Henry's land was dry enough to plant a few hills of squash and about a quarter acre of corn. He sort of hated digging into the meadow, for it was blooming with all sorts of wildflowers.

By the end of July, he was ready to start on his roof. He'd left a gaping hole that was ten feet wide in the living room for his fireplace. He'd also left an indention in the flooring ten feet long and three feet wide, for the hearth. Henry was once again proud of the limestone that lined the sides of the creek. He'd use them for his fireplace and chimney. He thought he'd make his chimney as tall as possible, so the sparks from the fire would be less likely to ignite his shingles.

Henry was so excited when he started on his roof! It would mean that he'd soon be out of the weather. He'd already built his fireplace and erected his chimney. He'd cut down on the laborious task of carrying the heavy limestone blocks from the creek bank. He simply made a ground slide and Buck pulled the blocks of limestone to his cabin. When there, Henry simply sawed the chalky substance the size he wanted. He was already cooking from the fireplace, and he was very pleased how it pulled the smoke up the chimney.

The squash he'd planted really produced well, and he was thoroughly enjoying them, cooked with strips of smoked pork. He wondered how he'd made it all that time on just fish. Henry would be glad when the corn ripened, which shouldn't take but a couple of more weeks. His Uncle Jesse wouldn't believe how tall the corn stalks were. Just seeing how the two vegetables produced, he knew he'd picked some good soil.

Henry started the very top of the house with larger poles, then decreased the size of the poles as he went down. Henry had also built eight-foot porches on the front and back of his cabin that ran the entire length of the building.

When it came time for the shingles, Henry once again used Buck to pull the cypress trees from a swampy area near the creek. He tried to find trees that had very few limbs near the bottom of the tree. Limbs would mean knot holes, and he didn't want that.

Stripping the trees to make the shingles was a slow go at first until Henry got the gist of things. To start with, he used a wedge and axe to split the trunk of the tree in half. He then used a froe (a metal blade with a wooden handle) and his axe to rive or split the shingles from the trunk of the tree. Luckily for him, due to the length of the first tree, he was able to rive eight long pieces from the it. This made it possible to nail a complete shingle down the entire length of the house and both porches. That way he could use regular sized shingles, ensuring the roof wouldn't leak.

Henry started at the front porch and worked his way up. Nailing the shingles wasn't a problem; making them is what took time. He thought of Tricademus and his family. He'd hoped he'd have time to build them something to live in, but he now knew he wouldn't have time. He was hoping he'd at least get something started and Tric. (Henry's nickname for him) could help him finish it. *"They'll just have to live in the wagon until something is ready for them,"* Henry thought.

As he reached the apex of his house, there was a certain spot where he could look over some short trees and see his neighbor's house. It had been long enough; Henry had made up his mind that he'd knock off earlier than usual and visit his neighbor that very afternoon.

Instead of riding Buck over, Henry decided to walk through the woods to his neighbor. He couldn't understand his feelings, but he was nervous as a cat. He kept telling himself that he, or they, were just human beings, the same as himself.

When he arrived at his neighbor's claim, it looked like the fellow's house was about as advanced as his own, except his neighbor's house was built in the "shotgun" style. This meant he had built his house long and narrow, whereas Henry's was square and more compact.

The young man was concentrating on his roof, so he didn't notice he had a visitor until Henry coughed to get his attention. When he did so, the young neighbor was startled, and he turned around so fast he almost lost his balance. The hammer he was using to nail his shingles dropped to the floor beneath the partially finished roof, and he grabbed a rafter to steady himself.

"Just thought I'd stop by and introduce myself. I'm your neighbor, Henry Smith," Henry said.

"Allow me to swing down from this roof, and I'll properly introduce myself," the young man replied.

"Sure, I'll just take me a seat on your front porch," Henry agreed.

"I'll be down in a minute," the fellow said.

Henry noticed right away that his neighbor had cut the trees down in front of his house, and the afternoon sun was uncomfortably hot.

"It's taking that fellow a mighty long time to get out here," thought Henry. He was wanting a drink of water due to the long walk and the hot sun. Henry also noticed while sitting

on the porch that the building was entirely too close to the ground. *"A big flood, and water will be inside the building,"* he thought.

Henry was shocked when the fellow stepped onto the porch. Right away he could see that his neighbor was wearing a clerical collar and a suit coat.

"Allow me to introduce myself. My name is Jesse Jordan; I'm an ordained minister from Putnam County, Georgia. I'm looking for this country to explode with people due to the homesteaders. I've been led here to be a minister and preach the gospel of the Lord," he said, as he held out his hand.

"Mighty nice to meet you, Brother Jordan. My name is Henry Smith, and I'm your neighbor. I'm sorry it's taken me so long to make it over here, but I've been awfully busy," Henry replied.

"No need to tell me about it; I've been busy with my church, too. Forgive me for not coming over to your place sooner," Preacher Jordan said.

"The only break I've had was when the flood came through," Henry told him.

"How well I remember! The only way I made it was, I have a wagon with a canvas top. I was still soaked, though," Preacher Jordan remarked.

"My brother and I went into Fort Claiborne for a couple of days, and stayed in a boarding house," Henry said.

"Fort Claiborne is a nice place, very reasonable with their prices, compared to little hamlets north of here. Unfortunately, though, my funds are limited, and I need to cut every corner," the preacher said.

"Oh, boy, do I know what you're talking about! My brother and I only brought the bare essentials. I knew it would be hard work, for we'd built log houses in North Carolina. I never thought about having several men pitching in to help. Here, you're all on your own," Henry said.

"So, you're here with your brother?" Preacher Jordan asked.

"Well, we made the trip together, but he's homesteading a place about twenty-five miles north of here," Henry explained.

"Well, it's nice that you have someone from back home here with you," Preacher Jordan smiled.

"Preacher, would you like to have some fresh squash for supper?" Henry asked.

"Are you kidding? I haven't had anything but grits and meal flap jacks for months," the preacher answered.

"Good; follow me home and I'll give you some. I planted a few hills and boy, did they produce," Henry said.

After the two men made the quick walk back through the woods to his place, Henry picked the preacher six yellow squash straight from the vines.

"This is wonderful. I have a Dutch oven; it'll really cook these things. Thank you so much! I'll say a special prayer for you, Brother Smith," the preacher said.

They then talked about Henry's house, and the preacher told him he thought that he'd done a remarkable job.

"Thank you. I didn't take a good look at yours, but from what I saw it looked all right to me, except you might have it a little too low to the ground," Henry said.

"Yes sir, you might be right," the preacher said, "During all that rain, the water came up to the porch, then rushed on down the hill. I sure had to do some tall prayers. It'll be small for a house of God; you see, I had to build me a small room in the back for somewhere to live," the preacher said.

"Of course. But the church will be big enough to start with; folks will start moving in and they'll need a place of worship, even me," Henry reassured him.

"That's my prayer," the young preacher said. He then added, "That and to cook this squash. Gosh, I'm suddenly ravenous!"

Henry laughed and said, "I'll soon have corn. It should be ready in about two more weeks. I can bring you some then."

"My goodness, where did you get the seed, and when did you find the time to plant them?" the preacher asked.

"I brought the seed from North Carolina, and I planted them after the flood," Henry told him.

"Well, I'll sure be obliged," Preacher Jordan replied. The young man then cradled the squash in the crook of his left arm, then thanked Henry again for the fresh vegetables. "I know we both have things to do, so I'll bid you adieu," he said, then shook Henry's hand.

"It's so nice having you for a neighbor," Henry remarked, then the preacher turned away and walked back toward his place.

After the preacher left, Henry surveyed his house. *"Alright, as soon as I get the shingles on the front, I'll be through with this sucker,"* he murmured to himself. *"Of course, I still have the shutters to rive, but thank goodness there's only three windows in the house,"* he thought.

Chapter Six

Henry knew he still had some tidying up to do, but by the fourteenth of August, he was through with the rudimentary structure of his house. He still had intentions of turning half of the loft into another bedroom, which would mean building stairs.

Henry's squash had long since stopped bearing, but he still had a few ears of his corn that were green and edible. He had to admit, the preacher and himself had eaten all they wanted of it, and there was still plenty on the stalks, left to dry for Buck. Buck would also have plenty of fodder, leaves from the corn that were stripped when it was green. Henry had no place to store it but in the house. He knew his storage place wouldn't go over with Phoebe once she arrived, but he figured Buck would probably eat it all over the winter months. Buck would also have plenty of corn to eat; it was stored in the house as well.

The house would have to do until Henry was able to put up a barn. He figured he'd cut down enough trees, and limb them for Tric and his family's house and the barn too. He decided he'd take the last of his green corn and squash to his brother James. He'd found the perfect refrigeration system. He'd simply put some of the squash in a sack, tied the top to a tree after filling it and dropped it into the cold water of the creek.

The day was Sunday, August seventeenth, if Henry's homemade calendar was correct. He didn't relish the idea of working on Sunday, so he thought it was a good day to pay a visit to his brother. He knew James would be glad to get the corn, and the squash, too. Henry was also wondering how James was doing with his own house.

Henry had stayed so busy he'd forgotten how beautiful the Alabama country could be until he set off for his brother's place. It looked like it was going to be a perfect day; there wasn't a cloud in the sky when he started his trip. He just hoped it wouldn't be such a scorcher, for he'd worn the new suit of clothes that he had bought when James and he had made their trip to Fort Claiborne. He'd invited the preacher, but Brother Jordan had declined, saying he wanted to just rest. Henry knew that the preacher had been building pews for the church all week.

Henry was surprised to see that all along the wagon trace, new log houses were in various stages of being built. It looked like his prediction to the preacher that the area would rapidly expand, would be correct. After seeing all the new construction, he felt better about bring Phoebe to Alabama. *"At least she'll have neighbors to visit,"* thought Henry.

After arriving at James' place, he was really surprised at what he saw. James was completely through with the main structure of the house and was adding on another room off the back porch.

He recognized Henry as soon as he came down the path to the house. James was sitting on his porch with his back leaning against the logs of the house. Of course, he stood up when he recognized his brother. Henry reined Buck to a tree in the front yard so that he'd have shade, then removed the sack of corn and squash.

"I brought you something to cook," Henry told his brother, as James rushed to him with a wide grin on his face. He put the sack on the ground until they finished slapping each other on the back.

"You're making me feel ashamed of myself; I've never even been to your place, and you've visited me twice now," James said.

"Aw, it's nothing to brag about, you're ahead of me on your house, little brother," Henry told him.

"Well, it's a long story, come on and let's get in the shade, I'll explain it to you then."

"Here, I've brought you something," Henry said, as he handed his brother the sack.

James opened the sack immediately. "Boy, I am glad to get this! Where in the world did you get this?" James asked.

"In my garden," Henry replied.

"Where did you get the squash seed?"

"I brought a few seed from North Carolina," replied Henry.

"Well, they'll make a fine supper; I'm sick of eating poke weed roots," James said.

"Poke weed?" asked Henry.

"Yes, poke weed. It goes along with my story. Come on, so I can get my supper in the shade," James said. He was lucky; he had a big white oak tree that shaded his house from noon until late afternoon. After they took a seat on the front porch, James began his story.

"The reason I'm so far along with my house is, I've had some help. I was cutting trees on the very back of my land when I found a wigwam. When I got there, an old Indian man and two of his daughters opened the door and stepped outside.

"Well, they didn't seem dangerous, so I spoke to them, and Henry, the two young women spoke the English language very well. The old man spoke English, too, although it was somewhat broken. I asked the old man what they were doing on my land. He told me it was his before I came along. I laughed and told him that I had filed claim to it and the federal government had given me a year to improve it and then I'd get a deed. "It will be mine free and clear after February of next year," I told him.

"'You'll never get it; you've done nothing but cut trees,'" the old Indian told me. Then he said, 'You must have land in two places; we watch as you fish and then jump in the water naked. We see you south of here, at the good fishing place.'

"I told them that was my brother they had seen," James laughed. "Whether you knew it or not, they've been watching you the whole time you've been skinny dipping!"

Henry blushed red at the thought of the old man seeing him in his birthday suit, much less the two girls, but he laughed along with his brother as James continued his story.

"Later, the two girls told me they were hiding out from the soldiers, because they didn't want to be sent off to a land they didn't know. So the old man and I struck up a deal; they'd help me build my cabin if I wouldn't turn them in to the Army.

"Henry, that old man never lifted a hand to do anything on the house, but instead, he foraged the woods and creeks. He brought in things to eat that I'd never seen, and the girls would cook it. Heck, I didn't have to waste time cooking. The bigger of the two girls helped me with the house; she was strong as a mule. The younger one, she mostly cooked and made pottery from the clay down by the small stream.

"They taught me so much! This might sound strange, but did you know your own urine was good for sores, earaches, and sinus problems? Willow bark is good for fevers, and mullein weed will knock out a chest cold fast. The old man made a drink out of blackberry leaves, and we drank it with our meals. He claimed it would purify your blood. You can only eat poke weed leaves when they're young, when the leaves start to turn; you dig up the roots and eat them. They're quite tasty, too," James said.

"Where are the Indians now?" Henry asked.

"Well, the old man found out that if you fought against the British with the United States, they would give you a land grant. He told them about his uncle that had helped Andrew Jackson fight, so he was deeded a huge land grant about eighty miles south of here. He was very excited about it, so they left from here nine days ago. The smaller girl, who was a beauty, had become attached to me and didn't want to leave. The old man offered to sell her to me, but I told him I already had a woman, so they left. I'll have to admit, I miss them," James finished his story.

"What were their names?" asked Henry.

"The pretty one, her name sounded like "Abi," and the one that helped me with the logs had a God-awful name, something like Auchoo. I could hardly say her name with a straight face; it sounded like I was sneezing! The old man's name was Homme," James said.

"It must have been just youthful folly on the young girl's behalf, to want to stay with an ugly cuss like you. I imagine she was just tired of hiding out, and hadn't come across anyone who was better looking," Henry teased. The truth was, both brothers were fine looking and had always had plenty of girls chasing them.

"Yeah, that must have been it," James laughed good-naturedly. "I know one thing, I learned a lot from them.

Unlike what people back home might think of Indians, they were very clean. They bathed every day, at least the girls did. The old man smelled like wet buffalo, mixed with mint. The girls smelled like mint too. It wards off mosquitoes," James said.

"Yeah, I smelled it on you, but didn't say anything," Henry remarked.

"It grows wild, all around here. Shoot, it works, too."

"I'm sure glad you told me! I'll have to try it; those things can be pesky. I'm constantly slapping at them," Henry said.

"Well, getting back to the subject of my house, after having help and not having to waste time cooking, or foraging for food, I decided to build the kitchen in another room, in back of the house. It'll mean building another chimney, but it'll also mean Mary won't get the rest of the house so hot in the summer months," James told his brother.

"That's a good idea. I'll do that when we return with our wives next year. Right now, I've started cutting and notching the logs for Tricademus and Precious' house. Lord knows, they'll need a place to live. They had six children when we left. No telling how many they'll wind up with," Henry laughed.

"Sol and Ruth have only four, all boys, as of when we left," James said. "I don't know about you, but I feel that we deserve a pat on the back. I think we've accomplished a lot in just six months," James said.

"It was a quest, for sure, picking up stakes and just heading out here. We had no idea how it would turn out, and our whole future hinged on it. But I must say, I never doubted you, little brother," Henry told James. He could tell that his brother felt the same kind of emotions he did:

pride, relief, and hope. It was a rare emotional moment between the two, as they seldom discussed feelings.

After a long moment, James said, "Well, I must admit, that bit in Grandpa's will leaving us just one silver dollar and no more, then mother marrying, put the icing on the cake for me. I knew I'd never be satisfied there anymore."

"I can't blame mother for marrying Mr. McMillian. She could have done worse. If I know Uncle Jesse, he'll keep an eye on things," Henry remarked.

"Yeah, I've thought of the same thing," James agreed.

"Well, I have a bit of news for you," Henry said. "It might not be as interesting as your story, but I've met my next-door neighbor, who is a preacher. He's built a little church, and he's very likeable. His name is Jesse Jordan."

"What kind of preacher?" asked James.

"I don't know for sure, but I think he's a Baptist," Henry answered.

"Well, that's nice. As you know, my land was the only parcel to homestead, so I don't reckon I'll have close neighbors. I'll imagine that'll change, though," said James.

Henry then said, "You know what?" I know this is projecting into the future, but I've decided my oldest son will be named William, in honor of our father."

"Well, there'll be two William Smiths then, because I've thought of the same thing," James remarked, and the two of them laughed at the coincidence.

After a few more minutes of talking, Henry said reluctantly, "Well, I'd better head on back home. Boy, it feels good having a roof over my head!"

"I know what you mean. Before you go, though, I have something for you," James told his brother. Going into the house, he soon returned with two ceramic glasses and a

46

ceramic bowl. "Some of the things that Abi made. They should be of use to you."

Henry put the bowl in the sack that he'd brought the corn and squash in, and the two glasses in each saddle bag.

"They're very nice," Henry said. "They'll be the first things to go in my kitchen. Thank you, James."

"Thank you for the vittles," his brother replied.

After their usual hugs and patting on the backs, Henry saddled Buck and headed back to his own house. He was smiling as he rode, thinking about the new people he and James had met as neighbors. With a minister close by, and the new information about living in the area that James had learned from his Indian friends, they were indeed beginning to put down civilized roots. He was looking forward to sharing his new home with Phoebe.

Had he known what was going on back home at that moment, he wouldn't have been smiling.

Chapter Seven

It was a long, cold winter, but not nearly as bad as Henry had experienced in North Carolina. He kept warm when he was outside by working, and of course, by his fireplace when he was inside.

Looking at his progress, he thought that he'd really outdone himself. He'd erected a barn with a loft to store his fodder. One side of the barn was used for the corn, and the other side was a as shelter for Buck. He'd also made a good start on cutting the logs for a cabin for Tricademus and his family.

James came to visit Henry at Christmas time. James informed him that he had finished his house, and had the logs cut for Sol's cabin. He and Henry made a foray into Fort Claiborne. They each bought one outfit of warm clothing, including coats and new boots. They knew it was nearly time to return home for their soon-to-be brides, and they wanted to be looking good on their trip back to North Carolina. They also purchased enough ticking fabric to make them each a small mattress. They would stuff the mattresses with the corn shucks from Henry's corn that they had shucked on Christmas Eve, 1823. The corn shuck mattresses sure slept comfortable for them that Christmas Eve night; it definitely beat sleeping on the hard floor.

Henry had made rabbit traps from pine limbs, and he checked them that Christmas morning. He had three traps set, and two of them had caught a rabbit.

James had spent the night with his brother, so for Christmas breakfast they had pancakes with honey. Their dinner meal was roasted rabbit and parched corn. They washed it all down with some of James' blackberry tea.

About the middle of the afternoon, James threw his corn shuck mattress over Daisy's back and headed home. The animal was skittish at first, but soon got used to the unusual load.

Henry finally settled down that Christmas night, after looking around in the house. He could see clearly at times from the flickering fire from the fireplace. He had a particular habit about himself. If he saw, felt or experienced an unusual or extraordinary event, he'd tell himself to "Remember this." That's what he did that night, lying there on his corn shuck mattress and listening to the stillness of the night.

He wondered what the next year would actually bring. He had so much to bring back from North Carolina: a set of oxen and farm implements to clear, stump, and till the land with, Phoebe herself and all her personal things, as well as all the multitude of other necessary things his own family would provide.

Uncle Jesse had told him and James he would provide the oxen and a stout wagon that would make the trip back to Alabama. Their mother had promised them each a cow with a calf, a sow with piglets, three hens and a rooster apiece, along with clothing, sheets and blankets, household implements and many other things. He also had to think about Tric, Precious, and their children, which would mean another wagon he'd have to pay for. Henry also wanted a dog, a hunting dog. It was a bit overwhelming, wondering how he would manage it all. *"Oh, well,"* he thought, *"It all can't be as tough and lonesome as the year I've just experienced. Just look what my own two hands have built."*

Finally, he just decided to concentrate on the necessities, and let Phoebe worry about the rest. He was looking forward to having her company next year, along with Tric and Precious and their children. *"Everything's going to be alright,"* he thought optimistically. Feeling good about himself, and hopeful for his future, Henry turned his back to the warm fire, said his prayers and went to sleep.

The second week of February, 1824, Henry made the trip into Sparta and had a meeting with Mr. Salter. Mr. Salter informed him he was working in the north part of the county that week but would get to him the next week. That meant it would be the end of the month before he could get the deed to his property and have it recorded. Then, at a minimum, it would take them another week to get back to North Carolina. He just prayed that Phoebe would still be waiting for him.

Henry didn't waste time when he returned home from Sparta. He kept busy. He'd sawn down some cedar trees earlier in the year. Instead of making the stairs and room upstairs from logs, he decided to use the froe and axe and make rough planks. He split the logs and made the steps the dimension his uncle Jesse had taught them. The risers would be seven inches high, and the steps themselves would be eleven inches deep by three feet wide. By the second day, Henry was nailing down floorboards. The downstairs would consist of two rooms, each fifteen feet square. The cedar had a few knot holes, but he figured he could cover them with some of the clay that he'd put between the logs. He loved the scent of the cedar, too; it reminded him of Christmas time.

Henry had started on nailing in the walls when Mr. Salter showed up the last week of February to inspect the property. The man was well satisfied with the progress that Henry had made, and also shared some news. He said that the Reverend Jordan had been called to preach at a church in the north end of the county. Mr. Salter offered to sell Henry the preacher's 165 acres of land, building included, for twenty-five cents an acre.

Henry knew that all the cash he had left on him was twenty-two dollars, but he definitely wanted to purchase the new land. He made a deal with Mr. Salter to pay twenty dollars down now on the land and pay the balance when he returned from North Carolina. Mr. Salter agreed to give him ninety days to finalize the purchase, so Henry followed him back to Sparta. He wound up paying eighteen dollars on the new property and two dollars to record the deed. Salter, in return, gave him a deed and a receipt of deposit for the 165 acres of land.

Henry left the courthouse that day in awe. It was unbelievable! He as good as owned 330 acres of good farmland. Tricademus and his family could make their home from what had been the church building. Henry would never reveal to Tric or his wife that the building was meant to be a church, for fear of Precious being superstitious. He just prayed that James had a few dollars on him to buy food on their way back to North Carolina.

If Henry's homemade calendar was correct, the next day was Friday, February 27, 1824.

He packed his saddlebags with what he thought he might need on the trip, and threw enough corn in a sack for both horses. He figured James wouldn't have any for Daisy. Mr. Salter had promised him he'd keep an eye on his property when he was in the area.

Henry had nearly made it to James' place when he met his brother coming in his direction.

"Did you get your deed?" asked James as soon as they got near enough to hear each other.

"Yes, did you?" asked Henry.

"Yep, yesterday, recorded and with the deed in my saddle bag," James replied.

After Henry reached his brother, he told him the news of the other land.

"My goodness, what luck! But how are we going to farm what we have? Do you realize we have more land already than what Mother has in North Carolina?" James asked.

"I know. I only hope you have a few dollars on you to get us back to North Carolina, for I don't have a penny," Henry said.

"If $9.50 will do it, then we're in luck," James replied.

"That'll do," Henry said, as they slapped hands. Then they turned and headed in an easterly direction.

They only stopped at James' place for a small while, and Henry was very impressed at what his brother had accomplished. He'd finished his kitchen and had the log walls constructed to his barn, but not the barn's roof. Henry took note that the barn was bigger than his, *"But mine is dried-in,"* thought Henry.

"I know poor Daisy is tired of staying out in the weather, but Sol and I will top that barn when we get back. Shoot, he and Ruth will probably have to live in there until we fix them something better," James said.

After replenishing their canteens with the cold water from the artesian spring, they struck out for North Carolina.

As soon as they crossed the Georgia line at Columbus, they noticed how the population had increased. James mentioned the difference to his brother.

"Well, Georgia has been a state for a lot longer. Just give Alabama time, she'll get there," Henry said, and they rode on.

Chapter Eight

Henry and James reached their mother's home in record time. They made it in six days, but they were both worn out, including the horses.

Needless to say, everyone was elated to see them. Mary actually swooned and fainted. After reviving her with a wet washcloth on her forehead by their mother and a kiss on the lips from James, Mary whispered, "We feared the Indians had killed you both."

Neither Henry nor James noticed the sharp look exchanged between their mother and her husband at Mary's words. If they had, they likely would have chalked it up to their mother's own anxiety and fear for her sons.

James picked his small fiancée's limp body from the floor and put her on the settee.

"They look quite the opposite, my daughter," Mr. McMillian said. "They look fit as a fiddle."

Their mother was beside herself, wanting to hug her only children.

"My boys, it's so good seeing you, but we've been expecting you for two weeks. We've been worried sick!" their mother exclaimed. She then added, "Poor Phoebe comes over every day."

"Yeah, well, she'll be seeing me before dark, but first I'd like to take a bath and put on some clean clothes," Henry told his mother.

"Y'all's bedroom is just like you left it, including your bath closet," the boys' mother said. She then added that she and Faith would add to the meal they were planning for supper and welcomed them home again.

Henry went into their old bedroom to bathe and put on his new suite of clothes. James stayed in the living room and continued to woo Mary.

As he prepared to take a quick bath, he thought that Mary had really blossomed since they had been gone. It was clear to see that she really loved his brother.

The boys' old bedroom joined the kitchen, and Henry could faintly hear his mother's voice as she hummed while she prepared supper. It brought back old memories, hearing his mother's happy voice, but it was just for a fleeting moment. He remembered Edmund McMillian standing in his father's living room. He then tried to make himself feel bad about his feelings toward the man, but he couldn't. He decided to swallow his feelings and let things be.

The first thing Henry did was to trim his long blond hair back to shoulder length, before washing it. He looked in the mirror and smiled. He had to admit that both James and he had white, straight teeth. Their mother said they both were the spitting image of their father, William Smith.

While bathing, his mind thought of many things. He considered the progress on their places in Alabama. He thought next of the ones he was most interested in seeing in North Carolina: Phoebe, his mother, and Uncle Jesse. He knew that his uncle had forsaken his own happiness, by delaying his own marriage to help raise them.

As Henry was putting his new suit of clothes on, he couldn't help but notice how his muscles rippled in his chest, stomach and arms. *"My goodness,"* he thought after looking at his body in the steel mirror that was tacked on the wall. Not having a mirror at his place, it was the first time he'd seen his image in a year. *"It must have been all that*

55

hard work." He smiled at himself in the mirror, and winked, then left the room with his new suit and boots on.

Edmund, who was now sitting on the settee, smiled at him and nodded his head, as his stepson walked by. Henry returned the nod.

"I think Mary and James went for a walk in your mother's rose garden," Edmund said, as Henry went out the door.

Henry didn't look for them; he walked straight to Buck and straddled him. It took only a few minutes to reach Phoebe's house. He heard someone playing the spinet inside the house and knew it had to be his fiancée.

Tying Buck to the hitching post, he then walked to the door and knocked.

He was shocked when Felix Evans (a "dandy," as his Uncle Jesse called them) answered the door.

Henry could see the smile drop off Felix's face as he recognized him.

"I've come to see Phoebe," Henry said, without acknowledging Felix.

"Sure, she's inside, but we thought you two were probably dead," Felix said.

"Well, do I look dead to you?" asked Henry.

"Clearly," Felix frowned, and reluctantly stepped aside.

When Phoebe saw him, she screamed, then ran to him.

"Darling, oh, Henry, it's good to see you! But we all had decided the Indians had killed both of you. We haven't heard a word," Phoebe cried, as she threw her arms around Henry.

"Yes, I can see that you thought so," Henry replied. He wasn't happy at all that the "dandy" Felix had been at his fiancée's house when he arrived.

Phoebe had the grace to look embarrassed. "I'm sorry..." she began, but Henry interrupted her with a hard voice. "Just exactly what is going on between you and Felix, Phoebe?" he demanded.

At that point, Phoebe began to cry, and hung her head. Before she could speak, her father, Lazarus Jones, came into the living room after hearing her scream.

"Henry!" the man said in surprise. "You're not...dead."

"I'm aware of that," Henry snapped. "Why is Felix here, is what I want to know."

Mr. Jones hesitated. "Well..." he stammered. "It's...uh..." Straightening his shoulders, the man gathered his courage and blurted, "The truth is, Son, he was here to discuss wedding plans with Phoebe. We hadn't heard a word from you, and they were due to be married later this week."

Henry's face darkened with anger. Then he caught sight of Phoebe's distress, and the tears on his face. Softening, he went to the young woman and knelt down in front of her. Lifting her chin in one work-roughened hand, he said quietly, "Don't cry, Phoebe. I understand. I'm sorry that I worried you so!"

As the two embraced, Phoebe's father turned to Felix, who had been lurking in the room's doorway.

"Felix, I think it's time for you to leave. These two have a lot to catch up on," he said.

"Yes, I can see that," Felix snapped, as he gave Phoebe a vulgar going over her curvaceous body with his eyes. It was clear from his demeanor that his only interest in Henry's girl was a physical one.

Felix grabbed his hat that he'd lain on a stool and stalked toward the door.

57

"Well, I've never been told to leave anyone's house before, don't think I'm going to forget this," Felix almost shouted.

"Just a minute, Felix. Don't you ever look at my future wife in such a way again. The only wedding happening with Phoebe this week, or ever, will be with me—and you're not invited. In fact, I want to give you something to remember me by," Henry said loudly, as he rushed to the open door where Felix stood. Using only half his strength, Henry drew back his big, hardened fist and punched Felix squarely on the nose. The force of the blow caused the other man to sail out through the open front door, landing with a thud in the dust of the dooryard. Stunned, Felix lifted a shaking hand to his broken nose, which was bleeding profusely. He said nothing.

Henry then quietly closed the door.

"Good riddance," Mr. Jones said. He didn't explain exactly how Felix had persuaded Phoebe to marry him instead of Henry, and Henry didn't ask.

"Well, I'd be willing to bet he won't be back," laughed Mr. Jones nervously, as they heard Felix's carriage rush off.

"I've been waiting a year for this moment, and to have it ruined by the likes of him was more than I could stand," Henry answered, with Phoebe close by his side, where she belonged. He then smiled, and said, "He did leave in a hurry though, didn't he?"

Mr. Jones came over and shook Henry's hand heartily.

"I'm glad that's over—and I'm thankful you've returned to take this moody girl off our hands. She hasn't been worth a nickel since you left," Phoebe's father remarked, as he put his arms around the young couple.

"Aww, Pa, you're going to scare Henry off next," Phoebe said.

"Ha, that's not likely, not after near killing myself, building us a place to live with my own bare hands," Henry said. He then added, "The quicker the better!"

Mrs. Jones came out of the kitchen, then hurried over and hugged Henry's neck.

"So good to see you, my goodness, poor Phoebe has just been overwrought with worry, especially the last month," she said. She didn't make any mention of Felix. She was just happy that the man her daughter truly loved had made it safely home.

"It's good to see you, too. I've been busy building a house for us to live in, and the state official was a little bit late inspecting things so I could get the deed," Henry said.

"So, you have got a house and your land?" Mr. Jones asked.

"Yep, I have a deed for 165 acres of good loamy farmland, and I'll increase it to 330 acres when I return. I'll be the first to admit, our house is more like a cabin, but it's dry inside when it rains and it's warm in the cold months. It doesn't get as cold down there as it does up here in the winter months, though," Henry said.

"Just long as we're together, Henry Smith. I've loved you since I was a little girl," Phoebe told him.

"Come on, Ma, let's go to the kitchen; it's getting syrupy in this room," Mr. Jones told his wife.

Mrs. Jones spoke with a long nasal accent, whereas Phoebe's father Lazarus was a big boisterous man with just a small amount of Scottish brogue in his words. Henry thought Phoebe was more like her father. She had his black hair, and at times Henry could hear the Scottish lilt in her

59

voice, especially if she was excited. Phoebe was short like her mother, but had her father's black darting eyes.

"Before we leave you two to yourselves, I just have one thing to say. I know beyond a doubt that when you take my daughter away, I'll never see her again. I'll never get to hold or rock my grandchildren to sleep. I know you two have to start a life just like Lazarus and I did, but why don't you just stay here? Make your home here," Mrs. Jones pleaded.

Lazarus interrupted, "It's the adventure of it, Ma, and Henry is too much of a man to want to stay here and farm my land. He wants a place of his own. Now, how would you have liked it if I'd moved in with your ma and pa?" he asked his wife.

Phoebe's mother smiled faintly, and admitted, "Well, I don't believe you and Ma would have made it very long!"

"Henry, you are staying for supper, aren't you?" Phoebe's father asked.

"No, Mother is expecting me back, but I'll be glad to come back tomorrow night," Henry replied.

"Good. We'll be expecting you, and tell that brother of yours I asked about him," Mr. Jones said.

"I sure will," replied Henry.

It was a nice afternoon for it to be March in North Carolina, so Henry and Phoebe walked out to the carriage house. There was an old bench just inside the building, so after a little kissing and embracing, Henry settled down to talk about their future.

"Now, you'll have to bear in mind that life in Alabama is a little more rugged than what you're accustomed to here," Henry said.

"What do you mean?" asked Phoebe.

"Well, for the time being, your nearest neighbors will be Tricademus and his family. There's very few places of business. Sparta, a little town north of us, is the county seat, but it's about fifteen miles away. There's Fort Claiborne…oh, you'll love it there. It's a bustling little town sitting right on a high bluff of the Alabama River. You can buy most anything you want there. They have mail service, and you can write your mama letters and the steamboat will pick them up. I think it goes to Montgomery, and couriers will deliver them from there. Fort Claiborne is in Monroe County, and it's about twenty-five miles from our house. Now, all this way of life is just for the time being. Honey, people are moving in fast, and you'll have plenty of neighbors before you know it. Where there's people, there's going to be places of business. You just wait and see, and we'll be there to watch it grow," Henry told her excitedly.

"Well, it sounds strange, but exciting. How far is the nearest church?" asked Phoebe.

"Gosh, I imagine it would be in Sparta," Henry replied.

"The Indians, what about them?" asked Phoebe.

'I never saw any, but James did; he said they were very friendly. I think they lived on his place for a couple of months, and they taught him all sorts of things. How to make ceramic dishes, medicinal herbs, wild things that grows on the land that are edible. I think they're still on the south side of the river, and the government has granted a few of them land to the south of us. The ones that helped fight the British," Henry said.

"You know, Henry, it's sad. I mean, after all, the Indians were here first, and the way they've been slaughtered and had to leave their homes," Phoebe remarked.

"Yeah, but that's the way of it. I imagine they'll eventually settle somewhere, though. I don't think they're much into farming; they seem to be satisfied to just leave things as they are," Henry told her.

"You know, have you ever considered, they just might be right? I mean, they've been here a long time," Phoebe said.

Henry didn't even have to think. "Nah, they want things as they are. Nothing stays the same. You've got to progress, and I intend on being on the cutting edge, and I'm taking you with me. There won't be a spinet to play, at least not right away, but I'm gonna be loving you so much you won't even think about a piano," Henry told her.

"You know, Henry, I've had year to think about things, and I really think I could face about anything with you by my side. I'm ready to make a life in Alabama. We'll make it," Phoebe reassured him.

"Atta girl, and I'll bet we'll have as many children as Tricademus and Precious," Henry told Phoebe, then he kissed her, and laughed.

"It's going to cost at first. We have to have food and clothing for everyone. Oxen, mules, farming implements, farm seeds…and if we head on back soon, we can take a variety of fruit and nut trees with us. Spring comes earlier there than here, so we need to get on back before then," Henry said.

"Baby, I'd marry you tonight and be ready to leave by morning," Phoebe promised.

"If it was only that easy! But we need time to get everything ready to take with us. Uncle Jesse has promised me a covered wagon with two oxen, and farm implements that's very expensive down there," Henry said. "Tric and his family will just have to find room in the wagon, along with everything else," Henry said.

"Father has a good, two-wheeled cart; it's covered, too. It'll be packed, but I can put my bare necessities in there. We can travel in it. It'll be easy to maneuver, too. I'm sure we can squeeze some fruit and nut trees up front with us," Phoebe mused. She then added, "Shoot, I'm an only child; I'll bet he'll throw in two obstinate mules to go with it. I'll be taking my dowry, too; I won't be leaving North Carolina broke," Phoebe said.

"My goodness, I didn't know I was marrying an heiress," Henry said.

"You can rest assured, it's not much. Maybe I can buy a few pretties for our house," Phoebe remarked.

"I have money, you can spend yours as you wish," said Henry, then continued, "Okay then, tomorrow we'll start digging up trees to put into the ground in Alabama. It's going to be a busy week. I'd like for us to be on the move within a week. We can get married at the church after services Sunday," Henry said.

"That'll give me two days; I'll be ready!" Phoebe said, excitedly.

"I hope you don't have objections to having a double wedding; I imagine James and Mary will be marrying, too. They'll be living about twenty-five miles north of us in Alabama," Henry said.

"No, I don't mind. Mary and I are the best of friends, and of course, I consider James to be my brother. It'll be a beautiful wedding, honey," Phoebe agreed.

"All right. I know you need to talk to your parents, and Mother will be upset with me for being later for supper. I hate to leave you, but I'm dying to see Uncle Jesse," Henry said.

They stood and embraced, then Henry climbed astraddle of Buck and left in a gallop, headed to his Uncle Jesse's.

Jesse, his wife Sarah, and their two young daughters still lived in Henry's grandfather's house. Jesse wound up with most of his father's property, including the house and furnishings. Henry's Uncle Jesse was as near to being a father to him and James as could be.

It was beginning to turn dusk when Henry galloped into Uncle Jesse's yard, amid a passel of yelping hound dogs. He hurriedly strode to the door.

One of Jesse's familiar hound dogs walked over and sniffed Henry's hand.

When Jesse opened the door and recognized Henry, he yelped, threw his arms around the young man and picked him up in a bear hug.

"Why, you rascal, you, the Indians didn't kill you after all! And your brother James?" Jesse asked.

"Nah, he's fine; they didn't kill either of us," Henry smiled.

"Come on in, we're about to eat," Jesse said.

"We just got in today, and I couldn't wait to come see you, Uncle Jesse. I'll just speak to Aunt Sarah and the girls, then be on my way. Mother is expecting me for supper," Henry said.

After his Aunt Sarah timidly hugged his neck, they all sat down at the kitchen table.

Henry talked while the others ate. He told his uncle briefly about everything they had accomplished in Alabama.

"Well, you look good, Henry; you've beefed up and made a man."

"Thank you, sir. It's from all the hard work, but we got her done. I have the deed for a hundred and sixty-five acres and will have another 165 when I get back," Henry told him.

"Whew! What about your brother?" Jesse asked.

"He has his house finished, but he only has a deed for a hundred and sixty-five acres. Of course, it all needs to be cleared of stumps and such, but it's excellent farmland."

"Well, I'll have to admit, I've missed you boys. I've held up to my end of the bargain, though. I have each of you a good stout wagon out there in the barn, and of course, your oxen," Jesse told him.

"Well, we'll be needing them, and I sure appreciate it," Henry said.

"It's the least I could do for my departed brother's children," Jesse told him. He continued, "Each wagon has a brand-new plow for tilling, and I'm going to throw in enough cotton and corn seed to get you going."

"Gosh, Uncle Jesse, that's great! It'll sure be put to some use," Henry said.

"Just holding up to my promise, and Henry, I think your mother did fairly-well marrying old Edmund. He'll be good to her," Jesse told him.

"Your word is good enough for me, and thank you for telling me that,"
Henry said.

"You boys just remember where and what you came from. Make your daddy proud and be good boys. Lead good, clean lives," his uncle said.

Henry almost teared up. "We will, Uncle Jesse, I promise," he said. He told them about the upcoming weddings before he left to go back to his mother's.

After returning home, Henry unsaddled Buck and made sure he had plenty hay, grain, and water before he went into the house to eat a late supper.

It was good to be home.

Chapter Nine

The Smith brothers married their new brides on March 7th, 1824, and left for Alabama the next day, amid tears, back slaps, and handshakes.

Henry and Phoebe led the train of wagons in the two-wheeled covered cart. Tricademus, Precious and their six children followed in the covered wagon that Uncle Jesse had bought. James and his new bride Mary were the third in line, while Sol, Ruth, and their four children followed to the rear. In order to have room for everything they took with them, James was forced to buy another wagon with his inheritance money that had been buried in the barn.

Every wagon was loaded to the hilt with household items. Each wagon had a cage built off the back that held four hens and a rooster. Buck was tied behind the two-wheeler, while a two milk cows was tied behind two of the wagons, each trailed by her calf. The four mules that Mr. Jones had given them pulled two of the wagons, while the others were pulled by oxen.

Uncle Jesse had given each of his nephews a set of bluetick hounds, which were about half grown. Henry knew he'd be having fun with them for years.

There was a commercial ferry that now crossed the Goshen swamp, so they gladly paid the price.

"Brr, it's a cold raw day, for sure," Phoebe remarked, and she pulled her shawl tight around her, as they crossed Goshen Swamp.

"It'll be nice and warm in Alabama, just you wait. Shoot, at times you can even feel a gentle warm breeze blowing from the Gulf," Henry said, as he put his arm around his wife.

Phoebe laughed, "Boy, will we have a honeymoon to talk about for years to come!"

Henry smiled. "Baby, you have that right," he replied.

He wouldn't dare admit it, but he was a little apprehensive while his loved ones and all their worldly belongings were crossing the wide swamp. He sensed Phoebe's nervousness, too, for she was about to squeeze his right arm off.

Tricademus' loud bass laughter at times really calmed the situation, though.

"I'll swear, I do believe Tricademus would laugh at the devil," Henry told Phoebe.

"Well, I guess they feel like they're on an adventure, too, so let him laugh," she replied.

They finally crossed the swamp without mishap, and late that afternoon, Henry turned south. They camped on a level piece of land. A campfire was built near a small creek, and all the women got together and cooked, while the men tended to the animals and checked on the equipment. They all dined on fried potatoes, smoked pork, and a pot of greens that Precious had brought with them.

Henry was tired, but his spirits rose as he heard the women giggling and laughing at everything as they worked together.

After things had been eaten and cooking utensils had been washed in the creek, they all found places to sleep. Everyone slept in the covered wagons except for Henry and Phoebe. The cart seat was barely wide enough for them to stretch out on. After padding the planks with quilts, it was possible for them to fall asleep.

Naturally, with the wagons and animals, they moved at a slower pace this time than the brothers had made on their outbound trip on horseback, but in a week, they finally crossed into Alabama, by going through Columbus, Georgia.

Henry went due east, then turned south on the ninth day of their journey.

"If the weather holds out, we should be home in four to five days," Henry told Phoebe.

"I see what you were talking about. It's so sparse here," Phoebe said, noticing how few people or buildings they passed on the way.

"It'll pick up as we go along; you'll begin to see little settlements here and there. Honey, you have to remember, Alabama has only been a state for a few years," Henry answered.

"It's beautiful country, though; some of the trees are already budding for springtime," Phoebe said.

While still in North Carolina, they had packed the fruit and nut trees with soil around the roots, and watered them occasionally while on the trip. Henry had noticed that some of the saplings were beginning to bud; he prayed they'd hold out for a few more days.

About the middle of the morning of the thirteenth day, they passed through the small settlement of Snow Hill, and not long afterward, the caravan pulled into the lane that led to James' house.

Of course, Henry was in a hurry to get home, but Phoebe wanted to see Mary's house first.

After a quick tour of the inside, and the immediate grounds, Henry and his crew left, with each lady promising visits.

"Well, what did you think?" Henry asked his wife after they were back on the trail again.

"It's hard to believe you two accomplished so much in such a short time; I think Mary's house is marvelous!" Phoebe exclaimed.

"Bear in mind, I'm not finished with the second floor at our house, but I can be through in a couple of days," Henry told Phoebe.

"It's the bedrooms?" Phoebe asked.

"Yes," replied Henry.

"Can we sleep there tonight, after we unload the mattresses?" she asked.

"Yep," replied Henry.

"Then that's all that matters, I am so ready to be alone with my husband," Phoebe replied, smiling softly.

Henry patted her on her thigh. "I love you with all my heart," he said.

Phoebe reciprocated Henry's words by crying, then, struggling to speak through her happy tears, she said, "I love you too, baby, and I can't wait to make our life together."

Chapter Ten

It was rough going for the first few years, mentally for Phoebe, and both physically and mentally for Henry.

Henry had finished paying for the preacher's 165 acres of land the week they returned from North Carolina. Phoebe made the trip with him to Sparta in the two-wheeled cart. A crude bridge made of logs was built over Burnt Corn Creek, and the team of mules pulling the cart crossed the bridge with ease.

After crossing the creek, there was a gradual incline for about two miles. Henry noticed a gradual oozing of muddy water flowing down the hill on the right and wondered what was taking place. At the very top of the incline, the land leveled off, and the place was littered with ponds of water. Henry imagined the ponds had been there since ancient times. He had learned from previous trips through the area that the mosquitoes were rough, so they followed James' advice. They smeared their exposed skin with crushed catnip, or mint leaves.

At the top of the hill was an intersection, and they saw that several buildings were being constructed around the crossroad. They noticed two young men near the crossroad who, by the use of two gray mules, were pulling a long log near an incomplete structure.

Henry pulled the mules to a halt near the intersection, so the two strangers stopped the gray mules.

"How do you do?" Henry asked, without leaving the cart. The two men introduced themselves. Henry learned they were brothers, and that their last name was Bell.

"We're draining the ponds around here so this area will be fit to cultivate. We're already constructing a grocery and mercantile store, thinking we can create a town," one of the brother's said.

"Goodness, that would be wonderful. We live about three miles east of here. I noticed the mysterious water flowing down the hill," Henry had said that day. Little did he know then that the brother's assumptions would be right, and that a small community would come to thrive there which would be named Belleville, in honor of the brothers.

By 1840, Henry had increased his holdings to over six hundred acres. Three hundred acres of the land was cultivated. A sawmill had been erected near Belleville, and Henry had plans for a spacious new two-story house. It was being built on newly acquired land that Henry had bought on the other side of the road.

Phoebe had birthed three children by then: two sons, William Lazarus and James (named for Henry's brother), and a daughter they named Phoebe Alabama. In that year of 1840, William Lazarus was fifteen, James was twelve and little Phoebe was six, and spoiled rotten.

Henry must have had a dominant gene, for all three of his and Phoebe's offspring had his long straight blond hair, blue eyes, and fair complexion.

Phoebe had never loved anything as passionately as she did her children. Henry would wait until bedtime to talk to Phoebe about her gentle nature toward the children, telling her she was going to spoil them. It was all said in good nature, though, for in their sixteen years of marriage, they'd never had a real argument.

All three of the children stood tall and erect, and each time one of the children passed Phoebe, she had a habit of touching or patting them. Henry took charge of the two boys and raised them in the fields and woods, as Uncle Jesse had done with him and James.

James and Mary had a house full of children, a total of nine offspring by 1840. As with Henry, James had named his oldest son William.

Tricademus and Precious had also continued to add to their brood; they wound up with twelve. Precious, who had plenty of experience, helped with the delivery of Phoebe's three children.

At the beginning, it was rough going, but with Tricademus' help and the oxen, they had stumped and cleared about sixty acres the first year. Both Henry and James had to really rely on their inheritance money for the first couple of years, as they had several mouths to feed. After the harvest of the third year, though, their hard work began to pay off.

Tricademus' oldest sons, Jasper, Sam, and Pete began plowing the fields at twelve years of age, the same as Henry and Phoebe's sons. There was one difference for the children of the two families, though. A small school had opened in Belleville, and the white children went to school from nine in the morning until noon every day. After school, however, the white boys were required to work the fields, just like the black boys were.

The school didn't open until Henry and Phoebe's son William (whom they called Will) was twelve, so he drove the carriage back and forth to school.

Henry was amazed at how quickly Will learned in school. He didn't know if it was because Will was the oldest or what, but in no time at all he was reading and could figure arithmetic. Henry's son James learned, too, but didn't seem interested like his brother was. By the third year, Will was reading advanced books that the teacher would loan him.

Several homes had been built nearby, just as Henry had predicted. There wasn't a church in their immediate area, so the families would take turn holding services in their homes. A big two-story church was being built in Belleville, for both races, although it was reported that the churchgoers of the black race would be sent to the gallery upstairs. Precious told Phoebe she didn't care where they sat. "Tricademus needs to be in church," she had said.

Phoebe and Mary's promised visits were very infrequent. They visited more often, though, when their sons become old enough to handle the carriages.

Phoebe was amazed at James and Mary's children; they all seemed bright and well mannered. Mary had two of Sol and Ruth's daughters as maids or servants. *"She certainly needs them,"* thought Phoebe, *"with the house being over-run with children!"*

Precious' oldest daughter Clairy helped Phoebe with her household chores. Sometimes, another daughter would come over, especially on wash day; her name was Suzy.

Everyone who was old enough had jobs. Even with all her children, Precious insisted on milking the cows herself, and taught each of her daughters to milk the cows, churn, and make butter. Someone always had to tend to the hogs as well. Pork was very important, not only for the meat, but the rendered lard of the animals was used for cooking and as an ingredient for making soap. Water wells had been dug at both locations, so water wasn't brought from the creek anymore.

There were orchards at both places. In the summertime, the fruits were gathered, peeled and sliced. The fruit was laid out on wide boards, a generous amount of sugar was poured over the fruits, and they were left to dry in the sun. Phoebe was convinced they made the best cakes and pies. All of the fruit trees they'd brought from North Carolina grew and prospered, except the apple. The cold climate just wasn't long enough for them to produce. The peaches, figs, and blueberries did very well, though, as did the watermelons.

Holes about three feet deep, six feet long and six feet wide were dug in the earth and a low shelter was built over them. A small door was built on one end. The indentions were filled with sweet potatoes when they were harvested in the late summer. The potatoes were covered with straw to prevent them from freezing or getting frostbite during the cold winter months.

The few chickens they had brought from North Carolina had multiplied into flocks, thus they supplied plenty of eggs and meat in both homes.

Another delicacy was the sugar cane syrup. Sugar cane was harvested before the first frost. The stalks of sugar cane were fed one at a time into a metal cane squeezer. The cane mill was attached firmly to a wide, stable post. The mill had a long pole attached to it. A mule was then hitched to the pole, and he would walk around and around the mill, squeezing the cane juice into a vat. The metal vats were heated by a fire beneath them, and the heat would cause the cane juice to thicken and turn into syrup. It took a craftsman to know how much heat to apply to the vats, and Tricademus was the "know how" man. The syrup was poured into clay jugs and stored away. Some of it was brought inside and stored in the pantries, along with the barrels of flour, corn meal, and other foods.

After the first frost, it was hog killing time. Everyone on the place pitched in and contributed to this event. Usually, six fat hogs were slaughtered. The bellies, front and back hams were salted and smoked over a slow burning fire in the smoke house, to cure the meat. No part of the hogs was thrown away. The entrails, including the liver, heart, and intestines were eaten. The intestines were turned inside out and thoroughly cleaned. They were cut into pieces and fried. All the scrap fatty meats were thrown into black pots with fire burning under them. The heat brought the fat, or lard, out and the lard was used to cook with throughout the year. It, too, was poured into clay containers and stored in the pantries.

Since the size of Tricademus and Precious' family was much larger, they got the proceeds of four hogs. Precious had her own pantry, and there was no doling out or controlling of food. Everyone was trusted to consume only what they needed.

Vegetables of all sorts were grown on the property, and most of them were preserved by drying, except for the early greens and potatoes. Of course, an abundance of corn was planted, not only for both families to consume, but the growing number of animals. It was the cotton that was king, however, because it was the cash crop. It was the proceeds from sale of the cotton that increased Henry's coffers, which he kept hidden in the bottom of a hollowed limestone block in the hearth of his home.

Over the years, Phoebe and Precious developed a bond that couldn't be broken, as did Tricademus and Henry. If Tric wanted to take a day off work and go fishing or hunting, nothing was said.

A grist mill had opened on Burnt Corn Creek. It sure made things easier for the locals. Usually, it would be Will that would drop the corn off, then go back the next day to pick up the milled or "hominy" grits.

The winter months were used for hunting and visiting, as there wasn't much work going on in the fields.

It was against the law for a black person to own or carry a firearm. Tric and his boys didn't seem to mind, though, for they still enjoyed going with Henry and his two sons, especially at night. That's when they killed possums and racoons. Phoebe refused to cook the two animals, but Tricademus and his family considered them to be a delicacy. Deer, squirrel, turkey, and rabbits were plentiful along the creek.

Phoebe still preferred to cook chicken instead of the wild meat. She had to admit, however, after tasting some of Clary's squirrel stew, that it was very flavorful.

Phoebe had gone with her husband to Sparta and Claiborne on several occasions. Henry and James began a tradition in 1840 that would last for years. They began to meet at Claiborne for Christmas shopping. Usually, only the youngest children would accompany them. In Henry and Phoebe's case, it was Phoebe Alabama. With James and Mary, it was Robert, Samuel, and Eliza.

Christmas gifts were bought, along with shoes, including shoes or boots for Tricademus, Precious, and their brood. Precious would put each person's right foot on a piece of paper and draw an outline around the foot. That's how the salesperson would determine the sizes. Coats were also purchased, and the sizes had to be written down for those. Luckily, both Precious and Phoebe were good seamstresses, thus most of their clothes were sewn at home.

Both families would leave their homes early on shopping day, and they'd always meet up at a café called Emily's Lunch and Brunch. Phoebe loved it there. The place had big glass windows that faced the river, and she could see the hustle and bustle of the docks.

The town had really grown since Henry and James had first gone there. There were boarding houses, mercantile businesses, grocery stores, and other businesses everywhere. There was a good, packed road in the town also.

A jewelry store had opened, and both Phoebe and Mary were surprised when, directly after lunch, their husbands took them there.

Phoebe had no idea how many gold coins Henry had brought with him, but she was shocked when she saw the bulging purse he pulled from his coat pocket.

The ladies didn't know which piece of jewelry to pick. Their husbands finally made the decisions for them. Henry chose a pair of diamond earbobs for Phoebe, while James chose pearl earbobs for Mary.

Phoebe whispered, "Honey, are you sure?" to Henry, as he gave the jeweler two twenty dollar-gold pieces.

Henry pretended he didn't hear her as he paid the smiling man, for he knew the jeweler was eager to wait on James and Mary next.

Phoebe twisted her diamond earbobs onto her earlobes, as James paid for Mary's Christmas gift.

After leaving the jeweler's, they continued with their shopping. Phoebe couldn't help but notice the difference in little Phoebe's behavior and that of Mary's children. Mary was constantly scolding them for their rowdy behavior. James even swatted Robert once for socking little Samuel in the face, and Eliza had a habit of sticking her tongue out at perfect strangers. Phoebe tried to ignore the children's behavior, thinking it was probably because they came from such a large brood.

Shoes, boots, coats, woolens, materials, and different colors of threads were bought that day. Their last stops were at the candy store and the fruit stand. An abundant quantity of oranges, apples, and raisins were bought by both families. The raisins were dried and still on the vines.

After their shopping and squeezing everything into the back of their carriages, the ladies hugged necks, while James and Henry did their ritual back slapping. They each knew they had to hurry in order to get home before dark.

James had squeezed the two boys into the back of the carriage along with the Christmas items. Phoebe had figured James had made a mistake allowing the children to ride there. Sure enough, before they left, Samuel had bit into an orange, without peeling it, then had thrown the fruit at their horses, startling them. Thus, they left Claiborne in a hurry.

Little Phoebe was squeezed between her mother and father. As they headed out of Claiborne, Phoebe felt a cold wind blowing across the yellow Alabama River, so she picked up her daughter, put her in her lap, then put her arms around her. "We're going to stay warm on the way home, aren't we, angel?" Phoebe asked her quiet, contented daughter.

Henry looked over at his wife and said, "Lord, we're lucky with our children."

Chapter Eleven

Much planning and patience had gone into building Henry and Phoebe's new house. Phoebe had walked across the road several times to look at the progress of the building. She had to admit that the place was beautiful. She had never seen a house with the same architecture.

The place had two gables, with a wide porch between the two gables. It had two stories. The kitchen was planned around a newly dug water well, thus there wasn't any more walking out into all kinds of weather to draw water.

The house sat east to west. Therefore, they could sit on the long back porch in the morning hours for shade, and on the front porch in the afternoons.

The double doors in front opened to a wide foyer that led to a spacious living room in the back. To the right of the foyer were two bedrooms, complete with bath closets and clothes closets. To the left of the big living area was the formal dining room, then the kitchen in the rear. A door opened to the outside from the kitchen and the big living room, resulting in the rear of the house having two back doors.

Few people knew it, but a cellar had been built directly under Henry and Phoebe's bedroom. A rug was pulled over the door to the underground room.

All of the long, wide windows of the house had glass windowpanes, along with vented shutters. The shutters could be fastened to the side of the house or pulled in and latched during bad weather.

To the left of the foyer was a wide staircase, with mahogany spindles and rail. Upstairs were four more bedrooms. They, too were complete with bath closets and clothes closets. Will and James were to sleep on the left, then Clary and Suzie on the right. The four bedrooms upstairs were separated by a wall that ran to the back of the house. The front of the second story had a door that opened to the balcony. Henry informed Phoebe that Clary and Suzy would become full time house servants and cooks. Ramona, another one of Tricademus and Precious' daughters, would be the wash woman.

"What am I to do?" asked Phoebe.

"You've been my wife for twenty years and have worked yourself to the bone, so you can plan the meals and see to everything," Henry told her.

Little Phoebe would occupy the front bedroom, while Henry and Phoebe would occupy the rear one.

Henry was usually frugal with his money, but when it came to Phoebe and the house, money wasn't an object.

Very few things were brought from the old house to the new one. Henry had ordered new furniture from Mobile, including a new piano, with sheet music. The piano, as was all the furniture, was painstakingly brought overland from Claiborne. When everything finally arrived, the piano was placed in the living room, along with the new divan and other new parlor furniture.

"Lord have mercy!" Phoebe exclaimed when she first saw the piano, "It's been so many years since I played, my fingers are stiff."

"Aw, you'll catch on, then you can teach little Phoebe," Henry told her, then swatted her on the behind, making sure no one was looking.

A long, curved lane led up to the house from the road. Magnolia trees had been planted on each side of the lane, so, sticking with tradition, Phoebe christened the new house "Magnolia."

Phoebe couldn't explain her feelings toward the new house. *"It's a mansion,"* she thought. *"Am I worthy of such a place with all its splendor?"* she wondered. She felt better about it, though, when Henry told her that James and Mary were building a new house, too.

Several things took place in 1844. A postal service was started, although they had to take their letters to Sparta or Claiborne.

Monroe County had changed its county seat from Claiborne to Monroeville. The little town had sprung from just a crossroads. The "Yellow Jack" fever had struck in Claiborne, plus Monroeville was the center of the county. Claiborne continued to be a thriving town, however, primarily because of the steamboat business. Local farmers shipped their cotton and other farm goods from there. Money was being made from the cotton. Some of it was being shipped to England, and not just to the northern United States. The steamboats would take it to Mobile, then it was loaded onto schooners. Most big everyday items, like flour, salt, sugar, whisky, and other household goods, were bought in Claiborne. Stores located in the north of the counties sold the same items, but they were at a higher price, due to the cost of freight.

The biggest change for their immediate area was that the Reverend Alexander Travis had begun preaching at the big two-story Baptist church in Belleville. Now they had a real church to attend. It had stairs on the outside that led up to the gallery and sure enough, Precious and her family sat on the front row. Tricademus was so big that he had to sit on a bench in the corner that had plenty of leg room.

Henry had always made it a rule that only household chores were performed on Sundays. He had also made a rule that he'd never sell or buy a black person, not knowing at the time that it would be a rule that he would be later forced to retract. He'd told Phoebe that if the resources he already possessed proved insufficient, then they'd just have to get by another way. He was making money, and plenty of it, with the help of Tricademus and his eight sons. Of course, Will and James worked just as long and hard in the fields, and Henry did, too, especially during cotton picking time.

Precious asked Phoebe if she and her family could move into the house that she and Henry had moved out of. The reason she cited was that after the Smiths had moved out, Precious and her family were just so isolated. "Eber since y'all moved out, we don't heah a thangs. Sides, our little house is so narrow and dem chillum hab done gots so big," Precious had said. Of course, Phoebe told Precious it would be fine with her, but she'd have to speak to her husband first. Henry agreed, and it took three afternoons of moving before Precious and her family were completely moved in.

It wasn't long after the move that Phoebe noticed welts and bruises on Ramona's legs when she came over one morning to help with the washing. Henry had built a wash house in the back yard, so clothes could be washed in bad weather. Ramona had come inside the house to get the soiled clothes. When Phoebe had asked Ramona about her injuries, the girl looked down at the floor and said, "That's where Muh whooped me."

Phoebe gently took Ramona by one of her arms and asked why her mother had whipped her.

83

"Well, it be's lack dis, when wese libed in de ole place, de woods, dey grows up putty close to de house. Since us's moved dare ain't no place to meet my boyfriend."

Phoebe saw where the conversation was going, and not wanting little Phoebe to hear it, she led Ramona onto the back porch.

"So, you have a boyfriend?" asked Phoebe.

"Yessum, his name be Rum, he libes up de road, he be Massah Hixon's boy. Muh , she say eyes gwine hab a baby," Ramona replied.

"Have a baby?" asked Phoebe.

"Yessum, Doddy, he say he gwine talks to Massah Smith today and if he won't buy him so's we can jump de broom, he's gwine kill Rum. I loves Rum!" Ramona cried.

"Well, I reckon you do. I'll speak with my husband about it," Phoebe told her.

"I don't want fuh Doddy to kills Rum, I loves him," repeated Ramona.

"Now hush your crying and go about your work; I'll see what I can do," Phoebe told the frightened girl.

"Yessum, but while eyes a talking, youse may as well know, Jasper, he in loves wit Rum's sister. He be wanting to jump de broom wit her too. Her name be's Cilla," Ramona added.

"My goodness, what next?" asked Phoebe as she turned and went back into the house.

The day was still young. Clary and Suzy were in the kitchen preparing dinner, for Phoebe observed they'd already tidied up the downstairs. Little Phoebe was lying on the floor reading a children's book.

"Poor Precious," thought Phoebe. She thought of little Phoebe. *What if she was in Precious' predicament?"* she sighed.

She knew all the menfolks were behind the house somewhere, clearing new land. She also knew she'd see Henry when he and the boys came in for their noon meal.

Phoebe thought of something Brother Travis had thrown in during last Sunday's sermon. "Try as you might, nothing stays the same except The Holy Scriptures. People shouldn't be so set in their ways; you must be willing to change with the times. Don't be like the mighty oak, hard and proud; be more like the weeping willow. The mighty oak will be stubborn when high winds come along and will topple over, while the willow will bend with the winds. It'll live to experience another day," the preacher had said.

Phoebe went upstairs and went out on the balcony, gazing toward Precious and Tricademus' house. She thought if she saw Precious on the outside, she'd go to her. Phoebe put her hands above her eyes to block out the early morning sun, but she didn't see a soul stirring in the yard. She thought she'd wait until she talked to Henry, then she'd know more what to tell Precious.

By now, it was late February of 1845. A stiff, cool breeze blew across the yard, so Phoebe pulled her shawl tightly around her shoulders. She enjoyed the quietness of the morning, though, so she chose to just sit there a while.

Before long, she began to reflect on the past. She thought back to their first night in the old house. The first time that Henry saw her naked, she put her hand over her mouth as she smiled. *"How young I was, and what a nerve I had, leaving the only life I knew to embark on such a strange land, but it turned out all right,"* she thought.

Phoebe thought of her children and of Henry. She was proud to be known as Mrs. Henry Smith. She considered her figure and was glad that she had maintained it. She saw lots of ladies, especially at church, who seemed to just let themselves go. The dress styles were ridiculous, with all those hoops and underskirtings. Phoebe could tell that most of the ladies wore tight corsets. Some of them nearly pushed their bosoms out of their dresses. *"How miserable they must be!"* thought Phoebe.

It was true that her waist was a few inches bigger than what it had been when she was first married. She wore one underskirt beneath her dress, just to keep her dress from dragging the floor. Henry seemed to like the way she dressed, and that's what mattered to her. Instead of wearing perfume, she rinsed all her clothes with crushed lemon leaves. The small lemon trees grew wild on their property. Other ladies had commented about the aroma she always projected, but she never revealed her secret. She just smiled and thanked them.

Her reminiscing suddenly came to an end when a cold gust of wind hit her in the face.

"Brr!" Phoebe said to herself. She then peered one more time toward Precious' house, but all she saw was gray smoke coming from the chimney.

Unconsciously, she mentally strapped the burdens of her life back onto her shoulders and walked back into the house, where it was warmer. Without realizing it, even though she had lived in the mansion only a short time, it had become her cocoon, her safe place.

After she had made her way back downstairs, she asked little Phoebe if she wanted to practice on the piano, and the girl readily agreed. Phoebe was teaching her daughter shape notes for the piano. She noticed the size of her daughter's hands, and how they had grown. *"She certainly has the Smith hands,"* thought Phoebe. In a way, she dreaded her children getting older. It was hard for her to believe that her daughter would be eleven years old on her next birthday.

James would be sixteen, and William, who was already liking a girl in church, was nineteen already. Both boys were excellent horsemen, and each had their own horse. Just the other day, Phoebe and Henry had sat on the balcony and watched as each of the boys would run beside their horse, then jump into the saddle as the horse was in full gallop. Also, they were so agile they could ride past something, then reach down and pick it up with the horse in full gallop.

"Who taught them all that?" Phoebe had asked her husband.

"I don't know," Henry had replied, "But they both are excellent marksmen, too."

It was strange to Phoebe that she'd think of that as she watched her daughter struggle with the piano. She then thought that it was a good thing, for it took her mind off Precious and Tricademus' dilemma.

As her daughter practiced "Mary Had a Little Lamb," Phoebe could hear the two servant girls as they walked from the kitchen to the dining room with the day's dinner.

There were three eating tables in the house. The long dining room table, with its candelabra centerpiece, was used when Brother Travis and members of the church ate with them. There was also a small table in the corner of the dining room where the family dined during the summer months to escape the heat from the kitchen. Phoebe's favorite one, though, was the table in the kitchen. The family ate there during the cold winter months. When the family had their meals in the kitchen, Clary and Suzy didn't have to tote the food so far.

In a few minutes, Phoebe heard voices outside. She went quickly to the back door and looked out. She saw that Ramona was almost finished hanging the clothes on the clothesline. She then saw her husband Henry and the boys as they stomped their boots on the ground, then again on the back doorsteps as they prepared to enter the house.

Phoebe went back to her daughter at the piano, and after running her fingers through the girl's golden locks, she told her to wash her hands for dinner.

Henry led the boys into the house. Phoebe was still standing near the piano. The boys headed straight toward the dining room, while Henry came over and kissed his wife on the cheek.

"I need to talk to you after dinner," he told his wife.

Henry looked so serious, Phoebe knew then that Tricademus must have told him about Ramona and Jasper.

"Sure, baby," Phoebe said, as she grabbed her husband's left hand and squeezed it.

They had fried chicken, dried green beans, collard greens, cornbread, and for dessert, the servant girls had cooked a marble cake. It was all washed down with cold milk that had been stored in the well.

Phoebe could tell from her sons' demeanor that they didn't know a thing about what had transpired. She knew that Henry was likely aware of it, though, for he barely touched his meal. He also wasn't his usual jovial self with their daughter.

Will and James were the first to push their plates back on the table, saying they'd had enough. As usual, little Phoebe just nibbled at her food and shoved it around on her plate. She always waited on her brothers to say the magic words asking to be excused from the table, before she, too, pushed her plate back.

The three young people went to the kitchen door and each of them complimented Clary and Suzy on the meal, as usual. Will and James made their way to the back door, while little Phoebe went to her room, leaving Henry and his wife alone. Henry looked toward the kitchen where the servant girls were cleaning up from the meal, then told Phoebe he needed to talk to her in private, so they wound up in their bedroom.

Once there, he told Phoebe about the same thing that Ramona had already confided in her, but she never let on that she knew a thing about it.

"I'm forced to go against a promise I've made. I'm going this afternoon and talk to Richard Hixon about buying two of his people," Henry said.

"It's the only thing we can do," Phoebe agreed, she then said, "Precious. I must go to her."

"Well, of course, you can do as you like, but I've yet to talk to Mr. Hixon," Henry said.

"I know. Under the circumstances it's the only thing we can do," Phoebe repeated.

After their dinner had settled, Tricademus and his eight sons tromped through the back yard and re-hitched the oxen. After Henry gave them his orders, he went back into his bedroom and made his way to the bath closet, while Phoebe waited for him.

When Henry came out of the bedroom, he was wearing a pair of his black trousers, a white shirt, a long green coat and a green cravat.

"My goodness, you look nice," Phoebe said.

"Thank you, but I couldn't go there wearing soiled clothes I had on earlier," Henry replied.

"That's probably about the same that Richard will be wearing," Phoebe said. She then asked Henry if he'd drop her off at Precious' house.

"Well, I was planning on just riding my horse to Richard's, but I can hitch up the carriage instead," Henry agreed.

"I can just walk back," Phoebe said.

Precious must have heard the carriage, for about the time Phoebe was to knock on the door, Precious opened it.

The two women hugged while standing in the doorway.

"Come set yoself by the fire," Precious told her, as entered the room.

"My, you have things looking good, everything is so clean," Phoebe told her.

"Well, dem boys, dey sleeps upstairs, foe to the room. Me and Tric, wese sleeps in de baidroom in de back. Judy and Ramona, deys de only ones dat sleeps in heah, so's it stays putty clean," Precious replied.

Phoebe decided to get straight to the problem.

"My husband has gone to see Mr. Hixon about buying Rum and a girl named Cilla," Phoebe said.

"Lawd have musy, dat Ramona, she musta tole you!" Precious exclaimed.

"Yes, she told me, and I saw the welts and bruises," Phoebe told her.

"Lawdy, Lawdy. If sumpkin aint done, I'm skeered Tricademus gwine kill dat Rum. He strapped Jasper good las' night, too. He tole Jasper dat Ramona had seed him and dat guhl, so she figured she could do de same thang," Precious told Phoebe.

90

"Our children, they've grown up right before our eyes," Phoebe said, as she took hold of one of Precious' hands.

"What's us's gwine do wit a baby? Dis place is full already," Precious fretted.

"I was thinking, if my husband can buy Rum and Cilla, they all can move into y'all's old place. Maybe another room can be added to it," Phoebe suggested.

"Lawd, I pray that he can buy dem," Precious said.

"Precious, just think, you and Tricademus are going to be *grandparents*," Phoebe told her.

Precious stopped dabbing her eyes, and a wide grin came across her face.

Chapter Twelve

By 1850, not only had Henry bought Rum and Cilla, but the remainder of Tricademus and Precious' boys had "jumped the broom," meaning that they had officially chosen their designated life partners. Henry had increased his holdings to twelve hundred acres of land and 27 blacks, including the four grandchildren of Tric and Precious. All of the children were married except Clary, Suzy, and Judy.

Phoebe had thought that Judy would have probably also "jumped the broom" with someone, but the girl stayed close to Precious. Henry never expected Judy to work for his family; he'd told Phoebe that Precious needed the girl to help her mother with her own household work.

Several cabins were built near Burnt Corn Creek to accommodate everyone.

Suzy and Clary visited their folks whenever they wanted to, usually on Sunday afternoons. They'd have the best time, too. If they were on the outside, Henry and Phoebe could hear them laughing.

Henry was so glad that everything ran with peace and harmony, and he felt like Tricademus saw to that.

With so many people living on his place, in order to feed and clothe everyone, more and more land had to be bought, and the crops had to be increased. Not only edible crops, but of course cotton. Henry was making big money with the cotton, but he had also spent it, buying more land, people, and animals. He now owned twelve mules, seven milk cows and over a hundred hogs, along with a multitude of chickens and turkeys. They all practically lived off the land. Very little was bought except for flour, sugar, coffee, and household items, such as lye, vinegar, and barrels of salt. Salt was a necessity, not only for seasoning, but for curing meats. Lye was used for cleansing, including making soap.

Henry had given Precious the job of doling out the cooking and household items. She kept things locked in a barn behind her house.

Tricademus was getting a little age on him, and Henry was beginning to notice that, even with his tremendous strength, he wasn't as fast and agile as he had been. As a result, Henry made him the overseer of his sons and in-laws.

"Now, Tricademus, overseers have to wear clean clothes each day, and you should just stay in the saddle. Try to find shade somewhere. I'm going to stick closer to the house and pay more attention to the books. It's a big responsibility for you," Henry told him.

"Yes sir, I'll tell Precious about de clothes, and I knows what to do," Tricademus assured him.

Henry still stayed aware of all the goings-on, though, even if it was through the books. Will and James also kept an eye on things, unknowingly to Tricademus, when their father wasn't around.

Some of Henry's older land was lying fallow, as the minerals in the soil had been used up, for cotton really took a toll on the soil. New land was constantly being cleared and planted. Manure from the animals was used for the gardens to fertilize the crops, for food was a dire necessity.

The summer of 1850 turned out to be a bumper crop for cotton, and two of Henry's fields didn't disappoint him; they were loaded with the white fluffs.

Henry had to weigh the cotton as it was picked in order to determine when he had a bale, so that year he had an idea. He told everyone they were going to have a race. Whoever picked the most cotton would get a prize. The ladies would get enough cloth to make them a new Sunday dress and the men would get an extra pint of syrup at the end of the week.

When Henry had bought Cilla from Richard Hixon, the former owner had told Henry that Cilla was a good cotton picker. Even with a young baby, that Precious was baby-sitting, and having to run to Precious' house a couple of times to nurse the baby, Cilla led the pack. By quitting time on Saturday afternoon, Cilla had picked 2,215 pounds of cotton. Ralph, Tricademus and Precious' youngest son had picked 2,422 pounds.

"Go to Precious and she'll give you two your rewards, and the same thing will be for next week," Henry told his workers.

Poor Jasper, who was big like his daddy, had managed to pick 1,200 pounds, and everyone laughed at him, although they managed to keep their distance.

"Don't make fun of Jasper or he'll womp you; he did very well considering his height and weight," Henry told them.

Henry, Will, James, and Tricademus took 26 bales of cotton to Claiborne that week, each bale weighing 1,200 pounds. Each pound brought eight cents. Henry tallied things in his head, and unless something went awry, he already had enough money to last another year. *"The rest will mean clear profit,"* he thought.

Henry met his brother James in Claiborne that day, and since he wanted time to visit with James, he sent the others on home before him.

James told him that he, too, was having a bumper crop of cotton. He then proudly informed Henry that his oldest son William was in Philadelphia, studying to be a doctor.

"Just think, we'll have a doctor in Snow Hill!" Henry exclaimed.

"Yep, that's his goal, and my son John, he's married to a girl that Mary is crazy about. Her name is Mary also," James said.

"Well, my William is still courting Tom Jones' girl. Her name is Frances, and we just love her. Phoebe and I look for them to marry pretty soon. I don't think my William has the aspirations that yours does. He's a hard worker on the farm, but every spare minute, he has his nose stuck in a book. Now James, he likes all the girls, and they like him. He has the makings of a darn good farmer," Henry told his brother, as they waited in line with their wagons loaded with cotton.

"What about your daughter, Phoebe Alabama?" James asked.

"Lord, Phoebe has tried her best to spoil that gal, but her brothers have taught her to ride as well as any man. When she's done with riding, she'll come inside and play the piano. If you didn't see her playing it, you'd swear you were at a concert," William told his brother.

James laughed, "I'll bet she's a beauty, too," James said.

"Naturally, I think so. Of course, the only social life we have is at church; she and her mother take turns playing the piano there. I've seen some old boys flirting, but so far, she hasn't asked any of them over," Henry said. He then asked James about his other children.

"Well, I've told you about William and John. All the others are still at home except Janie; she's moved in with

John and his wife. She said it was too noisy at the house. Of course, they just live right down the road," James said. He then added, "John keeps books and clerks at Mr. Purifoy's store, and of course, he farms a little too."

Henry was ahead of James in the line, so James walked back to his front wagon, telling Henry he would see them at Christmas time.

Letters were infrequent, to say the least. What few letters they received came to them at Sparta, and occasionally one would come to the post office in Claiborne. Henry decided to check while he was there, and sure enough, his hunch was right. The postmaster handed him a letter, and it was from his Uncle Jesse.

Henry waited until he was back outside and in his wagon before he opened it and read it.

Dear Henry and James,

It is with sorrow that I write you boys this letter. The typhoid fever hit here and took both your mother's and Edmond's life. His daughter cared for both of them but she never caught it. They willed what they had to her. I saw to it that your mother was buried beside y'all's father.

All three of our children have moved to Sumpter County, Alabama. We've decided to sell what we have and move in with or near to our son Ezekiel. Our daughters live down the road from Ezekiel, in Kemper County, Mississippi. I'm still in fair health, but we want to be near our children and grandchildren.

I'm proud of you two.
Love, Jesse Smith

Henry said a prayer, the gentle face of his mother flashing before his eyes. Then he went to find James, who was still in line with his wagons.

"May God bless her soul! She was a good mama," James said after he read the letter. He continued, "It pleases me that she was a Godly woman, so we know where she'll be going." James stared into space for a bit, then said, "It shocks me about Uncle Jesse, though. James continued, "I would have never thought he would leave North Carolina. Just think, he's probably in Alabama by now."

"We're getting old, brother," James remarked. "Ezekiel was born after we left from up there, and just think, he's migrated to Alabama too."

"I know; I wish we could go visit him sometimes, but finding the time is my problem," Henry said.

"Tell me about it! There's always something to do," James agreed.

The two brothers soon hugged, and parted ways.

The long miles ahead of him were filled with sorrow, and Henry wished he hadn't told the others to go ahead of him. He was glad that their Uncle Jesse had buried their mother beside their father. The letter broke all ties with North Carolina, though, and Henry felt a bond with Alabama, even more so than he had ever felt. He knew once and for all that he had made the right decision about moving to Alabama. *"My next move will be to my Heavenly home, and I'll see my mother there. Shoot, I'll even get to see the father that I never knew,"* he thought, and he found some comfort, thinking of that.

Henry also thought that he was glad that he had given Tricademus the gold coins from the sale of the cotton. He felt if there were roadside bandits, they'd never expect Tric to have the money.

The overseer must have been keeping a close eye out for his boss, for Henry barely had time to pull the wagon into the barn before Tric came inside.

"Heah's yo sack of money, Massuh Henry, I kepts it up front covered up with a burlap sack, jist lack you said. I sho was nuvous dough," Tric said.

"So, everyone made it in okay?" Henry asked.

"Yassuh, we'se alright, deys all gone home," the man answered.

"Good, go on home yourself now, Tric. No work tomorrow; I'll see you in church," Henry said, as Tricademus handed him the heavy bag of gold and silver coins.

"Yassuh, Precious, she done tole me we'se gwinna hab fried chicken fuh dunner tomorrow," Tric said, then he turned to leave.

"Tricademus?" Henry said.

"Yassuh?" Tric. answered, as he turned around.

"You remember my mother, don't you?" Henry asked.

"Yassuh, I members huh, she lookted lack young missy," Tric said.

"You know my daughter does favor her, doesn't she?"

"Yassuh, jist lack huh."

"Well, I received a letter in Claiborne; I'm sorry to tell you, she's passed away," Henry told his trusted friend.

It was the first time the two had ever touched, as far as Henry knew, but Tricademus put his huge left arm around Henry's shoulders.

"Eyes sho is sorry, Mr. Henry; she wuz a fine lady," Tric said, as he squeezed Henry's shoulder.

"Tric, I've never asked you this, but do you remember my father, by any chance?"

"Well, I was jist a lad of a boy, but yessuh, I members him," Tric answered, as he let go of Henry.

"What kind of fellow was he, and what did he look like?" Henry wanted to know.

"Lawd, I members all of dem peoples. Yo daddy, he wasn't hard lack yo grandpappy, he was mo quieter. He lookted lack you and Mr. James did when we'se comes to dis place," Tricademus replied.

"I see; thank you. And Tric, you've made a good overseer," Henry complimented, as he patted Tric on the back.

"Yassuh, thanky suh. Do you'se wants me to puts de mules up?"

"No, you get home to Precious, she'll be worried about you," Henry said.

"Yasuh, and eyes sorry bout yo mama," Tric said, then walked swiftly up the lane, toward his house.

After securing the mules and feeding them. Henry went into the house and showed Phoebe the letter.

Phoebe hugged her husband and said, "Honey, I'm sorry! she was a good woman. I know I shouldn't say this, but I know how you feel (for Phoebe's parents had died in a housefire, ten years prior.) She continued, "I must admit I felt guilty about leaving them, but after a while it wasn't too bad. You just trust in the Lord, my husband; he'll see you through," Phoebe suggested, as she hugged her husband even tighter.

At supper time, they told their children about the passing of their grandmother. Not knowing her, it was no big deal to them, but each one of them said they were sorry, and Phoebe Alabama hugged her father's neck.

"Well, I've often heard an idle mind is the devil's workshop, so I'm thankful we still have cotton to pick. It'll help keep my mind off my mother. Maybe," Henry said. He didn't tell them, though, that he still mourned about the passing of his father. *"And I can't even remember him,"* he thought.

They picked cotton for ten more days before they were finished. As Henry stacked the gold and silver coins with the rest of his stash in the cellar, he knew he'd made six thousand dollars that year.

He told Phoebe as he crawled into bed that night that they had $22,000 dollars hidden in the cellar.

Phoebe hadn't had any idea how much was down there. She asked Henry what he was planning on doing with so much money.

"Well, you never know what's up the road," was all he said.

The next week, they gathered all the corn, dug sweet potatoes, and stored them in their appropriate places. They had long since gathered the dried peas and beans, to eat during the cold winter months. By the first of September, the only things growing were the collard greens and the sugar cane.

It was unusual for a hurricane to blow out of the Gulf that late in the year, but it did. None of them had ever weathered such a storm. The winds were horrendous, not counting the lightning!

The eye of the storm must have blown right over them, for suddenly, after braving the strong winds out of the south for a full day, the winds stopped. It only lasted for a few minutes, though, then the winds started blowing from the north.

Henry had pulled the shutters in and latched them to protect the glass windowpanes.

No one was expected to work except for the cooks. Everyone else went to their rooms and listened to the howling winds outside.

The storm lasted from early morning throughout the night. It sounded as if the house might blow away with each strong gust of wind. Phoebe hardly slept a wink, even with the shutters closed, there were times when their bedroom would light up. Occasionally she could hear footsteps going up and down the stairs. Once, during a loud clap of thunder, she heard a scream which was undeniably Clary's.

How Henry slept through all the noise, Phoebe didn't know, but she crawled out of bed and lit the candle at her bedside table. She found Clary and Suzy crouched at the foot of the stairs.

"Girls, it's going to be alright," Phoebe said as she went to them, hugging each one of them.

"Lawd have mercy, Miss Phoebe, how long is dis stoam gwinna last?" Suzy cried.

"We must be getting close to the end of it. The winds started in the opposite direction hours ago, so quit your worrying," Phoebe reassured her. She then added, "If it'll make you feel better, put us on a pot of coffee. I could use a cup myself."

"Wese hab on our nightgowns! What ifs Mr. Henry comes inner de kitchen?" Suzy asked.

"He's not coming in here, unless you two wake him," Phoebe told them.

"Wese worried bout Pap, Maw, and de rest of dem, staying in dem little log cabins," Clary told her nervously.

"If the truth be known, those log cabins are put together better than this big place," Phoebe told them. She then walked softly over to Phoebe Alabama's room. After cracking the door and sticking the candle in the opening, she saw that her daughter was sleeping peacefully.

Phoebe then walked back into her bedroom to dress for the day, by candlelight. When she returned to the kitchen, the two girls took turns going up to their rooms and dressing.

Along about daylight, the winds seemed to decrease in their intensity, but it was still pouring down rain, when they heard a knock at the back door. After opening the door, Phoebe found it to be Tricademus, and of course, he was soaked with rain.

"Come in, Tricademus. My Lord how did you make it over here?" Phoebe asked.

"I'll get de flo soaking wet," Tricademus protested.

"Who cares? The girls can mop it up," Phoebe told him, for she was truly glad to see that he was all right.

The girls ran to their father, and even in his condition, he wrapped a wet arm around each of them, picking them off the floor.

Phoebe thought the sight was one of the most precious things she'd ever witnessed, and she dabbed at her eyes with her handkerchief, which she always kept tucked behind her belt.

She allowed them to have their moment. It wasn't long before Suzy pushed away from him, Clary soon followed.

"Ooo, Pap, you're soaking wet!" Clary exclaimed.

"Precious, how is she?" asked Phoebe.

"She be's alright. De fust of de night de winds blowed Ralph and Tensy's roof top off. Dey made it ober to de house doe, dey be's alrights too," Tricademus answered.

"What about the others?"

"Dey must be's alright I reckon, wese not hurd nuffin from dem. Precious, she sunt me ober heah to check on y'alls."

"We're fine, but I'm not sure how the house held up. I haven't seen any leaks, though," Phoebe told him.

"It be dauk out dare yet, but eyes didn't see anything, jist some limbs and thangs when I comes up de lane. I knows mostly deys a bunch of trees blowed down everwhere. Dem wuz some turrible winds dat comes through heah," Tricademus explained.

"We've witnessed hurricanes before, but nothing like this. I believe the center of it came right over us," Phoebe said. She then added, "I'm sorry, Tricademus, won't you have a cup of coffee before you go back outside and face this weather?"

"Well, maybe jist a sip, eyes needs to gits on back home, doe. Precious, she be worried bouts me ifs I aint back home soon," he answered.

Suzy ran to the kitchen, and soon she was back with a tin cup about half full of the black brew. Tricademus, by habit, blew on the coffee before he took a drink.

"Mr. Henry, and de chillun, dey be dosing awright?' he asked.

"Lord, I believe all four of them could sleep through a dynamite explosion in the very room they were in," Phoebe answered.

"Lawd, dey wouldn't sleeps round Precious, dat woman has nearly walked holes in de flo," Tric said, as he drank the last of the coffee in his cup.

Phoebe laughed, then said, "Well, you can go back and tell my friend that I'm just about as bad."

Tricademus smiled, then told his daughters he was glad they were all right. They came over to hug him again, but he pushed them way. "Y'alls is wet enough," he said. He then opened the door and left, muttering to himself.

Clary and Suzy sat at the table in the kitchen and drank coffee with their mistress until it began to get daylight. Phoebe talked of things that were funny, and surprisingly to her, they did too. They told Phoebe how scared they were when they first moved into the big house. "Wese wuz scairt dat we'd mess things up," Suzy said.

"Don't worry about that; I never had second thoughts about you girls," Phoebe told them. "In fact, if you like, after dinner each day, especially through the week, you can take turns. Before you start preparing supper you can take off for a couple of hours, go visit your folks are something," Phoebe told them.

"Miss Phoebe, you be so good to us," Clary said, and Suzy nodded her head.

It wasn't long before the girls put on another pot of coffee, and Suzy began to knead the biscuit dough, while Clary began to slice the bacon.

In about thirty minutes the boys came down the stairs; Henry was already in the kitchen. Phoebe had told him about Tricademus' visit.

"Well praise be to the Lord, we can always rebuild; maybe we'll come out of this unharmed," Henry said. He then walked to the kitchen window and cracked it enough to open the shutters so he could see outside. He called Phoebe to his side. "My goodness, what a mess! Just look at the trees down. The mules and the cow seem to be alright, and so do their stables. Have you seen any leaks in the house?" he asked.

"No, I've looked everywhere but the boys' rooms, and not a leak anywhere," Phoebe said.

"That's a blessing. We'll have to let this mess dry up, then we'll get Ralph and Tensy's cabin back in shape. Boy, am I proud we have everything in the fields gathered but the sugar cane; I hope it survived the winds," Henry said, as he slipped his arm around Phoebe's waist.

Together, they looked things over in the back of the house. He then said, "Go wake up sleeping beauty, and we'll open the other shutters."

It turned out that Ralph and Tensy's house had the worst damage. A few shingles were blown off some of the other buildings, but they were soon replaced. Ralph and his wife would live with Tricademus and Precious until their home was repaired.

The sugar cane sustained wind damage, but enough survived to make plenty of syrup.

Phoebe's magnolia trees had survived, but most of the leaves were beaten off or tattered, due to hail and strong winds.

It was during syrup-making time when William told them one Sunday night that Frances had set the date of their wedding date for December 14th.

"Gracious, we have a lot of planning to do!" Phoebe exclaimed.

Little Phoebe jumped from the table and hugged Will's neck. "I just love Frances! Finally, I'll have a sister," she said.

"Congratulations. I think you're marrying into a good family; you know that Tom and I are deacons together at the church," Henry told his son. James grinned and shook his brother's hand.

"It sure doesn't give us time to build y'all a house, but we'd better get started on it," Henry said.

"No need of that; we'll be moving into a small house on Mr. Jones' place. I'll be working for him, plus I'll be teaching school in Belleville. He's giving us eighty acres and the house for a wedding gift," William told them.

"Son, I don't think teachers make too much money, and who's going to work your land?" Henry asked.

"You'd be surprised how many children live in Belleville, and as you know, the parents of each student pay for them to go to school. Mr. Jones' men will work our property until I can afford to buy someone of my own," Will answered. Will continued, "Of course, I'm not too good to get behind a plough. Thank God you taught us pretty much everything there is to know about farming."

Henry was scared that Will was going to asked him for some of his people, but Henry had no intention of splitting up families.

"Of course, I'll be able to work on my place in the afternoons and Saturdays. It'll be slim to begin with, but we won't starve," William reassured them.

Phoebe looked at her husband with a pleading look in her eyes, and Henry had lived with her long enough to read her mind.

He cleared his throat and said, "Well, we're going to miss you around here, James will just have to pick up the slack. Your mama and I will give you two a wedding gift; it should be enough to give you a good start."

"Well, it will be appreciated," Will said.

"Son, you have earned it," Henry told his son.

"It'll sure seem strange around here with you gone," James mentioned.

Will laughed, "I've been putting Frances off for four years. Shoot, I'll soon turn twenty-six years old." He then continued, "I don't want to lose her to someone else."

It was only five o'clock, but William told them since he would soon be a man of his own, he believed he'd pay Frances a visit. "I've just got to tell her that I've told my family about things."

"Just be careful going over that bridge, it being dark," his father warned.

"Well, I guess that I can tell it now, but William has made many trips across that bridge at night," James laughed.

William socked James on his shoulder, then protested, "Big mouth."

Little Phoebe was the first one to laugh, and soon the others joined in, even James who was making an exaggerated rub on his shoulder.

"Tell me, how do you get back into the house, the doors being locked?" Henry asked.

"Simple: one day I got the key that hangs on the hat rack and made one identical to it at the blacksmith's shop located in the back yard,," Will confessed.

"Well, well, and I thought I knew everything going on around here!" Henry exclaimed, as he got up from the table. "You're still under my roof, so I guess I can say, 'Don't give Tom and his wife a bad impression. You come on in as soon as possible.'"

"I always do," Will laughed, then as he left the table, he hugged his mother and kissed her on the cheek.

Phoebe wanted to go sit on the balcony to contemplate things, but felt it was too chilly, so she joined her husband in their bedroom. Henry was sitting on the side of the bed pulling his boots off. Phoebe sat down beside him, and said, "Just think, we'll soon be grandparents."

Henry looked at her and asked, "Aren't you putting the cart before the horse?"

Phoebe laughed, then turned the covers back on the bed as he went into the bath closet. She remembered their stolen moments when they were courting, and how his Uncle Jesse didn't know about it, either. *"We sure couldn't do much, walking home from church,"* she smiled to herself, while she waited her turn in the bath closet.

Chapter Thirteen

December 14th was on a Saturday. Will already had a new suit, but Henry insisted on buying him another one, just for the wedding. Will was right about the little crossroad community. Belleville had grown into quite a little town. There were numerous big homes, built with lumber, too, instead of logs. Of course, many of the older homes were made from logs. Two general stores were in competition with each other, and sold not only groceries, but also dry goods. Ivey's dry goods store is where Henry bought Will's new suit.

Henry noted the price of several staple things that he bought in Claiborne, and he had to admit, they weren't too much higher in price in Belleville. Phoebe (who had no idea what the prices of things were) bought a few things.

It was a week before the wedding was to take place. Tom Jones and his wife Emma had sent the Smiths a formal invitation for a visit to their house, and William and Little Phoebe planned to accompany them on that day. Henry had been to their house before, due to church business. To Phoebe and little Phoebe, it was a big thing, for they seldom left their own house. Of course, they weren't completely reclusive. Once or twice a year they would go with Henry to Sparta, but it was usually on a business trip. They always went straight through the intersection at Belle, though, and never stopped. The places of business were to the right, and the church was on the left.

Henry had told Phoebe the night before that the Joneses lived in a nice house. "But nothing compared to Magnolia," he had said, goosing Phoebe in her ribs and making her jump. Phoebe didn't know what to expect, but it really didn't matter to her what kind of house Emma's parents lived in. *"Just so it's clean,"* she thought. She loved Magnolia but had always thought her husband had the thing built just for show; she had been just as happy living in the house where Precious and Tric now lived.

As it turned out, the Joneses lived about a mile south of Belleville. While they were still on the main road, William pulled up in front of a long skinny building and stopped.

"This is Belleville Academy, where I'll be teaching," he said.

"Can we go in and look?" Little Phoebe asked.

"Sure, I have the key. Come on," he agreed, as he dismounted his horse and tied the reins to a post.

Henry tied the reins of the carriage to the buggy itself, then helped the two Phoebes from the carriage.

All three of them remarked how clean the place was. "I'm amazed at how many benches and chairs are in here! Wouldn't it be wonderful if you could fill the place up?" Phoebe hinted, making it clear how much she hoped for grandchildren.

"That's my prayer," William said.

"I don't see a fireplace. How are the children going to stay warm?" Little Phoebe asked.

William walked over to the cast iron heater and thumped it. "Instead of a fireplace, you put wood into this. It puts out lots more heat than a fireplace, and you can cook on it, too."

"Henry Smith, I want one in the big parlor, and a smaller one in the kitchen, so the girls can cook on top of it," Phoebe informed her husband.

"Honey, your wish is my command," Henry said. "But personally, I think they're unsightly things. You have to cut a hole in the ceiling or wall, so the smoke can go out through the flue," Henry said.

"Oh, well, whatever you think, dear," Phoebe told him.

After looking at the school, they continued on their trip. William finally turned to the right down a well-maintained lane. After going about fifty yards, he stopped again. "This will be our house," he said, as he pointed to a small, whitewashed building to the right. The little house stood far enough from the road to have a nice yard.

"It was built for Frances' aunt, but she decided she'd rather move back into the big house with the Joneses. The land on each side and behind it is the eighty acres. My name will be on the deed after we're married," William told them.

"I'd love to go inside, but we'll wait until Frances can show us," Phoebe told her son.

"Okay, Mother, whatever you like," William agreed, so they continued down the curved lane.

Phoebe had to admit that she was anxious to see Emma's house. Just when it seemed the road was endless, the house finally came into view.

"Oh, I love it, and it's so logical. Look at that wide front porch that runs the entire length of the house! Boy, I'll bet you can catch a breeze there," Phoebe exclaimed.

"Well, I love the gazebo, with the red roses running up the trellis. I'd be willing to bet ol' William has sat under that thing many times," Little Phoebe laughed.

They were met on the outside by an elderly black man who was wearing black trousers, a long red coat, and a black top hat. The old fellow bowed after tipping his hat. "Eyes is to take yo hoss to de shed," he told them.

After Henry helped his wife and daughter from the carriage, Frances came running down the doorsteps, holding up her swaying hoop dress.

"Finally, y'all have come for a visit!" she said happily, as she bowed to Henry, then kissed both Phoebes on the cheek.

"Well, my goodness, where is *my* kiss?" William demanded, as he slid his arm around his fiancée.

"Oh my, you'll get yours when you place that ring on my finger next week," she said, but kissed William on the cheek anyway. Grabbing the Phoebes by the hand, she led them to the wide doorsteps.

"Mama and Daddy, especially Mama, are so nervous about y'all's visit, and I hope you're prepared for brunch. Mama has had all sorts of things prepared," Frances said.

"Oh, that wasn't necessary," Phoebe replied.

"What you're about to see…don't think we live like this every day. Mama just went out of her way to make a good impression," Frances whispered.

A house servant opened the door, and they all entered, one at a time. Emma Jones hugged both Phoebe and her daughter, while she bowed to Henry. Tom kissed both ladies on the hand and shook Henry's hand.

"We are absolutely thrilled to have y'all as guests," Emma said.

"We're glad to be here," Phoebe answered.

"Well, let's be seated, while Nervy and Lena bring out the refreshments," instructed.

Phoebe noticed that the large living room had more places to sit than they had at Magnolia. There were four rocking chairs and two settees, and two large chandeliers hung from the ceiling. Portraits and large paintings were hanging everywhere.

Emma, Phoebe Alabama, and Frances were wearing the fashionable hoop skirts, but Phoebe wasn't; she'd rather stay comfortable. It was clear that William's future mother-in-law had made a special effort on her appearance; she even thought she detected a hint of rouge on the woman's cheeks.

The two black servants soon arrived with trays of peeled fruits, crackers with cheese on top, and thin slices of caramel cake.

Phoebe could tell the two girls were nervous, for you could actually hear the porcelain dishes and cups clattering as they brought them into the room. Everything was set on a tall mahogany table with ornate carvings.

"We have hot tea or coffee; let's all get a snack and then we'll talk," Emma said.

William had to put his hand over his mouth to keep from laughing, for he'd never seen such "put-ons" in his life from his future mother-in-law. A quick elbow in his ribs from Frances straightened him up, though.

Just to be sociable, Phoebe put two slices of peaches, a slice of apple, and a cracker with cheese onto her dainty dish. After she was seated, one of the servants poured her about a half cup of black coffee. She noticed that everyone else piled their saucer with the refreshments.

"Well, what do you think about our children getting married?" Emma asked Phoebe.

"Well, both Henry and I think they're a good match. I must admit, we've been looking for it to happen," Phoebe answered.

"Truth be known, we were about to think that Frances was going to be like Emma's sister, Dorothea. You see, she never married. We built the little house that we gave to Frances and William for Dorothea, but she couldn't make it on her own, so she moved back in with us," Tom said.

"Well, it's such a lovely little cottage," Phoebe said. She then added, "I've never seen Dorothea in church."

Emma stuttered a little, then said, "Well, she's sort of a recluse. She reads her Bible, though."

Phoebe said, while nibbling on the piece of apple, "Bless her heart, I'll bet she's a darling."

"She was father's pick, and he spoiled her rotten," Emma said. "She's in her room, resting," she added. "We just love William! Why, he's already a part of the family. It'll be nice having them live right down the road."

"I know we'll miss him, but then, we'll be gaining another daughter," Phoebe said.

Everything sure was nice in the big room. All the furniture looked very expensive and comfortable, and there was a cheerful fire burning in the fireplace.

About that time, they heard a voice in the hall. It was a woman's voice, and she was loudly singing, "Camptown ladies sing a song, doo dah, doo dah…"

Emma almost shouted, "You were told to stay in your room, dear!"

The huge red-haired woman broke loose from the two servants who were attempting to hold her back and strode to Emma. She stood in front of her and exclaimed, "You're sitting in my chair!"

"Dorothea, dear, we have company, please, Emma told her with gritted teeth.

"Well, they'll eat everything, and I won't get anything," the big lady said.

"Girls, get Dorothea a regular size plate, prepare it for her and she can eat in the kitchen," Emma instructed. One of the girls led Dorothea to the table, while the other one ran to the kitchen for the plate.

"Damn, where's the meat?" Dorothea demanded, as she let out a loud fart, then shook the back of her dress, as if to turn the smell loose.

Emma burst out crying. Phoebe set her little dish on a small table near her and went to Emma.

"There, there, it's not worth crying about," Phoebe consoled, as she hugged Emma and patted her on the back.

"She ruined my party, as always. I'll swear we can't have anyone over, especially Brother Travis," Emma wailed.

"She didn't ruin a thing. Why, we're all still right her," Phoebe told her, attempting to come up with more soothing words, while trying not to breathe due to the lingering odor of Dorothea's flatulence.

"That's right, dear, Dorothea is just being Dorothea," Tom said, while he took a swig of his coffee, then got up from his chair, him being closest to the stink.

"I know, but she's the size of a whale and cusses like a sailor," Emma whined, then continued, "and now, to do *that* in public," as if Dorothea couldn't hear her.

Emma had hardly finished speaking before her sister let go of another one.

Frances set down the remains that was in her dish. "I'll bet no one can beat me to the porch," she said. Frances ran toward the door, and Phoebe Alabama, who was laughing, was right behind her. William soon followed, while the grownups stayed in the room, although Tom stood at the door, fanning the air in an attempt to let the smell escape.

Frances discovered that it was cool outside, and while pinching her nose, she ran back into the living room and brought two shawls out, one for her and one for Phoebe Alabama.

After the three were seated in rockers outside, William exclaimed, "My God, I wonder what Dorothea had been eating!"

"One of the slaves brought in a dishpan of peanuts and you know how she is, she doesn't know when to stop eating," Frances replied.

"Well, I hate it for mother; she was spreading it thick in there," Frances told them.

"I've never seen such fancy little dishes and silverware. We don't have such as that," Phoebe Alabama said, doing her best to change the subject to something more pleasant.

"Mama ordered all that stuff at Ivey's store, and this is the first time she's used them. Father told her she was going too far with this get-together," Frances told them. "She thought she was going to make a big thing out of our wedding, but I put a stop to it. I put it off on William, telling her he just wanted a short wedding."

"Well, your mother had that little thin sliced cake in there, but I have to say, your aunt Dorothea was the icing on the cake," William said.

The three laughed, then Phoebe Alabama told Frances that it was nice seeing where they lived. "You have a very lovely home, and the place where y'all are moving to looks like it came straight out a story book."

"Thank you, darling, and I'll be expecting you to spend plenty of time with us," Frances told her.

117

"Oh, I'd love that. I'm not much on handling a carriage, but I can sure ride the devil out of my horse, Birdie," Little Phoebe said.

"Good, I can ride, too. Get your brother to invite me to your house. I know how to get there, but he's never invited me. We'll just ride our horses," Frances told her.

"Father keeps me so busy; I haven't had time to invite anyone. The only day available is Sundays, and I always go to your house," William explained defensively.

"Well, you won't find all the fancy hoopla that I've seen here, but Suzy and Clary sure know how to cook. I'll have to ask Mother first, though," Little Phoebe told Frances.

"Sounds good," the other girl replied.

In a few minutes they could hear Emma and Dorothea arguing in the living room.

"If Mother would just leave Aunt Dorothea alone, she'd settle down. It's true that she can be awkward at times, but she has a good side, too. She can play the steam out of a piano; she taught me to play," Frances said.

"My mother plays beautifully. I can play too, but not as well as she can," answered Phoebe Alabama.

Their conversation was interrupted when everyone else filed out of the house. Phoebe told Emma what an enjoyable time they'd had, and Emma apologized profusely once again about the actions of her sister.

Both men laughed, shook hands, and said they'd see each other in church the next day.

Phoebe Alabama asked her mother if Frances could come for a visit the next day after church.

"Of course she can! We'd be glad to have her over anytime," Phoebe answered.

Little Phoebe hurried to their waiting carriage, picked up the shawl she had borrowed, then ran back to the porch and handed it to Frances.

"I'm so excited about your visit tomorrow," Phoebe Alabama said, as she kissed Frances on the cheek.

William told them he was staying for a while, so the others were soon seated in the carriage and heading home. Henry waited until they were out of sight of the Jones house, then he exclaimed, "Boy, what a mess!"

"Poor Emma," Phoebe agreed, as the horse made a fast clip down the road back toward Belleville.

"Well, *I* thought the lady was funny," Phoebe Alabama said.

"Darling, you're just sixteen years old; you have your whole adult life ahead of you. And you know what, I think you're right, Alabama. You're going to be acquainted with lots and lots of people, and we're all different. If you run into someone that's mean or just downright grinds on your nerves, simply extricate yourself from them, and always be yourself. Putting on airs, trying to be something that you're not, always catches up with you," Phoebe told her daughter.

"Like Mrs. Jones acted today?" Little Phoebe asked.

"Well, since you asked, I'd say so," her mother said. She continued, "I'd be willing to bet that Dorothea is a lot happier than her sister. Having a satisfied mind, that's what makes you happy and contented with your own self."

"Well, since you've brought it up, Mother, don't you think I'm a little too old to be called Little Phoebe, or Phoebe Alabama? I would like to be called "Allie," the girl said.

Henry laughed. "I *told* you she wouldn't like that name as she got older," he told his wife.

Phoebe thought for a small while, then said, "It's going to sound strange for a while. We'll need to tell a lot of people, but if you want to be called Allie, Allie it is."

As Henry turned the horse left at the crossroads and they went through Belleville, Phoebe said she prayed they'd find everything all right at home.

"It'll be fine; I left a good man in charge," Henry reassured her.

Phoebe laughed, and said, "Yes, it's true that James can handle just about anything. I'll have to admit, though, I'm going to miss William."

"Yeah, I will too, but he's getting us another daughter to go along with our Allie back there," Henry said.

Allie grinned and said, "Father, I love you!"

Chapter Fifteen

The wedding took place without a flaw. Two days prior, Henry had given his son $1,500 in gold for a wedding gift. The first thing William bought was a wide wedding band at the jewelry store in Claiborne. Things did seem dreary around Magnolia for a few days with William gone, but after the young couple had been married three days, they galloped up the lane toward the big house. Each of them was riding their own horse.

Phoebe and Allie were in the parlor, decorating the huge Christmas tree that James had brought to the house. They heard the horses as they galloped into the back yard, but figured it was James and his newfound friend, Daniel.

What a treat it was for them when Will and Frances burst through the door, smiling!

William was holding a large cloth sack. "Frances packed this thing with wads of paper, so maybe nothing is broken," he said, as he laid the sack on the floor. "Go ahead, open it."

Phoebe untied the string at the top and saw that the sack was filled with Christmas gifts. "Just look at all these! Your timing is perfect; we're just now decorating the tree," she said, as she and Allie took turns hugging the cold necks of the newlyweds.

"Goodness gracious, go stand by the fire, you two, and get warm," Phoebe told them, as she began taking the presents out of the sack. "Look, Allie, all the gifts are wrapped in decorative cloth, ribbons and all," she said as she started putting the gifts under the tree.

"Oh, how unique," Allie said, then she ran in front of the fireplace and hugged Frances again. "They are beautiful."

"Oh, by the way, we're inviting ourselves over for Christmas dinner," William informed them with a smile, as he rubbed his hands together in front of the fire.

"Now, that will be the best Christmas gift of all," his mother said. Phoebe cocked her head to the side, thinking. "I suppose I should consult with your father about this first, but why don't you two invite Frances' family here for Christmas dinner?" Phoebe said.

"What about Aunt Dorothea?" Frances asked with a sly smile.

"Especially her; she'll liven the occasion for us. Just keep the green peanuts away from her! Allie told me about it," Phoebe laughed.

"That's so sweet of you. Because of mother, the poor dear never gets to leave the house," Frances confided.

"Well, she's always welcome here. I just hope it won't be freezing cold weather," Phoebe said.

"Pa has a covered surrey; it's still cold in there, but at least you're out of the wind and rain," Frances told her.

"How well I know! We'll be making our annual pilgrimage to Claiborne Saturday, and we'll be sure to bring blankets for the ride, as usual," Phoebe remarked.

"Where are James and the old man?" William asked, as he sat down in the nearest chair.

"Your father has gone to Sparta to record another two hundred acres of land he bought. James has found a new friend; his name is Daniel Dean. They're supposed to be out cutting wood, but knowing them, they're just off fooling around somewhere, even knowing we need the wood," his mother answered.

"My goodness, how much more land does Father want?" William asked.

"Lord knows! I don't ask questions. All I know is he says it's virgin land and he's getting it at a good price. It adjoins ours in the back of the house," Phoebe answered.

"I know where it is; I use to ride my horse through that land, hunting. The hurricane blew several of the trees down back there," William recollected.

"Your father said he was going to get Tricademus and his crew on it before Christmas, and they'd be planting some of it by the spring of the year," Phoebe said.

"You were speaking about your wood. Knowing ol' Tric, I'll bet he already has his bunch working on it," William mused.

Clary and Suzy came out of the kitchen and curtsied at them.

"Lawd, I thought I hurd yo voice out heah," Clary said.

"Why are you two curtsying at me?" William asked.

Clary, who was the more outspoken of the two girls, said, "Well thangs, dey be different now, you be married. Wese wuz kirtsing fah yo wife too," Clary said.

"Well, that's mighty sweet of you. I met y'all when I paid a visit to Miss Allie," Frances said, as she took a seat next to William.

"Yessum, and wese said Mr. William wuz doing alright fuh hisself," Clary told her. She and Suzy then went back into the kitchen.

"When does school start back?" Phoebe asked William.

"Oh, it doesn't start back until after the holidays. It was turned out on the 13th; that's the reason we waited until the 14th to marry. They'll have a new teacher when they come back. Mr. Higdon, the teacher before me, will be teaching in Sparta."

123

"Well, I'll be praying that all goes well for you, son," Phoebe said, "but aren't you anxious about it?"

"Mother, I'm just following my intuition. I've always felt like I wanted to teach. I just hope I can find a way to further my education."

"You mean go on to college?" Phoebe asked.

"That's my intention. I plan on teaching a year or two first and, if I like it, I pray I can pass the examination and go on to the university in Tuscaloosa. If I graduate from there, I feel sure I can get a job teaching at the university. That way, I can make a pretty fair living just teaching," William said.

"Where is this university? Phoebe asked.

"Tuscaloosa. It's about a hundred and fifty miles north of here."

"Lord, wouldn't that be something, my son a college professor!" Phoebe exclaimed.

William laughed, and said, "Yes, ma'am, it would."

Allie spoke up. "I just want to know two things: how's married life, and sister, where did you get those riding breeches? I love those."

"Well, married life is wonderful because I have a wonderful husband," Frances answered as she reached over and squeezed William's hand. And the breeches came from Ivey's store in Belleville."

"Don't you be getting any bright ideas though about the marriage part, Miss Allie. You're too young," Frances told her new sister-in-law. She then added, "Look how long it took me to get your brother."

"No danger in that; there's not anyone interested in me. I'll probably wind up a spinster like your Aunt Dorothea," Allie said.

124

"Hmph, with that long blonde wavy hair, green eyes, and dimples, shoot, Allie, you're a looker and you know it. I wish I had your complexion," Frances replied.

"My complexion came from putting buttermilk on my face at night; Mother told me that's what she used to do," Allie replied.

"Oh, I've been meaning to tell you, I love your new name!" Frances told her.

"No offense to Mother, but Phoebe sounds as though it came from the Middle Ages, and as for Alabama...who in the world would name their daughter, Alabama?" Allie demanded.

"Well, your father named William and James, so I named you. Therefore, you can blame me," Phoebe said.

Allie went to her mother and hugged her, then suddenly she asked Frances if she wanted to do a duet on the piano.

"Sure, we'll try," laughed Frances at how quickly Allie jumped from one subject to the other.

Allie played the high notes and Frances played the low notes. They started out with, "O Little Town of Bethlehem, then played, "Joy to the World," and their last selection was "Jingle Bells." They ended up hugging each other's neck, then stood to a standing ovation. Of course, they turned around and did an exaggerated bow.

"Say, that was good!" William applauded.

"I must admit, we play well together. We'll have to play a duet at church sometime," Allie said.

"Well, I'm game if you are," Frances agreed.

William then told Frances they had better go. "It isn't getting any warmer out there."

"Okay, Darling, whither thou goest, I goest," Frances replied.

"Oh my, can't y'all stay and eat supper with us?" Phoebe asked.

"No, thank you, Mother," William said, as he put his coat back on, then held his wife's coat up so she could slip into it. "We're planning on eating with Tom and Emma; we're going to surprise them. They haven't seen us since the wedding. Besides, it's closer to the house. Tell Father, knucklehead, and Tricademus we said hello," William requested, hugging his mother.

Frances hugged Allie's, then her mother-in-law. As she did so, she whispered in Phoebe's ear, "Don't get Allie breeches for Christmas!"

Phoebe nodded her head, and the newlyweds went out the door to face a cold draft.

"*Brr*," Allie muttered as she hurried back toward the fireplace. "Reckon how they stand that cold wind out there?" she asked her mother.

"They'll be all right. They're young and in love; it's the best shield you can have. It's your father I'm worried about," Phoebe told her daughter.

"Father will be all right too. He's *old* and in love," Allie laughed, then asked, "What about James and the others?"

"James and Danny are too active to get cold, while Tricademus and his crew have sense enough to cut wood in the thicker part of the forest. The winds aren't so bad there," Phoebe answered.

"Uncle Tricademus and Aunt Precious have been so sweet to me over the years. I've never told you this, but I used to slip over there, and she'd always have a sweet treat for me," Allie confessed.

"Oh, I knew about it. I just never said anything," her mother said.

"Reckon how old they are?" Allie asked, as she picked up the fire poker and stirred up the fire.

"Well, let's see. Precious already had eight children when we moved here. She looked to be in her thirties then, so I would say she's in her early sixties. Tricademus, he's about the same age. Neither of them have ever worked for anyone but the Smith family," Phoebe answered.

"I can't fathom being owned by anyone. If I had the misfortune of being born as a slave, I'd run away," Allie said.

Phoebe put a finger to her lips and pointed toward the kitchen.

"Imagine if you were them…where would you run to?" she asked her daughter, in a lower tone of voice.

"Well, it's not right! Even the preacher tells them the servants are to mind their masters. They're not allowed to read and write. Not allowed to leave this property without written permission," Allie said.

"You've been reading that radical newspaper again. I just subscribe to the thing to see all the latest fashions. Honey, we live in the South, and it's our way of life. Baby, I can just see you scrubbing your own clothes, cooking, and cleaning house," Phoebe told her daughter. She continued, "We've always treated our people fairly. They eat the same things that we do; none of them have ever been flogged or beaten. Can you imagine your father whipping one of our people?" she asked.

"It's all right to say the word, Mother," Allie said.

"What word?" Phoebe asked.

"*Slave*," Allie responded.

"I guess about the best way I can explain it is, what would all our people do if we cut out their shelter, food, and clothing? And that's just three things. Why, they wouldn't know what to do. Your father isn't buying more land to farm for us, it's for them. They keep multiplying. When that happens on some plantations, they start selling them, but your father won't do that," Phoebe said.

"Oh, Mother, it's just so puzzling for me to understand!" Then, as was her way, Allie changed the conversation completely. "Can I start teaching Suzy some things about the piano? One day, while you were outside, I heard her tinkering with it. I believe she can learn to play, with a little bit of teaching," Allie said.

"Sure; just make sure it's her afternoon off, and your father isn't in the house. That poor man has so much on him, when he's in this house he needs all the peace and quiet he can get," Phoebe said.

Henry's reason for coming in late was that he'd done some Christmas shopping in Sparta, and also in Belleville. He told Phoebe that he'd had the deed recorded and the land was now theirs.

"Well, if you think we need the land. You've made good choices so far; we're all eating and we're warm, and we have clothes on our back," Phoebe said agreeably, then began a conversation about him doing the Christmas shopping, for she knew how he hated to shop.

"So *that's* why you took the carriage and didn't just ride your horse, so you could buy Christmas gifts," Phoebe said.

"Well, the gifts are for the children on the place. By buying such a large amount, I got a bargain. For the life of me I couldn't remember how many were on the place now. I bought a dozen rag dolls for the girls and a dozen toy horses with wooden wheels that can be pulled by a string. I got those for the boys. I dropped everything off at

Tricademus' for Precious to wrap. I left her plenty of paper and string," Henry told Phoebe.

"So, we're still planning our annual trip to Claiborne Saturday?" Phoebe asked.

"Of course we are; what I bought was just a little something extra for the children," her husband told her.

"Henry Smith, you are a sweet man!" Phoebe told him, as she looked at Allie and smiled.

Phoebe then told Henry about William and Frances' short visit, and about her inviting the Joneses for Christmas dinner.

"Darn, I hate I missed their visit," Henry said, but he didn't comment on Phoebe's plans to host the Joneses for a visit.

Not long after Henry came in, James and his friend Daniel entered through the back door.

"Mother, can Danny spend the night with us? He's never been coon hunting, so I thought he could go with Jasper and me tonight. He can sleep in William's old room, if that's all right with you?" James asked.

"Sure, that'll be fine," Phoebe told her son.

James had clearly been sure of his mother's answer, for he and Danny went back outside and brought in a small case containing his change of clothes, then they ran upstairs.

After hearing the doors close to the upstairs bedrooms, Phoebe asked Henry, "What do you know about this young man?"

"His family are good folks. They live about five miles up the road. His father is Hugh Malone. He bought the old Griggers place," Henry answered. He continued, "I believe they're Methodist."

"Oh," Phoebe said, as Henry opened the window next to the fireplace to get a piece of wood to throw on the fire.

"Boy, they've got the wood bin chock-a-block full," he remarked.

"That's good, because that wind is already like ice out there. How they can stand to go coon hunting in weather like this is beyond me!" Phoebe shivered.

"Hon, weather like this is when the racoons come out," Henry told her.

Clary came out of the kitchen and said supper was waiting, and that they'd be eating in the big dining room.

"Okay, thank you Clary," Phoebe said, glancing upstairs. "Allie, will you go upstairs and tell the boys it's time to eat?" she requested.

"Of course," Allie answered, and went upstairs.

Phoebe couldn't help but laugh at her daughter's attire, for she was like her. Allie didn't care much about the latest fashions, and never wore her wide hoops and crinoline dresses around the house. "They are for guests and Sundays," the girl often said. Instead, she dashed up the stairs wearing a dark blue pleated dress, with just knee length bloomers beneath, instead of the more fashionable but bulky undergarments.

Everyone knew to wash and dry their hands in the kitchen before they ate. Henry and Phoebe were already seated at the table by the time the three young people hurried into the kitchen.

The family had a consistent routine regarding where they each always sat for meals. Henry sat at the head of the table, Phoebe at the foot, while James and Allie sat on opposite sides. It was just by chance that Danny chose the chair next to Allie.

130

Danny was tall and had long legs. Everyone, including Allie, noticed the unusual way Danny took his seat. He simply pulled the chair away from the table, spread his legs over the back of the chair and sat down, while everyone else came in from the sides of their chairs.

As soon as everyone was seated, Henry blessed the food, and they began passing it around. They had sliced roast pork, creamed potatoes with gravy, mustard greens, dried peas, cornbread and bread pudding for dessert. They enjoyed cold milk, fresh from its storage in the well, to drink with their meal.

Allie noticed how Danny made himself at home, eating some of everything on the table and filling his milk glass twice. She couldn't help herself, but she really took notice of James' friend, and wished she had dressed better. Danny's hair was cut like James' was, shoulder length, but his hair was a lighter shade of blond. *"About the color of mine,"* she thought. He had the same green eyes as she did, only his lashes were almost black. To be so tall, he wasn't raw-boned either; he seemed well built.

"I know your father. I see that you've inherited his height," Henry told the young man.

"Yes, sir, we're all tall: my father, my two brothers—even my mother and sister. They're all married and have left home," the young man said.

"Even your mother and father too?" asked James.

"No, stupid, just my siblings," Danny told James.

Everyone laughed at James' silly question.

"Then, you must be the youngest?" Phoebe asked.

Danny wiped his mouth with the cloth napkin and said, "Yes, ma'am. Mama was forty when I came along. I barely remember any of my siblings being at home. My sister and one of my brothers live in Selma, Alabama. He's a steamboat captain, and sometimes he comes to Claiborne. My oldest brother is a blacksmith; he lives in Camden, about forty miles from here."

"Well, at least y'all live fairly close to each other," Henry said.

"Yes, sir. Pa and Mama are from Putnam County, Georgia. They've been living in south Alabama for a while, though. He has a pile of slaves and couldn't get enough land to take are of everyone until we moved here. I like it, but it's a little bit isolated," Daniel explained.

"Well, he has some good land where he's at," Henry said.

"Yes, sir, and he believes in hard work. I don't understand it. We have all those slaves, yet I have to work just like they do," Danny said, as he finished his last bite of the bread pudding.

"Well, it'll make a man out of you. Just from the looks of you, it doesn't look like you're missing any meals," Henry said.

"No, sir, we have women in the kitchen. One of them cleans, and the other two of them are great cooks. They definitely keep me well fed," Daniel smiled.

"Well, you're getting off to go coon hunting, so you must have some free time," Henry said.

"It's because James is handy as I am with a buck saw. I'll bet we cut nigh on a cord of wood, then had to take it to all the cabins, and of course, our house," Danny said.

"I see. I sure hope we have plenty," Henry said as he looked at James.

"Everyone does. We made sure to go by Jasper's and ask before we came here," the young man reassured his father.

Pushing his plate away from him since he was through eating, he changed the subject.

"I noticed presents under the tree; Father must've brought them back from Sparta," James said to his mother.

"No, your brother and Frances brought them by. William said to tell you hello," Phoebe answered.

"I hope they're doing well, and enjoying married life?" Henry asked.

"Well, they didn't say, but they certainly acted as though they are," Phoebe replied. "I do have news, though. William said he planned on teaching at Belleville Academy for a year or two and, if he likes it, he's going on to the university."

"Surely he doesn't expect to teach up there?" Henry said.

"Not yet, but if he can pass the examination, he wants to further his education, and maybe eventually get a job up there as a professor," Phoebe replied.

James and Daniel soon bored of the conversation and went back upstairs to dress for the hunt.

Back at the table, the first thing that went through Henry's mind when thinking about William's education was the money it would require. He thought about his brother James, and how, even with how many children he and Mary had, he'd managed to send his son William to medical school. Henry suddenly felt ashamed of himself, worrying about how he would pay for just one child's future when his brother had so many to support.

"Well, we'll certainly have something to boast about Saturday to my brother, won't we," he said to his wife.

Phoebe just smiled at the expression on her husband's face.

The Christmas shopping that Saturday in Claiborne had gone about the same as in the past. They again met at Emily's eating establishment and had a nice meal before they started their shopping. They learned that James and Mary's son William was now also married. His bride was a girl from Kempville, Alabama, and he had brought her to meet everyone. Her name was Sarah, and they loved her immediately.

"Who would have thought when we made that long trip from North Carolina as newlyweds that we'd one day have grown children of our own, getting married themselves?" Mary mused to Phoebe. "It didn't cross my mind at the time."

"I know; the only thing *I* thought about was seeing my house, and what Henry was going to think when he saw me completely naked," Phoebe whispered.

"Lord, me too! They must have liked what they saw, though, because look at the children we produced," Mary chuckled.

"What are you two giggling about over there?" Henry asked.

"Oh, nothing!" the women said in unison, laughing even harder at their identical response.

Knowing better than to try and get the truth out of his wife in front of everyone, and that she would likely tell him later what it had been about, Henry dropped the subject.

"We have news about our William," he said instead. "He told Phoebe the other day that he might be going to the university."

"Well, congratulations! What's his goal?" Mary asked.

"He wants to be a college professor," Henry answered.

"Better have a fat purse," James told him, then added, "Knowing you, brother, you have one, too."

There was silence at the table for a moment, as each of the pioneer couples contemplated how far they had come in building a life, in what seemed to be such a short time. The years had gone by so fast!

Finally, Mary said, "Well, I imagine we'd better get busy with the shopping. We're not as young as we use to be."

Phoebe looked over at Mary as she spoke. The two women only saw each other once a year, which made Phoebe really take a good look at her sister-in-law. *"My goodness, look at the weight she'd gained over the years! she even has a double chin,"* observed Phoebe to herself.

Quickly dismissing her observation, though, and feeling ashamed of herself, Phoebe thought that if she herself had birthed eight children, she'd probably be just as big. She'd loved Mary since childhood, and nothing could change that. It was plain to see that James still loved her, too.

For once, both couples were alone on this trip. When they were planning for it, Allie had confided to her mother that she'd rather stay home and teach Suzy some things on the piano.

"Alright, but only until Clary starts supper. It's not right for Clary to do all the work," Phoebe had said.

Shopping was about as usual. Most of the objects bought were for the workers and children on the two places. The jewelry store was the first stop, and Phoebe picked out a beautiful emerald necklace for Allie. "It matches her eyes," she told Henry, as he paid for it.

James and Mary bought each of their girls a gold cross necklace. Mr. Loetz, the store owner, even had someone wrap the gifts in colorful Christmas paper.

Their next stop was at the dry goods store, where Phoebe showed the clerk thirty-two outline drawings of feet so they could purchase boots and shoes for everyone.

A man by the name of Levi Straus had come out with a material called denim. It had proved to be very durable and strong, so Phoebe bought ten bolts of it, complete with a variety of buttons. She also purchased four bolts of cotton material for shirts, pantaloons, and socks.

She intended to keep about ten yards of the denim material to sew James some trousers and shirts. For Allie, she bought ten yards of red crinoline to make the girl a couple of dresses. She also saw an emerald green ready-made dress with huge red roses imprinted on the material, which she thought would go perfectly with her daughter's green eyes. The bodice of the dress was very low, but Phoebe figured she could sew a piece of lace there to help conceal Allie's bosom. As she bought the dress, she thought about how Allie had filled out to have the body of a young woman. *"I don't have a baby anymore; she's no longer 'Little Phoebe."* The thought made her proud and a bit sad, all at the same time.

She bought James an olive green suit to wear to church, while Henry bought him a pair of knee-length brown pull-up boots. He also threw a pair of knee length brown lace-up boots on the counter, as a gift for William.

The store managers loved to see the wealthy plantation owners come in for holiday shopping, and they called in plenty of clerks to assist their favored customers.

Phoebe felt responsible for Suzy and Clary too, so she bought them two dusters each to wear over their clothing while they cooked. She also chose each of them a pair of pearl-colored barrettes to go in their hair.

Phoebe decided she'd return to Loetz's Jewelers as their last stop, and buy Frances a gold cross necklace, too. Before that stop, though, they all bought groceries, fruits, and holiday candies.

As she surveyed their purchases just before heading home, Phoebe could see that they'd bought a ton of Christmas items. She noticed that James and Mary had driven a wagon to Claiborne, and it was level full also.

"My, my, we're in for an uncomfortable ride home!" Mary whispered in Phoebe's ear as they hugged before their departure.

As usual, they left in separate directions, the two women waving their handkerchiefs at each other.

Henry couldn't help but laugh as they passed the blacksmith's shop.

"What are you laughing about?" asked Phoebe, taking hold of her husband's free arm.

"I was just thinking about the first time James and I went into the blacksmith's shop back there. We really thought we were spending some money when we bought a few dollars in nails. Now, look at this carriage—it's stacked as high as it can go! My goodness, you're almost sitting in my lap," Henry said.

"I know; the Lord has really blessed us, and it'll keep us warm sitting this close on the ride home," Phoebe told her husband.

The two horses had to climb a steep hill about a mile away from Claiborne. The hill was about two miles long. They'd made it about halfway up the hill when two black men ran out of the woods, blocking their way. They were ragged looking and neither one was wearing shoes.

The bigger of the two had a machete drawn back, while the other had a sturdy looking tree limb in his hands.

Henry looked in front of them and behind, but he didn't see another soul on the road. The horses reared, and Phoebe was scared the carriage might tilt over.

"Wese gwine takes out what bee's in dat carriage, and y'all's pockets," the one with the machete growled threateningly, as he attempted to grab the reins of the horse on his side.

"I don't think so," Henry told the man calmly, then Phoebe witnessed something from her husband that she'd never seen.

From out of nowhere, Henry brandished a pistol, and fired it over the head of the man with the machete, causing the horses to rear again.

"Dat gun, hit won't shoots buts one time," the man said as he attempted to grab the reins again.

"You're right, but *this* one will shoot, and this time it's aimed straight at your head," Henry said, his voice deadly calm as he wielded another pistol, aiming it at the black man.

With that being said, the one with the limb ran toward the woods first, then the one with the machete threw his weapon in the middle of the road. He hurried after his partner into the thick woods.

"Hold the reins while I pick up the things that fell out of the carriage," Henry said, his voice still quiet and steady.

With hands that shook, Phoebe did as her husband asked.

When Henry had put everything back into the carriage, he threw the abandoned machete on top to weight things down. He then climbed back into the carriage, grabbed the reins from Phoebe, and clicked his tongue at the horses. They left the place in a trot.

Phoebe waited until her heart had settled down, and they had topped the hill, before she said anything.

"My Lord, I didn't know you had a pistol on you, much less two! You would have killed that man, wouldn't you?" she asked, her voice trembling along with her still shaking hands.

"I intended to, with the second pistol. I thought maybe I could have just scared them away with that first shot, but they meant business," Henry replied. He then added, "The person that owns them is the one that needs shooting. Did you noticed how they were dressed? They didn't even have shoes on, and it being nigh Christmas."

At the first house they came to, Henry stopped and reloaded the pistol he had fired. A fellow came out of the house and walked toward them. Henry reported the incident to the man and told him he might want to be on the watch for the would-be robbers.

The man seemed amicable enough, and when Henry described the highwaymen to the fellow, who introduced himself as being Lee Peacock, the man told Henry that he and Phoebe had been very fortunate to escape with their goods and their lives intact. "That sounds like Big Jack and his partner, Tea Boy. They ran away from their master a couple of years ago. He lives across the river, and they've been stealing and living off the land since they ran off. Big Jack can be dangerous; they claim he's killed a couple of white folks. Y'all sure were lucky, Peacock repeated.

"You folks live near Monroeville?" he asked.

"No sir, we live near Belleville," Henry answered.

139

"Well, the sheriff needs to know about this," their new acquaintance said. He then told Henry that he'd get his son to ride into Monroeville to inform the lawman of this latest incident.

"Whatever you think is right," Henry agreed, they then shook hands and Henry told him they'd better get a move on. "We need to get home before dark."

"I understand," Peacock said, as they tipped their hats to each other, and Henry and Phoebe left for home.

As they made it down the road a bit, Phoebe said, "Just think, my husband fought off Big Jack!"

"Yeah, well, I've never heard of him, but I could look in his eyes and see he meant business. No telling what he would have done if I'd just thrown up my hands," Henry answered.

Phoebe had to admit that she had been scared, but it seemed that her husband had nerves of steel, and she was glad of it.

"Just don't mention this to anyone, unless it's someone that's planning on making a trip to Claiborne," Henry told his wife.

"I won't, Honey. I'm so thankful you knew what to do; your actions surely saved our lives, not to mention everyone's Christmas," Phoebe said, squeezing her husband's arm a little tighter. She was actually glad that the packed carriage required her to sit so close to him the whole way home.

That Christmas, Clary and Suzy put the big pots and the little pots to cooking, and there was plenty on the table that year. It seemed that everyone appreciated their gifts, too. Allie just swooned at her emerald necklace and told her mother she absolutely loved the green dress.

Henry and Phoebe each received get a nice pair of bedroom shoes from William and Frances.

As everyone else opened their presents and made happy remarks about them, they got down to the last few gifts and there was nothing for Phoebe from her husband, for the first time ever. She told herself she didn't care that she didn't get anything personally from Henry, and that her true gift from him was the look in Tricademus' eyes as he picked up the gifts early that Christmas morning, and the look on their children's happy faces. Phoebe was glad that she had thought of Frances' gift, too, for the young woman exclaimed she'd always wanted a cross necklace.

Once the last present was opened and Phoebe was about to get up and start tidying up the remnants of wrapping paper and ribbons, however, Henry suddenly stood up and cleared his throat. Everyone looked at him in surprise as he made a show of looking around under the tree, then patting his pockets one after another. Finally, he said, "Ah. Here it is," and reached into the inside of his vest pocket.

Standing in front of Phoebe, he took her hand and gently brought her to her feet. No one else said a word; they just watched and listened as Henry began to speak.

"Phoebe, you have been everything I could have wanted in a wife and a mother to our children. I know I haven't told you enough over the years how blessed I always felt that you were willing to give up everything you'd ever known and make the journey to the wilds of Alabama, not knowing what you'd face on the way, or when we got here.

"There's no way I can repay you for all you've done to make our lives so rich and full. You have the spirit of a pioneer, that's for sure—and I never would have made it without you. I guess this will have to do," he said softly.

He placed a small red velvet box into her hand.

Opening the box with tears in her eyes, Phoebe gasped. Nestled on a soft bed of cream-colored satin was an exquisite carved ivory cameo brooch. She knew at a glance where Henry had purchased it, for she had seen it in one of her magazines and pointed it out to Allie. He'd had to special order it all the way from Paris, France!

"How did you…?" she stammered, looking up at her husband's smiling face.

Before he could answer, Allie clapped her hands and jumped up to hug her mama's neck. "It was me!" she exclaimed proudly, laughing. "I could tell how much you liked it, but you'd never ask for such a thing. You always put yourself last, Mother—and as for you, Dad, you probably would have just gotten her a pair of new gloves or something boring like that."

Phoebe hugged her daughter and her husband at the same time and smiled over at William. She didn't have to say a word to Henry to show how she felt; her arms, and her heart, and her life, were full to the brim at that moment.

She didn't know at that moment that the special cameo brooch would end up becoming a prized family heirloom, passed down from mother to daughter for generations. All she knew was that every hardship she'd faced by leaving her home and building a life as a new bride in an unknown land had been worth it. She wouldn't have changed a thing.

After the emotional opening of the gifts, Aunt Dorothea provided a welcome relief with her relaxed personality. It was clear she could relax and be her real self when she was able to get out from under her sister's constant criticism. Other than attempting to eat everything on the table,

142

Dorothea had perfect manners that day, and enjoyed conversing with everybody on a surprising number of topics.

After everyone had eaten, they gathered around the piano and listened to hear Dorothea play Christmas hymns. Frances had been right; her aunt played beautifully. The only trouble they had with her was when it was time to go; she refused to get into the carriage. She was clearly dreading going back "home" to her sister's house. She eventually agreed to leave only when Phoebe had Clary to prepare her a big platter of food to take home with her.

Emma didn't put on airs the whole time she was there, nor did she say one negative remark regarding Dorothea. Frances had whispered in Phoebe's ear that she had dared her to.

Phoebe thought it was nice seeing the comradeship between Tom and Henry, too, and she knew they both had an enjoyable Christmas.

Phoebe told Clary and Suzy they could spend the afternoon with their own parents after they'd finished cleaning up. She told them to just spread a sheet over the food that was on the left on the table.

"Yes, ma'am, can wese wear our new white dusters ober dare?" Clary asked.

"They are yours to wear as you like," Phoebe told the girls.

After the Joneses left, Danny Malone came galloping up the lane, with two of his hound dogs trailing behind him.

Allie heard the commotion outside, and after seeing through the window it was Danny, she dashed upstairs, carrying her new green dress.

Not bothering to even put on his new suit, James went outside to welcome his friend. The day had turned out to be unseasonably warm, so James asked Danny what he was doing with a coat on. "It looks like your suit is made from wool, too. I know you're burning up!" James exclaimed.

Stammering, and trying hard to think of a reason he could say out loud, Danny finally said, "My mama insisted I wear it."

"Oh," James said, never thinking his friend was coming to let Allie see him all dressed up.

"If you're hungry, there's plenty of food on the table," James told Danny.

"You know, I was full as a tick when I left the house, but after riding five miles, maybe I could eat a little something," the young man agreed."

"Well, come on in. You can pull that coat off and hang it on the coat rack just inside the back door," James told him.

He and Danny were still in the kitchen when Allie came back down the stairs in her new dress, sporting her new emerald necklace. She was wearing a pair of soft ballerina shoes. Phoebe could only see the toes of them occasionally, due to the long dress.

Seeing the look on Allie's face, Phoebe realized all at once that her daughter had feelings for Danny.

"My dear, you are just stunning in that dress, and it's definitely your color," Phoebe told Allie as the young woman descended the final stair.

"I just love it! I needed you to tighten the stays, but I was able to tighten enough of them to fit into it," Allie said. She then sat down at the piano and began to play.

Danny, hearing the piano, hurriedly finished the piece of pecan pie he was eating and almost rushed into the parlor.

Instead of sitting into one of the comfortable chairs, he chose to sit on the hard piano bench beside Allie.

James couldn't believe his eyes when he came out of the kitchen and saw his friend on the piano bench beside his sister, looking oblivious to anyone or anything else around him.

"I figured when he brought his dogs, he could borrow some of clothes and we'd go hunting," James said quietly to Phoebe. "Doesn't much look like he has coons on his mind right now, that's for sure!" He then sat down beside his mother and stuck his legs out as if he was inspecting his new boots.

"That young fellow couldn't squeeze into anything you have," Henry laughed.

Phoebe looked at her husband, as if getting his approval, then said, "James, why don't you go into the kitchen and take that marble cake to Precious? It wasn't even touched, and there's several mouths over there to feed." She winked her son as she said it.

"Yes, ma'am," James replied, quick to take the hint.

"Dear, it's such a nice day, would you like to go upstairs and sit on the balcony?" Phoebe asked her husband.

"Sure, it suits me, but only for s short time, it *is* December," Henry said, as they got up and headed toward the coat rack before they went upstairs.

Phoebe and Henry had just gotten settled in their rocking chairs on the balcony when they saw their son walking up the lane, carrying the cake with both hands.

"Shrewd trick honey," Henry told his wife.

"Well, I had to pick something that he couldn't take over there on his horse. Something that would take a little time, and just look at how he's kicking those rocks with his new boots on," Phoebe said.

Phoebe stopped rocking and laid her hand on Henry's arm.

"Did you know you're my hero, in many ways," she told her husband.

Henry stopped rocking, and asked, "Yeah, in what ways?"

"The way you handled those beasts on the way back Claiborne. I'll bet you wouldn't have resisted as much if all the things in our carriage had been yours," Phoebe said.

"Oh, yeah I would have," Henry replied.

"Really?" Phoebe asked.

"Sure, because you were in that carriage too, and you're my world," Henry told her.

Touching the beautiful new ivory cameo brooch pinned to the collar of her red Christmas dress, Phoebe smiled at him, her eyes showing all the love she felt for her husband in her heart.

"And you are mine," she responded, and kissed him.

Chapter Fifteen

So many changes can happen in just five years!

By 1855, James had married a young lady by the name of Wanda Kay Ryland. Her people lived in a booming little town named Bermuda. Bermuda was a unique little town, which had homes and businesses on each side of the road. One side of the road was in Conecuh County, and the other side was in Monroe County. Wanda Kay taught school there She was an only child, and her father had a lot of land, so James stayed on to oversee Mr. Ryland's property. James and Wanda Kay lived in a nice little house near the school, which was at the end of the Ryland property.

Henry told Phoebe that James got a pretty good deal. "He gets twenty-five percent of what the place makes, and he doesn't have to worry feeding and clothing anyone," Henry said. Bermuda was about fifteen miles away, so they could visit each other occasionally. Wanda Kay's family was very nice, and so was Wanda Kay. Phoebe thought she was a very pretty girl, with her long, wavy brown hair and bright blue eyes.

Allie had married Daniel Malone. Like James and William had done, she had moved out of Magnolia, in her case onto the Malone property. Phoebe was really worried about Allie to start with, but after a few visits with both Allie and Danny's parents, Phoebe accepted the fact that her baby had grown up and seemed happy. Hugh Malone, Danny's father, was older than most parents Danny's age, and was pretty feeble. Danny's mother Sarah Danny's mother was frail, also, thus they relied totally on Danny to make all the decisions around the place. Allie and Danny moved into the big house with them, and Allie became the lady of the house, which suited Danny's parents. Sarah Malone spent a lot of time in her bed, due to crippling arthritis. Hugh Malone passed his own days sitting in his chair on one of the two porches, or near the fireplace.

William and Frances were the parents of William, Jr., who was three years old, and of course, the Smiths thought he was the spitting imagine of his daddy. They'd only seen their grandson two times, since William and Frances had moved to Tuscaloosa. William graduated from the university the spring of 1855. The dean of the school told William if he'd go for his doctorate, he would get him a job teaching at the school until he'd earned his doctorate. William was thrilled to death and jumped at the opportunity. It would mean they could move on campus, which meant they could cut down on expenses. William's father could stop sending money, as well as Frances' parents, although the amount they sent was meager in comparison to his own parents' contributions. Tom just sent the money their eighty acres cleared each year.

Henry and Phoebe experienced a first that year. They rode by carriage to Camden, Alabama, then caught a train that took them to Tuscaloosa.

It was a heck of a trip. It seemed that the train stopped at every little town, and it was blazing hot inside. The train had windows, but none of the passengers dared to let one down, for the soot and burning embers from the smokestack would come inside. Phoebe felt that it would be worth the trip, though, since they'd get to see everyone. *"Especially little William,"* she thought.

Henry's thoughts were of a different nature. Since his sons had left home, he had to rely more on Tricademus and Jasper. Spring was a crucial time of the year for a planter. The farming operation was in the full swing of things, for it was planting season. Henry knew that Danny had his hands full with his own planting. To ease his father-in-law's mind, Danny had told Henry that he'd keep a check on Magnolia until they returned.

Phoebe had told Clary and Suzy they could just stay with their parents until they returned, but when given a choice, they chose to stay at Magnolia.

"Dis bees our home," they both had replied, and then Suzy asked if it would be all right if she practiced on the piano while they were gone. Of course, Phoebe had told her it would be fine.

William, Frances, and Little William met them at the train station.

"Look at our son! I can remember when you use to carry him around on your shoulders, the same way he's carrying our grandson," Phoebe told Henry.

Will and Frances rushed to them as soon as they stepped off the track.

After hugs all around, William handed his son to his proud grandma. "I'll help Dad with the baggage," Will told his mother. Of course, it was just what Phoebe wanted, to get her hands on her squirming grandson.

It was a task to unload everything, for it seemed as though Phoebe had packed everything but the wash tub. They finally packed all their things into the back of the three-seated carriage that William had rented.

Not knowing the carriage was rented, Phoebe elaborated about what a nice carriage they owned.

William replied, "Mother, we don't own this carriage. Shoot, I don't even own a horse. No need of it; everything we need is in walking distance from the apartment."

Surprisingly, Little William seemed very contented sitting in his grandmother's lap, with Henry dangling his pocket watch in front of the child's eyes to entertain the child.

William knew his parents were probably worn out from the trip to Tuscaloosa, but he decided to show them a small portion of the town.

"My Goodness, look at the oak trees, they line every road! I know they're a gorgeous sight in the fall when the leaves change colors," Phoebe remarked.

"Yep, water oaks line the sides of almost every street up here," Frances answered.

"Well, they are gorgeous, and I've never seen so many brick buildings in my life, and just look at the people! They're everywhere," Phoebe remarked.

William laughed, then said, "It's a far cry from things back home. My goodness, you had to travel three miles to Belleville, just to get to a grocery store. Here, you only need to walk a block or two and you can find almost anything you need."

"I'll be the first to say, William and I love living up here," Frances said.

"It's almost a different world, that's for sure," Henry chimed in.

Before William took them to their apartment, he decided to show them the river.

"My goodness, what a sight," Phoebe said as they neared the wide river. "Is this the Alabama River?"

"No, Mother, this is the Black Warrior. It's swelled right now due to the spring rains. This is where the local farmers bring their cotton and other farm goods to be shipped."

"Yes, I figured that from the looks of all the warehouses along the river," Henry said.

"There's just as many across the river too. Once you get across the river, though, it's actually another town. It's not incorporated like Tuscaloosa is; it's known as Northport," William answered.

"You should see some of the steamboats! They're so fancy that people around here call them floating palaces. They serve food, and even liquor. Passengers leave here on Mondays, shop in Mobile, then they're back in Tuscaloosa, ten days total," Frances told them. She then continued, "William has promised me one of those extravagant trips once he saves up enough from his teaching job. The people claim the food is top notch, and you're treated like royalty while you're onboard."

"Oh Henry, we should plan on making a trip up here when Will is off for Christmas!" Phoebe suggested. "We can all make the trip to Mobile together. Tricademus and Jasper can handle things while we're gone. You're not busy that time of the year. I've always wanted to see Mobile.".

She could read her husband's facial expression and could see that he was thinking.

"Well, that's too far off to make such a decision, but I guess we could buy the others their Christmas gifts early and store them at Magnolia. Tric could pick them up on Christmas morning. Allie, Danny, James, and Wanda Kay could pick their gifts up early. We'll just have to see," Henry concluded, as he patted Phoebe on her arm.

Henry knew his wife's face, too, and knew that she was thinking about spending Christmas with their only grandchild.

William left the river's bank and headed for their apartment, which was located on the campus. Frances knew what direction William was going, so she spoke up.

"Let me forewarn you: our apartment is cramped; it's a far cry from being Magnolia. There are two bedrooms, though, and we're lucky that it's on the ground floor," she said, as they neared the apartment.

"If we have to sleep on a two-by-four, it would beat that train! Of course, I saw things that I would have never seen. Those tall Indian mounds we saw, I'll bet it took a while to build them, and Greensboro...my, did that town have some beautiful homes," Phoebe said.

"Yeah, a lot of wealthy planters live in Greensboro, but have their plantations out in the country," William said.

He had to pull on the reins to stop the horses in order to allow rows of military cadets to cross the street. They marched to the music of a fife and two beating drums.

"My goodness, what young-looking soldiers! Their uniforms look so snappy," Phoebe remarked.

"Well, you know the university is really a military cadet school. The students train to be in the military, while they get an education at the same time," William answered.

"Are you in the military now, too?" his mother asked.

"Sure, but I chose to stay on an be an instructor," William answered. He then continued.

"There are several branches here in Tuscaloosa you can major in. There's artillery, telegraphy, engineers, infantry, and cavalry, which is the one I majored in. We have physical training, as well as mental training. We mount our

152

horses and rush toward each other two at a time. Right before we meet, I've learned to lean one way or the other and knock my foe off his horse. You know, about the same things that James and I did back at Magnolia.

"There's a lot of pomp and circumstance to it, which I find is ridiculous, but to get an education, I'll put up with it. Of course, the new recruits get the rough end of it. With me graduating tomorrow, they hardly fool with an old hand like me. I've finished with all my tests and have started to teach already. Shoot, in a couple of years I'll have my bachelor's degree, then my masters, and of course, the last is the doctorate.

"Anyway, to make a long story short, you can stop sending money. I'll start getting paid tomorrow," William said.

"We're thrilled to death about it," Frances remarked.

"As you should be. To get a diploma in the Smith family is a big deal, son, much less a doctorate, and I don't mind saying, I'm proud of you," Henry said.

"Thank you. That means a lot," Will told his father. His face lit up with a new thought. "Oh, there's news I have for you about your Uncle Jesse!"

Henry was taken aback. "How in the world?" he asked.

The cadets passed from in front of them, and William slapped the horses on their sides with the reins, but he continued with the conversation.

"Well, you know Smith is a common name. There's a young man here named Smith. He's just a first-year cadet, but definitely a stand-out, and a superior horseman. I began to take notice of him, so one day last week I began to question him. He said his father's name was Ezekiel and his grandfather was Jesse. I asked him if they hailed from

Duplin, North Carolina. When he said, yes, I liked to have cut a somersault, and then I told him about you. He wants to meet you," Will told him.

"It's a small world! Of course I'd like to meet him," Henry replied enthusiastically. Then he sobered somewhat. "Please tell me that Uncle Jesse is still living," he said.

"Not only is he still living, but he's very wealthy, as is his son Ezekiel. It seems they invested in a railroad that runs from York, Alabama to Birmingham. It then connects to other railroads that runs along the East Coast, then on to New York. He said they freed all their slaves, and even bought some of them five acres of land each and deeded it to them," Will answered. Then he smiled.

"Guess what his name is?" he asked his father.

"I have no idea," answered Henry.

"Shoot, I thought you'd guess it right away. His name is William!" the young man exclaimed, laughing.

"Well, well, Ezekiel named him after our grandpa," Henry smiled. "Seems like that's become a real family tradition. He was a good old man; he fought in the Revolutionary War, you know. I must get Uncle Jesse's address from this friend of yours."

"I figured y'all would be too worn out to invite him over tonight, but he's coming for supper tomorrow night," Will said.

"What does your friend look like?" Phoebe asked.

"Oh, he's a Smith, all right. He's tough as a lightard knot, and very muscular built. He's taller than James and me, but in my opinion, he favors James in his appearance. He's in the cavalry, like I am, and he's very bright," Will answered.

"Well, I'm dying to meet him," Phoebe said.

"Me, too," Henry agreed.

"Well, here we are, the old homestead," Will announced, as he stopped the carriage in front of a huge brick building, then jumped out and tied the horses to a hitching post. He then helped Frances and William Junior down, while his father helped Phoebe out of the carriage.

"After we get the baggage inside, I'll go with you to take the horses and carriage back," Henry told his son.

On the way back to the livery stable, Henry couldn't help but notice the hustle and bustle of all the strange people.

"Boy, could you imagine all these people meandering about back home? I wonder what Tricademus would think of it." Henry remarked.

"I imagine that wondering what the folks around here would think about Tricademus would be more appropriate; he's such a giant," William replied.

Henry laughed, then said, "Yeah, I guess you're right, but ol' Tric would sure have himself a time in Tuscaloosa."

"Mother seems to like it up here," William said.

"Son, your mother would love it anywhere that grandson would be at. That boy is all she talks about," Henry replied.

"He is a pretty boy, if I say so myself. In fact, Frances has an appointment for all of us to have our images struck tomorrow. She will mail you yours, and that way, Mother can show that boy off to folks back home," William told his father.

"I'm sure your mother will like that," Henry replied, as he automatically opened his purse to pay the man at the livery stable.

"Dad, that's not necessary," Will whispered.

"I'm sorry; it's just automatic for a father to think he has to pay the fare," Henry told his son.

"I know, and I'm sure my day is coming. Shoot, Frances already thinks Junior must have all the latest things," Will replied.

The stable keeper didn't care who paid, but he took the gold coin from Henry after giving the two horses and carriage a going over.

Father and son didn't have to walk but two blocks to make it back to the campus apartment.

On the way, Will asked how James, Allie, and Tricademus were doing.

"Well, as you know, James' wife Wanda Kay is a teacher; I've heard she teaches quite a few students. As for James, he stays busy being the overseer of Mr. Riley's land. Poor little Miss Allie, she stays busy seeing to Mr. and Mrs. Malone, as well as keeping the household on an even keel. She seems to be happy, though, as does James." Then Henry told his son that Tricademus was still Tricademus. "He does his part and more, but Lord knows he and Precious have so many grandchildren, I don't think Tric knows half of their names. Tric is the so-called overseer and will hold that position for as long as I live, but Jasper actually runs the place these days. Of course, they both make sure I have the final say on things. With farming, you never stop learning. For instance, the most barren land will produce if you use enough fertilizer. Thank God, I shouldn't have to keep buying land, not since I've started using fertilizer. It's expensive, but so is land."

"How many acres do you own now?" Will asked.

"Almost two tracts, about eleven hundred acres," Henry replied, then continued. "You know we own a grist mill on Burnt Corn Creek now; Robert operates the thing. I'm making a few dollars on my trees, too. Belleville has two sawmills now," he concluded.

"Well, my dream is to own a place near the campus, you know, where Frances can have a flower garden. I can grow a few vegetables, and Junior will have a yard to run and play," Will told his father.

"I get that you have a different life than we do. Who am I to tell you what to do? You're educated, doing what you always wanted to do. Things are different now. My brother and I did the only thing we knew to do, and that was farming. Now, though, things are different. There are a lot more places to work and make an honest living. Not so many in our area, but I've read that there are plenty of places in the cities where young folks can work. Nothing stays the same, Son, except the Bible. Thanks be to the Lord, you have an education to fall back on, that can't be taken from you. A farmer depends on the weather; little rains mean little crops.

"I'm so glad to hear that Uncle Jesse and Ezekiel aren't relying strictly on farming. People on a farm just keep multiplying, meaning you always have more people to feed and clothe. It's an endless cycle, because as you know, I'd never sell anyone. I intend it to be if you're born on Magnolia, you'll die on Magnolia. I've been reading about folks up north, especially some of these politicians, they're wanting to free the negro. Lord, can you just imagine the ones on Magnolia being set free? They wouldn't know what to do. Like I said, though, nothing stays the same, and you must adjust to the times."

"Father, I've never known you were such a deep thinker," Will said.

"Well, enough of the serious stuff! I'm wanting to spend some time with my grandson," Henry told him.

"We're almost home; it's about another fifty yards, and I must say, you can walk at a fast gait."

"It's due to hard work and all that country air," Henry said, slapping his son on the back as they entered the apartment.

When they got inside, Henry and Will heard the girls laughing and clapping their hands.

"What in the world?" Henry asked Will, who shook his head. "Your guess is as good as mine, Dad."

The two women were sitting on the sofa with Junior, who was on his mother's lap.

"Say Grandmother," they would instruct the boy.

"Gandmubber," the child would say, then clap his hands along with Frances and Phoebe.

"Hey, that's not fair," interrupted Henry. "What about me?"

Will laughed, then said, "William, say Grandaddy."

"Gandiddy!" the child exclaimed, then clapped his hands along with the rest of them.

After a round of hugs, the child was put on the floor to demonstrate how he could ride his stick pony. Of course, that brought on another round of applause. As little William kept entertaining them with his antics, time slipped by them.

Due to the hour, the girls couldn't cook a decent supper. Frances told them there was a nice restaurant down on First Street, so they all agreed to go there for supper.

Phoebe and Henry couldn't believe all the food choices on offer at the restaurant, for it was the first time they'd ordered buffet style. There were three types of meat to choose from: chicken, beef, and pork. The meats were accompanied by a colorful array of different vegetables, green salads, and tempting desserts.

"Boy, you could get spoiled living in this town!" Phoebe remarked happily, as she sat down with her food, which was still on her tray. After seeing Will and Frances remove their different plates and saucers from their trays, Henry and Phoebe did the same. Little William sat in a high chair next to his mother.

"All the main dishes and vegetables are hot, too, and I didn't see a fire anywhere," Phoebe remarked.

Will laughed. "Mother, you'll like this part: beneath the containers that hold the food is a big tray of water which is heated by oil, and that keeps the food hot. We have oil lighting, heat, and an oil stove at our apartment, too. No need for a fireplace."

"Well, do tell. Now I've heard it all," Phoebe answered, then added, "I wish we had oil at Magnolia."

After Will said grace, they all dug in. No passing of bowls or platters was necessary, as everything was already on their plates.

After they had all eaten, Phoebe said she was going to make a recommendation.

"What's that, dear?" Henry asked, as he wiped his mouth with a cloth napkin.

"We'll be here for two more days and nights. I recommend we eat supper here every night. There's no need of Frances getting in that kitchen and cooking for us," Phoebe suggested.

"I'll pay for it," Henry said.

Frances and Will looked at each other, then said, "It suits us, but remember, Uncle Jesse's William is coming tomorrow night."

"The conditions still apply," Henry replied.

"We have Will's graduation ceremony tomorrow at two o'clock. Before then we have that appointment at eleven to have our daguerreotypes taken, so we'll have to be looking pretty," Frances said. "The photographer recommended that we wear something dark in color, and we're not to smile," she added.

"My goodness, why is that?" Henry asked.

"Because you must stay in the same position for a full minute, so the daguerreotype won't come out blurry. That's why it's almost impossible to capture a child's image," Frances informed them.

"My goodness, I'm so excited! But I admit I'm a bit disappointed, too; I wanted a picture of my grandboy," Phoebe said.

"I know, I'd love to have one of my big boy," replied Frances.

"Well, he certainly has a good appetite, and he's the spitting image of his father," Phoebe said, as little William ate one grape after the other.

"Thank goodness, he'll eat most anything. He loves jellied toast and scrambled eggs," Frances smiled.

They waited until little William had his fill of the fruit, before they left to walk back to the apartment.

"I must admit, you've picked a good profession, with a location like this place. My goodness, the town is so compact you can simply walk everywhere you need to go," Henry told his son, on their walk back.

"It's ideal, except for in rough weather. You definitely have to wear a slicker when it rains, or a long coat when it's cold," Will replied.

"Yes, I can attest to the fact that it gets colder here than in Belleville," Frances said.

Little William loved riding in his stroller, but Henry and Phoebe insisted that they'd take turns with him, so Frances let them carry the boy. He was fine with Phoebe, but he seemed to enjoy riding on Henry's shoulders the most.

After they'd returned to the apartment and everyone had loosened their belts and got more comfortable, the conversations began in earnest. Of course, Frances wanted to know about her folks, especially her father and Aunt Dorothea.

"You know, I hope you don't think less of me, but Lord, was I glad your son came to my rescue! My mother would grate on anyone's nerves," Frances admitted. How are my father and Aunt Dorothea doing?

Neither Henry nor Phoebe knew quite how to respond to Frances' comment about her mother, so they didn't say anything for a minute.

"Oh, they're doing fine, just like myself, staying busy," Henry finally answered.

"Dad, I know this is the busiest time of the year for you, and I really appreciate you coming to see me graduate," William told him.

"Are you kidding? You're my son, and my children come before anything. I have Tricademus and Jasper tending to things. As I've already said, Danny said he'd keep an eye on things, too," Henry repeated.

"You know, I really miss ole Tricademus. We'd sneak off and go fishing in Burnt Corn Creek and you'd never be the wiser. Why, he even taught me to swim," William said.

"Oh, I knew about it," Henry replied.

"Really?" asked Will in surprise.

"Sure. Not much went on with you children that I didn't know about."

"You never whipped any of us either, even when I knew we deserved it, especially James and me," Will said.

"No, I always tried to keep my temper. I can remember that while I was growing up, Uncle Jesse's stern words were more effective than a good whipping, so I just used his strategy when it came to my own children," Henry told his son.

"Well, I just pray I'll make as good a father as you," William said.

"You will, Son, without a doubt. You know, I think young people might have a better opportunity of amounting to something in a city than back home. It's so remote there, there's only one thing to do, and that's farm," Henry said thoughtfully.

Phoebe and Frances had gone into the other bedroom with Junior, and therefore they couldn't hear Henry and William's conversation, or vice versa.

"So, Danny and Wanda Kay…what do you think about that?" Will asked.

"Well, they both come from good families, but while Wanda Kay is quiet and reserved, Danny is right opposite. He's so clumsy, he trips on almost anything in front of him. I think his size has something to do with it; he doesn't know his own strength, either. He's a good farmer, though; I can give him that. The best thing is that I know he loves our Allie. If Allie says jump, he asks, "How high?" Henry laughed. "I'm proud of Allie. She has her hands full, taking care of Danny's parents and seeing to her own affairs, but she never complains about it.

"And James is working his tail off managing the Ryland plantation. They both seem happy, that's the important thing," Henry said. "As for you...I have to tell you that on the day your mother and I left Duplin County, North Carolina, we never thought we'd have a son graduating from the University of Alabama!"

"Well, it's taken me long enough, but thanks to God, your money, and a loving wife and family, I've made it. Now, on to my doctorate and I will soon be making some real money. I can afford that house in the country then. It'll be a better place to raise your grandson," William said.

"If that's what you want, then, good," Henry told his son.

Phoebe and Frances returned to the room. "Well, we have Little William's room all prepared for you, and we have a busy day planned for tomorrow," Frances said.

"So, you're saying it's time to hit the sack?" Henry asked.

"Well, we're turning in. Junior is already asleep. He'll be sleeping in the bedroom with Mommy and Daddy tonight," Frances told him.

She then hugged Henry's neck, and Phoebe's. "Good night, sleep tight, don't let the bedbugs bite," she laughed, before heading to the bedroom she and Will shared.

"Well, I guess I'd better join my wife, but it's been so nice talking to you, Father," William said, then he, too, hugged his mother and kissed her on the cheek.

Both Henry and Phoebe bathed the best they could in the cramped bath closet, then Henry pushed the window open to catch a breeze. Afterwards, they crawled into bed.

After lying in bed for about twenty minutes, Phoebe said quietly to her husband, "Well, it's certainly not like Magnolia. There's so much noise outside!" Henry didn't answer her, so she knew he must be sleeping already. Phoebe kissed him softly on the forehead, then she, too, fell asleep in a short while.

Phoebe had always heard the expression, "You're never too old to learn," and she once again was shown the truth of that statement the next morning. She had never heard of French toast, much less made it. That's what Frances was cooking them for breakfast when Phoebe entered the kitchen that morning. At Magnolia it was always biscuits or flapjacks, but never anything made from yeast bread.

She watched carefully as Frances simply sliced the bread, dunked the slices into scrambled eggs and fried them in butter. She placed two slices in each in a saucer for each member of the family, and offered their choice of syrup and honey to pour over the French toast.

"It sure is good with black coffee," thought Phoebe as she finished her second slice. She noticed that Henry seemed to like it, too.

After the ladies cleaned up the kitchen, Frances jotted down the recipe for the yeast bread, then they all dressed to have their images made.

Like everything else in the town, the daguerreotyper's studio was just a short walk from the apartment. The place was quite elaborate, with colored velvet tapestries on the walls and a fancy frescoed ceiling. There were several examples of daguerreotypes hanging on the walls of the studio. While Henry spoke to the proprietor, Frances took a closer look at the framed photographs. Most of them featured fairly ordinary-looking people, but she noticed that

164

there was even one of Queen Victoria. A few of the images had been hand painted in color, while the rest were in a grayish tone of black and white.

An elaborate poster on the wall described the history of the daguerreotype along with information about its inventor, as well as details of the photographic process itself. Reading it with interest, William learned that the daguerreotype was invented by a man named Louis Daguerre and was presented to the public in Paris, France in 1839. The special "camera obscura" used mercury vapors to capture the image onto a highly polished, silvered copper plate, resulting in an extraordinarily detailed photograph that looked almost three-dimensional when viewed in the right light. Reading over William's shoulder, Phoebe was impressed that the process had become popular on a world-wide level in just a few short years after its Paris debut.

The daguerreotyper, Mr. Silva, was an odd little man with an olive complexion, dark hair, slightly bulging eyes, and a small black goatee. He wore black trousers, a stiffly starched white shirt and a long black cloak that tied around the neck. A long, funny-looking covering over his head completed his unusual outfit.

The thin little man was a bundle of energy as he bustled around the fairly good-sized space of his studio. When Silva spoke, they noticed his thick accent, which was unlike anything they had ever heard before.

He practically shoved Henry and Phoebe down onto a hard narrow bench across from the camera. Silva reached out and immediately removed Henry's hat, and muttered, *"Shade!"*

Standing with his wife and son, William hastily removed his own hat before the strange little man could do it for him, even though the daguerreotyper was some distance away. Frances stifled a nervous giggle which she immediately turned into a very fake sounding cough so Silva wouldn't notice. She glanced across at Phoebe and could tell that her mother-in-law was actually holding her own breath to try her best not to giggle out loud.

There were metal clamps on the back of the bench. Silva reached out and adjusted the clamps, so that the backs of Henry's and Phoebe's heads were pressed firmly against the headrest of the bench to his satisfaction. He folded his arms across his thin chest, then stood back and studied the composition of the scene he was about to capture on the special copper plate in his mysterious device on its tall metal stand.

Finally, he moved behind the black box and dramatically whisked off the black fabric covering the front of the machine. He removed the lens cover and looked through the lens at the couple. Silva then paused theatrically for a long moment. Everyone held their breath.

"*Perfecto!*" he exclaimed finally, startling Phoebe with his loud volume and causing her to jump a little on the hard bench. He cast her a stern look, making his huge, bristling eyebrows pull down over his large, dark eyes. *"Do not move!"* he snapped, glaring at her.

"Do *not* move until I tell you to," repeated the unusual little man, shaking one pointer finger in Phoebe's direction. "Don't even bat an *eye*, I tell you!"

They both sat perfectly still. Though it wasn't yet their turn to have their picture made, Frances and William stood motionless also. To be honest, they were all afraid to move so much as an eyelash, much less an eyelid. Even little William sensed the tension in the air and was unusually quiet all of a sudden, and the ladies weren't laughing anymore. Neither of them wanted to upset the daguerreotyper in the slightest degree; they both found the man's intensity intimidating.

After what seemed like an eternity but was in reality only about a minute, the fellow finally put the covering back on the front of the lens.

"Okay, you can breathe now," Silva said. He smiled, and his face was immediately much more friendly looking.

William laughed, and both women breathed a sigh of relief that the ordeal was halfway over with.

"Well, I guess it beats sitting for a painting," Henry chuckled, as he put his black felt hat back on, then walked over to the long wooden secretary desk that stretched across the front part of the studio. Phoebe picked up her grandson and held him close while William and Frances took their turn on the bench. Frances, especially, was relieved to get through their sitting without any further admonitions from the excitable Mr. Silva.

After studying the available options and discussing it briefly with his wife, Henry ordered one portrait-sized print and four smaller ones. The smaller daguerreotypes would be placed in decorative bronze frames that could be set on a table or fireplace mantel. Henry also paid for William and Frances a portrait size and four of the table sizes.

Afterwards, William offered to pay his father, but Henry told him to just send them a copy of the smaller portrait when he picked up the finished product.

When all the business was eventually concluded and they had said their goodbyes to the daguerreotyper, the four of them paused for a moment outside the studio before they walked back toward the apartment.

"My gracious!" Phoebe exclaimed, laughing. "That was quite an experience, wasn't it?"

If she was honest, she was still a bit shaken up by the whole thing. She had never in her life encountered anyone like Mr. Silva and his portrait studio.

They all burst out laughing. "I know what you mean," giggled Francis. "I thought Henry was going to sock 'Meester Seelva' right in the nose when he ripped the hat off his head like that!"

"You did very well, honey," Phoebe reassured her husband. "I thought you showed admirable restraint, all things considered."

"I agree, Dad," said William.

"Thank you for noticing, son. I have to admit, I swear I'd rather pick an acre of cotton by myself before I go through that again. I hope the finished product is worth it!" Henry grinned. Then he said, "But what *I* want to know is, what the heck was the deal with that outfit?"

"So, does that mean I shouldn't get you your own black velvet cape for your birthday?" Phoebe teased him, and Henry gave her back a glare worthy of the formidable Silva.

"CAKE?" exclaimed little William. "*I* want cake. I'm hungry!"

They all laughed once again at the child's misunderstanding of the word cape.

"I think he's got the right idea," said Henry. "I think it's high time we all got something to eat."

They barely had time to stop at a street vendor and get frankfurters for their lunch, since William had to rush back to the apartment and change into his cadet uniform for

168

graduation. Phoebe promised her grandson that if he was a good boy and ate all his lunch, she would make sure he got cake later in the day. The little boy came through like a champ, polishing off two hot dogs before he was full.

It was such a warm day that it had been decided to have the ceremony outside. A huge circle of chairs five rows deep was arranged on the athletic field. All the graduates were at the south end of the field. Their names were called out alphabetically.

The dean of the college, along with two other individuals, stood on a podium in the center of the chairs.

There was so much noise from the audience that Phoebe could barely hear her son's name called, but finally she heard it. William Lazarus Smith, Bachelor of Science degree. William walked to the podium, shook the dean's hand and one of the helpers handed her son his rolled-up degree.

Suppressing her tears, Phoebe glanced over at Henry, noticing that his own eyes were moist. She put her arm around her husband and squeezed him.

"It's a good day," Henry said proudly, as he looked lovingly at his teary-eyed wife.

It was a good thing that Phoebe was holding her grandson, for Frances was absolutely boo-hooing. Finally, she said through her tears, "William has worked so hard for this, and just think, he'll be getting a monthly salary. It won't be much, but we should be able to live comfortably enough. I'm just so proud of him!"

After each graduate received their award, they were free to leave the ceremony. Henry, who was now holding little William, saw a familiar-looking young man loping across the field, headed in their direction.

"That's got to be Uncle Jesse's grandson, another William," said Henry to Will.

"That's him, the brightest yet clumsiest cadet here," Will said.

There was so much activity going on around them that no one paid them any attention. The young cadet first congratulated his cousin, then hugged Phoebe and Frances.

"So, I assume you're my cousin Henry?" the "new" William asked.

Henry was in awe as he took in the young man's appearance. "My God, it's as though I'm looking at a ghost. You're the spitting image of your Grandpa Jesse!" he told the young man, as he took him by both shoulders and pulled him forward for a closer look.

Phoebe hadn't seen such a grin on her husband's face in a long time.

"My grandpa has always told me I was the spitting image of your father. That's why he named me William. He said I had the same build, hair, eyes...everything," the young cadet said. "I'd give anything if he could see you and your brother James. He talks of you two often," he told Henry.

"When will you graduate from this place?" Henry asked.

"Well, I have my first year behind me, so that means I'll graduate in 1858. That is, if everything goes well, sir."

"Well, you can tell your father and grandfather we'll plan on coming to your ceremony; we can see them then," Henry said.

"I'll be going home for a month after today, and gosh, he'll sure be glad to hear that. He's mentioned several times about wanting to visit you and your brother, but he's always traveling from place to place on one of his trains. I don't think he'll be satisfied until he gets railroad tracks from the Atlantic to the Pacific," the young William said.

Junior was becoming fretful from being in the heat, and Will noticed it.

"I'll tell you what: we're going to the apartment, and you're welcome to come along. You know, you're invited for supper," he told his cousin.

"I know where your apartment is. Just give me time to run to the barracks to change clothes. This uniform must be made from wool, it's so hot and scratchy!" the young cousin said.

"Sure, go ahead; we need to get this child out of this sun," Will agreed.

After hugging the ladies once more, then patting Henry and Will on their shoulders, the young man began galloping across the field towards the barracks.

"What a treat! I wish James was here to see him," Henry remarked, as he pushed the stroller back toward the apartment.

Will laughed, "It's a good thing we're eating at the buffet and it's a set price. That young man knows he can eat!" Will told his father.

"He's a big, muscular boy; It's only natural that it takes a lot for him," Henry said.

"Well," Will suggested, "all I can say is, let's make sure we get our plate full before he does, otherwise we'll all go hungry!"

Chapter Sixteen

As expected, when the train pulled away from the depot in Tuscaloosa, both Frances and Phoebe were crying. Phoebe held her grandson until the very last minute, then reluctantly turned and stepped onto the train.

After they were seated, Henry put his arm around Phoebe, and in an attempt to console her, he said, "Now, now, don't cry, dear, we'll be coming back."

"Yeah, in three years. By then, my grandbaby won't even recognize us!" Phoebe sniffed, with her handkerchief to her nose.

"Aha, so it's *little* William you'll be missing," Henry teased.

"Of course, Will and Frances are included, too," Phoebe answered.

"Oh, well, I feel sure *they'll* recognize you, honey," Henry told his wife, trying to cheer her up. He then tried a different tack. "Boy, that grandson of Uncle Jesse's is a mess. I do believe he can out-eat Tricademus!"

Phoebe smiled. "You know, if you look at him from one direction, that boy looks like our James, then the next time, he looks like our William," Phoebe said.

"Well, he did say that Uncle Jesse told him he looks like my father," Henry said.

"I wish I could have known your father; then I could say I know who our children resemble. He definitely had a dominate gene, that's for sure, because neither of them favor me, not one iota. Look at little Junior: that boy his daddy all over again," Phoebe smiled.

"You don't know the nights I'd lie awake thinking about my own father, especially when I was younger," Henry told her. "I didn't consider at the time how Mother must have been suffering, too. I know now that we would never have made it if it hadn't been for my grandfather. Then, later on, after we were big enough to work, Uncle Jesse took over with helping raise us."

It was Phoebe's time to comfort her husband. Patting him on the leg, she said, "You know, for two young'uns, I have to say we've done all right for ourselves. I won't ever forget that dreadful trip from North Carolina. All our possessions in that two-wheel cart! I had confidence in you, though; my thoughts never wavered. Now look at us...we've been truly blessed. We have three grown children and a grandson, and Heaven only knows how many more grandchildren will come along," Phoebe said.

Henry snapped out of his somber mood and thought how like her it was to think of only family as accomplishments, and not the material things they possessed. He recalled to mind all the backbreaking work of clearing stumps from the land. How he would lie awake at night, praying for rain. The way he had constantly wondered whether he was making the right decision about buying more land, and of course, about building the "mansion," as Phoebe called it.

Then he thought of his brother and said, "You know, Snow Hill isn't far from Camden. Let's stop by James and Mary's on the way home and tell them about Uncle Jesse's grandson."

"It would be good to see them," Phoebe agreed, "but I thought you were in a big hurry to get home."

"It'll only be a couple of hours out of the way; besides, he'll be thrilled to have word of Uncle Jesse," Henry replied.

The train trip back to Camden wasn't bad as the outbound journey to Tuscaloosa. Phoebe knew to dress in cooler clothing and to sit as far back from the smokestack as possible. Even with the discomforts, both Henry and Phoebe thought the train trip was amazing. To think that their transportation could travel at speeds of fifty miles an hour was surreal to them.

"We'll certainly have something to tell when we get home! Not many people from Belleville can say they've ridden on a train," Phoebe said.

"It cost enough, but it sure beats riding on that old two-wheel cart," Henry laughed.

They left Tuscaloosa at nine a.m., and due to all the stops at different towns, it was noon by the time their train pulled into Camden. Phoebe remained at the depot with their luggage until Henry returned from the livery stable with their horse and carriage.

Henry knew he had to hurry if he and Phoebe wanted to have time to visit James, so he didn't waste time getting back to the depot. After loading their luggage into the back of the carriage, it was nigh on one o'clock when they pulled out of Camden.

Snow Hill was about fifteen miles from Camden. Knowing it was another twenty-five miles to Magnolia, Henry ensured that the horses kept up a good pace with the carriage to ensure he would have every possible moment to spend with his brother before heading home.

When he and Phoebe arrived at James and Mary's, they found the house was about like theirs, seeming pretty much abandoned now that the children had married and moved away.

Their son, William, was now a practicing medical doctor.

"At least his office is near here, but the others are scattered from Camden to Selma. We're the proud grandparents of twelve grandchildren, and we seldom see them," Mary said.

"We understand how you feel," Phoebe told her sister-in-law, then she went on to tell Mary about their trip to Tuscaloosa.

Both James and Mary said they were proud of Will.

Henry didn't waste time telling James the news about Uncle Jesse, and his grandson William.

"Boy, our grandpa's name continues on," James said.

"That's for sure. We have near about decided just to call our grandbaby 'Junior' so it won't be so confusing, what with four 'Williams' running around.

"You'd really like Jesse's grandson," Henry continued. "Phoebe thinks he looks like you, but the young man said that Jesse told him he looked like our father," Henry told James.

"Well, I'd sure love to see him," James said.

"We're making plans to catch the train to go back to see Will get his doctorate degree in three years. Uncle Jesse will be there, too, to see his grandson graduate. Maybe you two can go with us," Henry said.

Phoebe looked at Mary's huge "belly lap" and swollen ankles, and she knew the other woman wouldn't be able to make the trip.

James was like Henry when it came to keeping up his health; Phoebe thought that her brother-in-law was aging well. She was so glad that neither brother used tobacco or alcohol. They both had remained about the same weight as when they had all left North Carolina and each had only a few wrinkles in spite of their many hours in the sun, wind and weather.

"Gosh, it would be great to see Uncle Jesse again," James commented, not giving Henry a commitment one way or the other.

Both James and Mary knew that Henry and Phoebe's visit would be short, so they could make it back to Magnolia before dark. It wasn't long before it was time to say their goodbyes.

James helped his wife to her feet, and Mary waddled as far as the front door, then held to the door frame, while Phoebe hugged her. James followed them to their carriage, then the two brothers did their regular thing by slapping each other on the back. James then said, "Allow me," so he ran to the other side of the carriage, gave Phoebe a big hug, then helped her into the carriage.

"Y'all come back as often as you can! Believe it or not, it gets lonesome around here," he told them.

"We will, and the same to you two," Phoebe replied, as Henry popped the whip next to the horse's ear. They left in a jolt, with both Mary and Phoebe waving their handkerchiefs at each other. Phoebe didn't know at the time, but she would never see Mary alive again, for her sister-in-law would die in her sleep that very night.

Chapter Seventeen

Henry and Phoebe received word the next day about Mary's death. One of James' slaves had carried a note to Danny and Allie's, and Allie brought the short message to Magnolia early that morning.

A graveside funeral was held at four o'clock that afternoon, and Mary was buried at Snow Hill Cemetery. Henry and Phoebe barely had time to make it to the services, but they did, and they were accompanied by Allie.

Henry and Phoebe were to attend two more funerals that year, as both Mr. and Mrs. Malone died. Mrs. Malone passed away one hot July day, while Danny's father lingered on until the day after Christmas before he died. They ended up leaving everything to Danny and a hugely pregnant Allie.

Allie's son was born May 27th, 1856, and they named him Daniel Lazarus Malone.

James would accompany Henry and Phoebe to Tuscaloosa in April of 1858, where they all witnessed Will receive his doctorate degree and cousin William get his diploma from the university. Neither Henry nor James could get over seeing their Uncle Jesse again, and how prosperous looking he was. Of course, Jesse was just as overjoyed at seeing his nephews as they were at seeing him. He promised them that he was finally going to visit their neck of the woods now that he had a spur of railroad built from Birmingham to Tuscaloosa.

Of course, Phoebe and Henry were delighted to see their grandson again. They had been wrong about Junior not remembering them, for he ran to greet them at the depot.

Neither of them could believe how much the boy had grown.

They had a wonderful time in Tuscaloosa for three days, but they couldn't stay longer than that. As with their previous visit, it was in the middle of planting season and the brothers needed to get back to farming. Also, Phoebe was anxious to get back home to see little Danny. She considered it a good problem to have, that she had to leave one grandson in order to go and spend time with the other.

As they boarded the train to come back home, they were all happy. It had been good to see Uncle Jesse, and it was also good to know that the family was moving forward.

After the birth of her second grandson, Phoebe (and sometimes Henry) would visit Allie two or three times a week. If Henry couldn't go with her, Phoebe would put on her gloves so the reins wouldn't chafe her hands. She'd then get Clary or Suzy to go with her to see her daughter and little Danny. Allie was genuinely glad when her mother came; it gave her a break. Phoebe could tend to household chores, or spend a little time with the child in order to allow Allie time with Danny Senior, even if she had to saddle her horse and meet her husband in the fields.

Most times, if the weather permitted, on their way back home Phoebe and Henry would stop and visit with Precious, and sometimes Tricademus would be there.

Their son James and his wife Wanda Kay seldom visited, as James was like Henry when it came to hard work; he stayed busy on the plantation of Mr. Ryland. Wanda Kay still taught school in Bermuda, too. Occasionally, Henry and Phoebe would find time to visit them.

Taxes from the federal government on farm products kept increasing year after year. By the time 1860 rolled around, Henry and the other cotton farmers barely cleared enough money that year to pay for the fertilizer, due to the crippling taxes.

Henry talked to Tricademus and Jasper about it, explaining the situation to them. He thought they understood why things seemed to be getting slimmer on the place. "Christmas is going to be poor this year, until I can figure out what to do," he told them.

They both nodded their heads, indicating they understood that the circumstances were unavoidable.

"Next year, we're going to plant more edible things. Looks like we're just going to be forced to live off the land," Henry informed them. Again, they just nodded. They all knew that in farming, the profitable years were a blessing to help sustain them and their families when the lean years came around.

No one but Phoebe knew about Henry's stash of money in the hidden cellar, but he was forced to dip into his savings for just the necessities.

In November of that year, Abraham Lincoln was elected President of the United States. His name wasn't even on the ballot in ten Southern states. The South didn't feel like they were being represented in Washington, and eventually, one by one, the southern states began to break away from the Union. South Carolina was the first to secede, in December of 1860. Alabama followed on January 11, 1861.

Jefferson Davis was chosen to be the President of the Confederacy on January 6th, 1861, and he immediately called men to arms against the North. Montgomery, Alabama was designated as the Confederate capital on February 4th, 1861. On April 12th, the Confederate Army fired on Fort Sumpter off the Charleston harbor in South

Carolina, and the Union Army personnel stationed in that area surrendered in less than thirty-four hours. Thus, the War Between the States had begun in earnest.

A flood of young men began to leave their homes to join the military, both the Union and Confederate armies. They were accompanied by many older boys who were officially too young to fight, and older veterans of earlier combats who knew all too well what war would bring.

The Northern states were led to believe the Southern states rebelled because Lincoln had promised to free the slaves. Little did they know that the slave population had grown so that it was actually a burden on the Southern farmers. Hiring farm labor would have been less expensive, as the owners of the slaves had to furnish them a place to live, plus food and clothing. Half of the slaves owned were too young to do any meaningful work or were too sickly.

The true reason for the conflict was the heavy taxes the Northern states had imposed on the South. Just because a person owned slaves didn't mean they were inhumane; only one in ten actually sold their slaves, and it was a point of pride to treat their people well. Many of the owners had grown to love their workers as family, and thus, they felt it was their responsibility to take care of the young and feeble. To sell a slave was frowned upon by their neighbors and kin.

Henry tried to not get too involved in politics, but he knew things couldn't continue as they had been. The old system was being strangled by the overflowing population of the slaves.

Both he and Phoebe prayed fervently that William and James wouldn't get the "war fever" and join the army. Henry believed strongly that it was the politicians who egged on the young men to leave home and join the military. They felt a little better about Danny, as he couldn't be called up to duty because he had a small child and didn't have anyone to manage the farm if he wasn't there.

Meanwhile, back at Magnolia, Tricademus and Jasper knew the Civil War business was serious when Henry only planted a minimal amount of cotton. In April of 1861, they planted more peanuts, corn, and sweet potatoes than usual. Of course, the regular vegetables such as peas, beans, okra, tomatoes, and greens were also planted.

Tricademus taught Robert and Jasper how to make fishing nets from wire and string. The supply of fish helped to cut back on buying fertilizer, and the eating of pork. "We'se gwine plant lack de Injuns did," Tricademus said, as he and his family threw down fish in the rows as they plowed to use as fertilizer.

The War Between the States, if nothing else, really gave people in the area something to talk about. It had even become a big topic at church. The preachers began to give blistering sermons aimed toward the black race, saying the Bible spoke of slaves being loyal to their masters, even in Biblical days. All over the South there were stories of runaway slaves, as well as wild rumors of a possible slave uprising. All the wild gossip only made some of the slave owners tighten down on their people that much more, making the slaves' lives even more miserable.

Henry believed he had squirreled away enough money for his to live comfortably for the rest of their lives. *"But what about Tricademus and his family?"* he wondered. He knew they hadn't been taught to fend for themselves. *"So, what would become of them if they were set free?"* The topic was a constant source of worry in his mind and heart.

One Sunday afternoon in May of that year, Henry told Tricademus to get word to his extended family to gather at his and Precious' house at six that evening. He and Phoebe had talked things over, and the time had come to share their decision with everyone else. They even had Clary and Suzy there.

Henry stood on the front porch of Tricademus and Precious' home as he spoke.

"Dear friends and neighbors," Henry spoke. "Due to the outrageous demand of taxation the north has levied on the export of cotton, it has become impossible for Magnolia to carry on as it has in the past. I've had you all to gather here today to let you know that I'm willing to set you all free."

He waited for the surprised gasps and murmured words to die down, then held up a hand so they would allow him to continue.

"If you choose to be set free," he went on, "it will mean you'll have to leave from here; I'll no longer be responsible for you. Once I sign papers giving you your freedom, I don't know how you'll make it to the Northern slave-free states. I have no idea how long this war will last, but it's nigh impossible for Magnolia to keep feeding and clothing you without money coming in. I will tell you this, though, if you choose to stay, we will all survive together, by the will of God."

Rum, Ramona's husband, was the only one to step forward.

"Yassuh, Mr. Henry, eyes would sho lacks to be free, dat is if you'se can takes care of my fambly tills I gits a job up dare, den I'll sends fuh dem," the man said.

Henry took a deep breath, knowing that he'd be stuck with taking care of Rum and Ramona's extended family.

182

"Well, Rum, I must say we'll miss you here at Magnolia," he said.

"No!" screamed Ramona, as she burst through the crowd with a baby in her arms. She fell to her knees in front of her husband, begging him not to leave.

"Don' leave, Rum. Massuh, he been good to us! 'Sides, you mights git kilt on de way to dem free states," she begged.

"Ramona, eyes gots ter do's what I thanks is best fuh our fambly, an' I thanks it's up nawth," he told her.

"Mr. Henry, you's sho you gwine sets Ramona and my cheerun free when I sends fuh dem?" Rum asked.

"That's the deal, yes. I'll do the best I can by them, but like I said, Heaven only knows how this thing will end up. You just be sure to hang on to your freedom papers I'll give you. If you get caught without them, you'll just be picked up by the patrollers and be put back into slavery. If that happens, no telling where you'll be," Henry told him.

"Yassuh, I'll travels at nights," Rum said.

"Okay, then. We'll need to go to the courthouse in Sparta tomorrow so they can stamp your paper, to make it official," Henry said.

"Ok, eyes be's waiting," Rum said.

"I'll pick you up in the carriage after breakfast," Henry told him, then he stepped off the porch, disappointed that more people weren't leaving. As Henry made his way back to his carriage, he heard Tricademus scolding Rum.

"I knowed you wuz a no-account when you's fust comes to dis place. Now, you's gwinna takes off with Precious' gal and grandcheerun," Tricademus said angrily, clenching his massive fists at his side.

183

"Eyes doin' it fuh Ramona and my fambly," Rum said, as he pulled his wife, who was still holding their baby, up from the ground. He wanted to say a lot more, but he kept his head, knowing if he sassed his father-in-law there would be hell to pay. Their older children followed them as Ramona and two of their daughters walked slowly back to their cabin, crying.

That evening, against her wishes, Ramona packed Rum's best clothes, and his other pair of shoes. Later that night, she heard a knock on the door, when she opened it, she didn't see anyone. She did find a small sack, though. After she walked back into the cabin into the light, she found the sack contained food. There was a slab of bacon and some cornmeal, along with dried beans and peas. Ramona knew that her mother had instructed someone to send the food over. She also knew the food came from the larder behind her parents' house, and was meant for Rum.

The next morning, Rum stood alone in the road, waiting on Henry. When his soon-to-be former owner arrived, Rum crawled into the back of the carriage with his sack of clothes and food.

Henry spoke to Rum and told him that he was a good worker, and reiterated the fact that he would be missed at Magnolia.

"Thank you, Massuh Henry. I wants you to know I 'preciates you buying me so's I could be's wif Ramona. I'm only leaving cause I wants me and my fambly to be's free," he said.

Henry turned left at the crossroad that led to Belleville, then to Sparta.

"Rum, I'm going to take you as far north as I can after your papers are probated. Do you know how to read the stars?" he asked.

"Yassuh, I believes mos' black folks unnerstan how, dey jist don't wants de white folks ter knows it," Rum said.

"Good. When I put you out, you go north, and try to travel at night, so you can read the stars. If you do get caught by the patrollers, show them the paper that you're about to get at the courthouse," Henry instructed. "When you cross Kentucky and get into Ohio or Illinois, you can say you're a free man, and maybe you can get a job of some sorts. I've watched you work in the blacksmith shop; you'd make a good smithy."

"Yassuh, I likes werking in de shop too," Rum said.

Henry was shocked when it came time for Rum to mark the usual "X" on his free man paper; instead, he printed Rum Smith in precise, neat letters.

After the signing, Henry walked across the street to the same café where Juanita had worked years ago when he and his brother James had first visited the town. He purchased both himself and Rum a ham sandwich and an apple.

Rum sat stoically on the back seat of the carriage, while Henry ate his early lunch.

"I believes I'll wait to git down the road a bit foe I eats mine. I ain't never seed so many white folks, and it looks lack dey all looking at me," Rum said.

"Have it your way, but I'm hungry," Henry replied.

After Henry had finished his lunch, he left Sparta. Rum noticed they were going down a strange road. He didn't know it, but after leaving Sparta, Henry had turned right and started going northeast on the old federal road. After traveling for about an hour and a half, they reached the outskirts of a village called "Old Texas."

Henry pulled the carriage to the side of the road. He then reached into his pocket and gave Rum a ten-dollar gold piece.

"Now, Rum, I hope you know I'm breaking the law by giving you this. You make sure and keep it hidden, and don't dare try to spend it until you get into a free state. It'll give you a little something until you're established," Henry told him.

"Yassuh, don't wurry, I'll hides it good," Rum said.

"Try not to worry about Ramona and your children; I'll look after them. Now, hit the woods on the left. Hide there until dark," Henry said.

"Yassuh, thanks you, Massuh Henry," Rum choked out in a strangle voice, as he swallowed the gold piece, then stuck the free man paper on the inside of his shirt. He then looked both ways before he jumped from the carriage and scurried toward the woods.

Henry could have sworn that Rum was crying as he ran across the road.

On the way back home, Henry really thought about the Southern planters. He didn't know what the future held. All he knew to do was just carry on. He could somewhat understood why the Northern states were in such an uproar. A woman by the name of Harriett Beecher Stowe had written a book titled "Uncle Tom's Cabin." Allie had brought them the book, and she was quite upset about its contents. It portrayed the life of a black slave in the south. The slave, "Uncle Tom," was beaten, lied to, made fun of, and just about everything inhuman that you could think of.

"If only the folks up north could see the real life of the slave," thought Henry, *"Maybe things would settle down some."*

Henry wanted to see his brother James, and discover how he was handling the situation. He thought he'd drop Phoebe off at Allie and Danny's, then after spending a little time with his grandson and daughter, he'd go up the road to visit James. He knew that Phoebe would want to stay on at Allie's, especially since Mary had died. Planting season was over for the year, and he knew Tricademus and Jasper could handle the situation at Magnolia. *"I'll plan on going tomorrow,"* he thought to himself.

It was near sundown when Henry neared his house. He saw Jasper and a couple of his young sons, as they crossed the road. Each one of them were leading a mule. Henry knew they'd been plowing in the south field and had left the plows and the mule's gear in the field.

Henry stopped and asked Jasper if everything was all right.

"Yassuh, Ramona, she not carrying on as much, but Pap, he still be mad at Rum," Jasper answered.

Henry then told him his plans for the next day, and informed him that Rum was a free man and on his way up north.

"I be glad fuh him. I'll let Ramona and maw knows, and don't wurry bout tomorrow. If any white folks comes around, wese just act dumb. Suzy and Clarry, dey knows better dan lets anybody in de house. All Suzy gwine do's is bang on dat pianny," Jasper replied.

Henry chuckled and tipped his hat at Jasper, then headed towards the house.

Chapter Eighteen

The next day, Phoebe was thrilled as always to see little Danny and Allie. It was unusual to catch Daniel at home, but he greeted them at the door.

Henry had always pronounced Daniel's name, "Dan'el."

"How in the world did you manage to be home on such a pretty day, when I know there's plenty things you can be doing?" Henry asked.

"Red, my overseer, can handle things. Today, I'm taking my lovely wife and son to the creek for a picnic," Danny answered.

"Oh my, we've come at a bad time," Phoebe said.

"Nonsense! I'm sure there's enough cooked for you to come along. I'd sure love to dunk my father-in-law's head into that cold water," the young man laughed.

"Twenty years ago, I'd have given you a run for your money, but I'm planning on dropping my wife off here, then go to my brother's," Henry said.

"Gonna talk about Abe, or the damn Yankees?" Danny asked.

"Both, along with the perplexities of being the owner of so many black folks," Henry answered.

"You too, huh?" Danny asked, then continued, "There's so many young'uns on my place, it's taking twenty-five chickens a week to feed 'em. Not mentioning pork, flour, sugar, rice, and other things."

"I know the feeling. I gave all my people a chance to just leave. I'll have to admit, the older ones seem like family, but only one chose to be free," Henry told Danny.

"If I didn't have a family of my own and so many to look after, I don't mind telling you, I'd join up myself. I sort of look for the Confederacy to start conscripting, if that happens, we won't have a chance to decide. I've made up my mind, if the Yankees get into Alabama, I'm going to fight," Danny said.

"I pray it won't come to that, but there's no telling how this thing will end. I have a feeling it's going to mean the death of the life that we know now. Shoot, it already has! Just look at the taxes we're forced to pay on our exports now," Henry said. He paused. "Well, my old grandaddy fought for us to be free of England; now, we're being forced to be free of the Northern states. One thing's for certain, though, the Almighty is still in control of things," he concluded.

"Of course He is, but we can't just sit back and allow the Northern states to control us like puppets," Danny argued.

"I'll agree, but let's not get ahead of ourselves," Henry advised his son-in-law.

"Well, when I see what's going on around us, it gets my dander up," Danny replied.

"Well, today's a day just to enjoy; you're about to go on a picnic with your family. I won't stay any longer, but you can dunk your mother-in-law instead of me, if you'd like," Henry laughed.

"*Henry!*" Phoebe exclaimed.

"No, if I did that, I'd have Allie to fight too," Danny laughed. "And she scares me more than the whole Union Army!"

Their grandson, who was the spitting of his father, kept tugging on his Daniel's hand.

"I'm ready to go swimming, Daddy," little Danny insisted.

"Just a minute," Daniel kept telling his son.

189

"You ought to see how this rascal can swim, and he's barely four years old," Danny told Henry.

"You little rascal," the proud grandpa said, then reached down and picked up the boy. "Hug my neck, then I'll leave, so you can go swimming," he told the child. He barely had time to get the words out of his mouth before his grandson threw his arms around Henry's neck and gave him a tight squeeze.

After putting down his grandson, Henry walked over and gave Phoebe a peck on the cheek. "I'll see you about the middle of the evening," he told her, then hugged Allie's neck before he went out of the door.

It took about an hour and a half before Henry reached James. He noticed that his brother's crops on both sides of the road looked neat and freshly plowed.

Henry tied his horse to the hitching post to the side of James' house. The beauty of the two-story mansion was indescribable. Henry thought the house was built to looked like a showboat that was stranded on land. The balcony had decorative grapevine metal railings. Henry thought it was a shame that, after Mary's death, James lived alone in such a beautiful place.

There was a metal clapper on the double front doors, so Henry rapped on the door. A servant soon opened the door, and she must have recognized Henry, for she directed him to the library, after she spoke to him. She tapped on the door, and James answered.

"Mr. Smif, I believes yo brother is here to see you," she said.

"Well, tell him to come in, by all means," James said.

The brothers met, mid-way of the library.

190

"My goodness, you're dressed fit to kill," Henry told his brother, after they did their ritual of back slapping.

"Yeah, I went to Monroeville on a little business this morning, and just haven't taken time to change clothes," James replied. After checking to make sure the door was closed, he indicated for Henry to have a seat. He then asked his brother if he wanted some water, but Henry declined, saying he had a full canteen in his carriage.

After the usual formalities of each one of them asking about children and grandchildren, James immediately got down to business.

"Henry, what are we going to do? I have barns full of cotton, and I'm not going to sell it. After all those blasted taxes, there's not enough profit left over to buy fertilizer for this year's crop."

"I saw some of your fields on the way here; looks like you have lots of corn growing," Henry replied.

"Yeah, I just planted forty acres in cotton. The remainder is in crops that can be eaten," James said.

"I sold my cotton. I didn't make anything on it, though. Tricademus and his boys have been using fish from the creek to use for fertilizer in some places, to try and save some money," Henry told his brother.

"Is ol' Tricademus still able to get around? You know, it sure was a blessing when Uncle Jesse gave him and Precious to you," James replied.

"Yep, he's still with me and he's still the boss," Henry replied.

"You're lucky; all my old timers are dead. I have plenty of their offspring though. In fact, too many."

"Same here. I think I'm feeding about sixty-five of them, when I left the house, that is," Henry laughed.

191

"Yeah, they become family to you, don't they? I just don't see how some people can split up families and sell them," James remarked.

"You're right, little brother, it's beyond me," Henry replied.

"So, what is your plan of action?" James asked.

"Well, I gave them a chance for freedom, and that failed spectacularly, so all I know is to tighten down on things. We'll just live off the land as much as possible," Henry answered.

"I could have told you that none of them that have a brood of children were going to leave," James said. "Shoot, how are they going to leave with a bunch of children?".

"Well, I just didn't tell them to leave, I gave them a chance for freedom," Henry told his brother.

"That might fly if we were in North Carolina or Virginia, but we're in the Deep South. Maybe Uncle Jesse had the right idea: give them five acres and set them free," James mused.

"He didn't have as many slaves as we do, evidently," Henry told his brother.

"Well, I'm going to do like you said, just do the best I can," James said.

"It's settled, then; we'll just continue on as always. I don't know about you, but I doubled my sugarcane this year. We can use syrup to sweeten things instead of buying all that sugar," Henry said.

"Funny how we think alike; I did the same thing," James laughed.

"I'm going to get off the subject and ask how your children are doing."

"Well, thank goodness, none of the girls married a planter! They're all businessmen. Two of my sons work at a munitions factory in Selma, and of course, William practices medicine and lives about a mile from here," James replied.

"Well, you already know about mine," Henry said.

"Yeah, I've thought a lot lately about my namesake that lives in Bermuda. If he's still getting twenty-five per cent of Ryland's profit, he's not getting much, if anything," James replied.

"Well, his wife Wanda Kay is still teaching school, and James has gone into the mule breeding business. I understand he's selling them to the Confederate Army. Of course, he's still working on the Ryland place too," Henry elaborated.

"And little Allie, how's she?" James asked.

"Happy as a lark, and my grandson Danny is his father made over. I do believe that Phoebe would move in with them if I gave the word," Henry smiled.

James laughed, then said, "At least you get to *see* your grandchild; you know how young folks are. They stay too busy to visit, and my goodness, the last count I had, I have seventeen grandchildren. Too, I think coming here makes them miss their mama. I know I sure miss her," James said in a low voice.

"I can't fathom living at Magnolia without Phoebe. It sure worked on all of us about Mary's death," Henry told his brother. "I'm sorry for you, brother."

"It's rough," James admitted, "especially at night. And when I come in from the fields, I forget for a few seconds and always look for her."

"I'm sorry, brother," was, again, all Henry could think to say.

"I know you are, but it's part of life, I reckon. Something we've all got to do," James replied. Then, changing the subject, he asked, "Well, do you think the Yankees will make it this far south?" James asked.

"If it continues, there's no way of knowing. The politicians...they're just fanning the fire. It has the young folks in a frenzy; that's about all that's in the paper. If those politicians were in an actual battle, I imagine when the first shot was fired, they'd turn tail and run," Henry answered.

James came out of his melancholic mood somewhat, and smiled a little, though the pain was still visible in his eyes. "I imagine you're just about right," he agreed.

As they continued to converse, the two brothers chuckled at times, and were saddened again at times, especially when they talked about their mother and her death.

"Well, at least we're not still living in a cave, or a tent. I won't ever forget your tent with that snake in it," Henry said, and they both laughed.

"Yeah, me either," James agreed. "I swear you jumped about five feet when that sucker stuck out his ugly head!"

"Thank God, you made short work of him, that's for sure. He picked the wrong tent to shelter in, that day. That's the last bad move he ever made."

They had always enjoyed each other's company, and must have talked for at least another hour, when Henry glanced at the clock on the mantel and noticed how late it had gotten.

"Well, little brother, I just had you on my mind, and decided I'd pay you a visit. I'd better get going. I've got to pick up Phoebe at Allie's," he said, as he got up from the chair.

"Well, I've enjoyed your visit. You're always welcome, you know that," James said, as he followed Henry to the door. "Don't be a stranger."

They hugged each other, and James said, "Brother, we've come a far piece together, haven't we."

"Yes, we have," Henry replied. As he walked across the wide porch toward his carriage, he was reflecting on the many years that had passed since two much younger versions of himself and his brother had departed from North Carolina in order to seek their fortunes. He also couldn't help wondering, and worrying, about what the next few years would bring to them both, and the people they loved.

Chapter Nineteen

Later that month, Henry read that the capital of the Confederacy was moved to Richmond, Virginia, and he was glad of it.

In the time since their visit, Henry had done as he'd told his brother, James, that he would. Everything at Magnolia carried on much as it had in the past.

The war really picked up when, on July 21st, 1861, President Lincoln sent General McDowell with thirty-five thousand soldiers on a trip to Richmond. Lincoln thought he'd put a quick end to the uprising by surrounding the Confederate capital, then capturing it.

Things didn't work out that way, however, because when they were twenty-five miles out from the Union capital, McDowell and his soldiers were met by a force of twenty thousand Confederate troops. The Southern soldiers were commanded by P. T. G. Beauregard.

Several spectators from Washington had followed General McDowell to watch the events as they unfolded.

The two forces met at Bull Run Creek, and a bloody battle ensued. The rebel General Thomas Jackson earned the moniker "Stonewall" that day, because the Union forces couldn't budge him and his troops.

The battle lasted all day, then, despite being vastly outnumbered, General "JEB" Stuart's cavalry troops routed the Union forces, forcing them to head back to Washington with their tails between their legs.

There were approximately three thousand Union casualties, and two thousand losses on the Confederate side.

The spectators (those who were sober, though they were in the minority) also quickly made their way back to the capital. Some of the more intoxicated ones didn't make it back until the next morning.

After the disastrous battle of Bull Run, President Lincoln immediately replaced the too-cautious McDowell with General George McClellan.

Lincoln had previously thought that he'd send General McDowell to the Confederate capital and squash it quickly, ending the rebellion. It was a rude awakening, and afterwards, he knew they were in for a long and bloody war.

That fall, after the cash crops at Magnolia were gathered, the cotton was sent to Mobile by steamboats at Claiborne. The peanut crop, along with its fodder, was sent to Montgomery and Selma. Since the blockade runners had to sail the cotton to London, they correctly claimed they were taking a big chance of being blown out of the water, which they used as an excuse to pay only a minimal price for it. The peanuts were paid by a Confederate draft.

Henry wouldn't dare say anything to anyone about it, but he didn't have much confidence in the paper money, so he spent it before he used any of his gold coins. The blockade runners paid off in gold, even though it was a small amount.

Meanwhile, the war continued, even if it was just small skirmishes, the Southern army seemed to be the most dominant of the two. Young men in the area were continually leaving to join the Confederate side.

One Sunday after church, Henry and Phoebe decided to visit their son James and his wife, Wanda Kay. Knowing how busy James and Wanda Kay were, so they had planned for their visit to take place after that year's harvest.

They both thought their sons and their daughter had made good decisions in choosing their mates, for all three of their children clearly loved their spouses.

When they arrived, Henry began the conversation with his son about the price of farm products, and the progress of the war. Phoebe and Wanda Kay talked about social events in their churches and in the area.

Phoebe noticed that Wanda Kay seemed a little happier than usual, so when her daughter-in-law went to the kitchen for refreshments, Phoebe followed her.

Wanda Kay had an assortment of mints and a big bowl of tea cakes on the counter.

"Boy, those tea cakes look delicious," Phoebe complimented.

"James loves them. I made them yesterday, so they should be soft and not so brittle by now," Wanda Kay said.

"I can't wait to have some. I haven't made any in ages; there's no one to eat them, anymore," Phoebe said.

"I can only imagine how you miss your children," Wanda Kay told Phoebe, then added, "but at least you have your grandchildren."

"Yes, I see little Danny two or three times a week, then little William about twice a year. It's not the same as them living in the house with us, though. I think a mother's happiest times are when their children are little," Phoebe replied sadly. Then she glanced up and saw the bright look on her daughter-in-law's.

Wanda Kay grasped Phoebe's hand and asked her to have a seat at the table. After the two were seated, she continued to hold her mother-in-law's hand in her own.

"I'm so happy, Phoebe! I'm quite sure James and I are going to have a baby. I've missed two months. He's taking me to see his cousin, the doctor, tomorrow," Wanda Kay said excitedly.

"Oh, my goodness, what wonderful news. You've simply *got* to get word to me somehow tomorrow!" Phoebe exclaimed.

"I will," Wanda Kay agreed, as she turned Phoebe's hand loose and kissed her on the forehead.

"We'd better get these snacks in there before they suspect something, I've promised James I wouldn't say a word to anyone. You're the only one I've told."

"I won't tell a soul until I hear from you," Phoebe promised.

"One other thing, Phoebe, your son is so good to me. He still enjoys going hunting and fishing at night, but that's about the only time he's not working at something or other," Wanda Kay told her.

"Yes, his father would take them hunting at night. James loved it, but William had rather read a book," Phoebe laughed. "And by the way, I think it's high time you started calling me 'Mom,' don't you?"

After wiping her eyes on the corner of her apron and embracing her mother-in-law, Wanda Kay went to the sink. She and James had a water well in the kitchen, just as Phoebe and Henry had at Magnolia. After drawing cold water from the well, she and Phoebe carried the tea cakes and the water pitcher with its matching glasses into the living room on a silver tray.

Neither Phoebe nor Wanda Kay breathed a word about the wonderful secret they had shared in the kitchen. Henry and James acted as if they'd never missed the ladies, for they were still talking about the war and the price of things when their wives came back into the living room.

The men soon noticed the tea cakes, however, and everyone dived in. All four of them agreed they were perfectly delicious, and they all very much enjoyed the time they spent with each other that afternoon.

Henry and Phoebe had to leave at four o'clock in order to make it back to Magnolia before dark. On the way home, Phoebe commented about what a pretty dress Wanda Kay had been wearing. "That dark red color with the candy-striped top was just gorgeous, wasn't it?" she asked.

"Hon, I don't know. Men don't notice things like that. James must be good to her, though, she seemed mighty happy about something," Henry said. Phoebe just smiled and kept Wendy Kay's secret to herself.

The next afternoon, while Henry and Tricademus were out fishing, Roscoe, one of Danny and Allie's old slaves, tapped on the back door of Magnolia. Clary answered the door.

"Tells Miss Phoebe dat Massah James from up de road done sent dis note to her. Miss Allie, she tole me ter brang it here," the man said.

"Thank you, I'll see dat she gets it. Would you lack some water foe you goes home?" Clary asked.

"No, I specks I'd better gits on back, 'sides, I done drunk some outta de creek," Roscoe announced.

Clary thanked him again, then took the note directly to her mistress, who was sitting on the balcony.

"Thank you, Clary," Phoebe said, as she reached for the short note that read, "YES. Sometime in April. I'm so excited, Mom. Or should I say, Grandma? Love, Wanda Kay."

Phoebe was so thrilled that she could hardly wait until Henry came in from fishing. She decided to stay on at the balcony a while longer, because it meant she would see Henry that much sooner. She knew he would be coming from Tricademus' direction.

She knew the young couple probably stopped on the way home from the doctor somewhere between Snow Hill and Bermuda, to buy their first baby items. She remembered how she herself and Henry were when they found out about their babies, especially William.

Another thing that Phoebe was pleased about was that she knew how much her children and their chosen life partners truly loved each other. She was so pleased that Wanda Kay had told her how good James was to her, not that Phoebe had entertained doubts about her son on that score. She knew how busy James was on the plantation, and he had his mule business as well. She also knew that James was different from his brother William, in that he loved to go fishing and hunting at night. *"Evidently, it doesn't bother Wanda Kay,"* Phoebe thought.

Phoebe was so excited about the new grandbaby coming! She couldn't wait to share the good news with someone, so she decided to walk across road and tell Precious.

Even though she intended on walking, Phoebe still put on her riding boots when she went downstairs.

The walking distance to Precious' house was only about a hundred and fifty yards. She knew that Precious was too busy with children to pay her a visit, and she was also too heavy to walk the distance. Even though Tricademus was twice the size of Precious, he still had to almost shove his wife up the long flight of stairs at church, since it was clear she could hardly make it on her own.

The yard was full of children of all ages playing, and they scattered though they noticed Phoebe. A big red hound dog ran towards her, but after sniffing her hand, he seemed satisfied and plopped down into the dirt of the dooryard, beginning to scratch a floppy ear with one of his back legs.

Due to the alert from the children, Precious met Phoebe at the door.

"Lawd have mercy, is everthang alright?" she asked in a worried voice.

"Yes, everything is fine. In fact, everything is absolutely wonderful," Phoebe reassured her.

After a brief hug, Precious shooed the children away, and said, "Let's set out heah on the porch. Judy be cooking in de house and it's hot in dare. 'Sides, it's sich a cool breeze blowing out here."

Phoebe didn't waste time, for soon as they were seated, she told Precious about the baby James and Wanda Kay were expecting.

Precious grinned, showing her perfect teeth. "Lawd have mercy, Little James. I members when him and Jasper use to run dese woods at night hunting coons and possums. Running through briars and brambles didn't slow dem down. Sometimes they'd comes in bloodier dan de coons or possums," she chuckled.

"They were all 'boy,' that's for sure," Phoebe said.

"Well, I'm proud fuh dem, but Lawd, yo cheerun didn't multiply lack mines and Tric's. I done lost count of all of dem! I feels sorry fuh Ramona and her bunch doe, dey sho misses Rum. You knows I believes Tric woulda kilt dat boy if it hadn't been fuh me," Precious said.

"Tricademus is a loyal ol' soul. I guess Rum did what he thought was best for his family," Phoebe remarked.

"Dat's what I tole Tric," Precious agreed.

"I was hoping he and Henry would be back, and cleaning fish by now," Phoebe told the other woman.

"Tric, he say dey start digging de sweet potatoes tomorrow, so I reckon dey making a day of it whiles dey can," Precious laughed.

"I guess so. Well, I guess I'd better be getting on back to the house, before the girls come looking for me," Phoebe said.

Precious laughed again, and said, "Lawd, chile, dem gals loves you and Mr. Henry to death. I don't knows what wese do's iffen de Nawth set us free and wese have to leaves." The smile died on her face at the thought.

"Don't you worry about it; Henry has promised me if it ever comes to that, whoever wants to stay, can," Phoebe told her friend.

"Dis here is our home eber since we lef Caroliny. Wese don't wants to leave, so dat makes me feels better," Precious said.

"Hopefully, our rambling husbands will get back safely before too much longer. I'd better get on back home," Phoebe said, as she walked down the doorsteps.

"Miss Phoebe, you sho gits round good," Precious said, as she watched Phoebe's still-slender figure gracefully make its way across the familiar yard.

"Poor Precious," thought Phoebe, *"Her big bosoms hang down to her stomach. Maybe if she could manage to heist them up somehow, she'd have better balance."*

As she made her way down Magnolia Lane, she noticed, as usual, that Precious and Judy had continued to keep the house and the yard spotless. The sheep that Henry had bought years earlier had really multiplied, but the grazing habits of the animals kept the lawn looking good in the summertime, and Phoebe was glad of it. Neither she nor anyone else on the place would eat any mutton, as they considered the sheep to be biblical creatures. The men sheared the sheep, however, providing Precious and Judy with wool to spin for warm clothing and blankets.

Henry made it in by suppertime, and he stank like fish. In spite of her eagerness to share the good news, she knew a quick bath and a change into some clean clothes would have to take priority.

Finally, while he was dressing, Phoebe told Henry the news that James and Wanda Kay were to be parents in April.

Henry hugged his wife and exclaimed, "Goodness, if it keeps going like this, we'll wind up as prolific as Tricademus and Precious' bunch!" He then kissed Phoebe on the lips and said, "I know they're two happy people tonight. I can remember how it was for us," he told Phoebe tenderly.

"I'm so happy for them," Phoebe agreed. She then asked Henry if he and Tric had managed to catch any fish.

"Yes, ma'am, a bunch of them. After we cleaned them, Tric gave them to Ramona."

The very next day a letter came to the post office in Belleville. Henry had ridden his horse to town to buy a sack of salt and decided to check the mail while he was there. The outside of the envelope had Henry's name and address, then on the top left side was printed a single word: "Rum."

Henry could hardly wait to get the letter to Ramona. He put the thick sack of salt in front of him on the saddle, then left town at a trot.

Ramona was outside laying some of the freshly dug sweet potatoes in the sun to dry, before they'd be put into the potato bunker.

"Yassuh," Ramona greeted him, as she looked up at Henry.

"I have a letter here; it says that it's from Rum," he told her, leaning in the saddle and handing Ramona the envelope.

With a trembling hand and a worried look, Ramona passed the letter back to Henry.

"Reads it to me, massuh," she requested. "I'se caint read. I sho' hopes he's alright!"

Henry carefully opened the small envelope and, unfolding the piece of paper, he read:

Dear Ramona, I'm getting someone to write this for me.

This is Rum. Tell Massuh I made it to Ohio, and got a job in a wagon wheel factory, making wagon wheels. I'm in good health. The boss man is letting me sleep in the back of the place. I'm saving money to buy two mules and a wagon.

I should have enough by the spring of the year, and I'll come after you and the children.

Love,
Rum Smith

Henry folded the letter and stuck it back into its envelope, then handed it back to Ramona.

She quickly stuck the thin letter in the bosom of her dress.

"Thanky, Massuh Henry. I been praying I'd heah sumpin from Rum, and to hear he be's alright."

"I can imagine," Henry said. He then pulled the left rein to turn the horse so he could take the sack of salt to Precious, who would put it in the pantry to be issued out.

"Massuh Henry," Ramona called up to him before he could go.

Henry pulled back on the reins for it to stop.

"Yes?" Henry asked.

"All dis is so scary to me. Iffen I gits up dare and don't lacks it, can I comes back?"

Henry looked at the frightened woman, and said, "Sure, even Rum, and all the children."

"I jist been thinking, I'd sho miss my mammy and pappy; dis here is de only homes I knows," she said.

"I understand that better than you know, Ramona," Henry smiled, climbing down off his horse so they were eye to eye. He then told her about him leaving the only life he'd ever known in North Carolina, as a young man, not knowing what life would be like or whether he and James would even live to tell the tale. "You'll miss your family here, but you chose a life with Rum. Things have a way of working out, if you keep working hard and loving one another. You'll be all right up there," Henry reassured her.

"Yassah, I hopes you're right," Ramona said. She then went back to sorting the potatoes, with a soft smile on her face that suited her looks much better than her earlier worry had done.

Henry dropped the salt off with Precious and made his way home, thinking he was glad that Rum had made it safely to Ohio. He prayed his hopeful words to Ramona turned out to be true, and that she and her husband would be blessed with a long and happy life together.

Chapter Twenty

That Christmas of 1861, there were so many people coming that Phoebe was worried that Magnolia didn't have enough places for everyone to sit, so all the chairs and benches were brought inside from the porches.

Jasper and Ralph knew just the right sized Christmas tree to cut, and after they brought it in, Phoebe, Clary, and Suzy decorated it on the 22nd of December.

Will and Frances had written that they'd be coming. James and Wanda Kay planned to be there, along with Allie and the two Dannys. Tom, Emma, and Dorothea would also be visiting. Even Henry's brother James had sent a runner that he was coming and was looking forward to seeing everybody.

Clary and Suzy, along with Phoebe, had started cooking three days before the big day. Phoebe baked most of the cookies and prepared several types of candies and other sweets. Henry knew his wife was thinking mostly about the children, leaving the main Christmas meal to Clary and Suzy. Henry had confidence in the two girls, though, for they'd successfully managed to provide a wonderful annual meal for years.

In his letter home, Will had written that he'd rent a horse and carriage in Camden so Henry and Phoebe wouldn't have to waste time coming after them. After Mary had died, they'd stopped making the forays to Claiborne, and instead, Henry and Phoebe Christmas shopped in Monroeville and Belleville.

Only shoes, material, sugar, coffee, and flour were bought that year for Tricademus' extended family. Of course, every household had been given a larger ration of food for the holidays.

Phoebe insisted one day while Henry was in Belleville to buy sixty big peppermint canes. "They're children, and looking for Santa Claus too," she had told her husband.

Precious had made the smaller girls rag dolls, while Tric had whittled the boys different animals from wood.

Will, Frances, and little William arrived on the 23rd. It was a rainy day, but Will had managed to rent a covered carriage, so they had stayed somewhat dry on their forty-five-mile trip from Camden.

'Little William' wasn't so little anymore. The first sentence out of his mouth to his grandmother when he walked through the back door was, "I'm in the third grade!"

"My, my," Phoebe said proudly, as she handed everyone towels to dry themselves as they came in the back door, along with handing out hugs, of course.

"We didn't get wet until we got out of the carriage here," Will said, as he shooed his small family toward the warmth of the fireplace.

The first thing he and Frances noticed was the portrait-sized daguerreotype that Henry and Phoebe had made that day in Tuscaloosa. Phoebe had it framed and hung it on the wall near the fireplace.

"Well, just look at that! Old Mr. Silva actually captured your beauty and Mr. Henry's handsome self," Frances said.

"I thought he did a very good job," Phoebe remarked. She then asked how theirs turned out.

"Oh my, it was terrible! You know how light the color of William's eyes are. Well, it looks like that silly photographer wasn't satisfied with the color of Will's eyes, so he decided to color some in! I tried hanging it on the wall, but I couldn't stand to look at the thing. I swear, it seemed like those spooky eyes followed me around in the room, so I put it away," Frances complained.

Both Henry and Phoebe laughed about it.

They had the best time that night and, as always, Clary and Suzy had cooked a fine meal.

After supper, Frances played a tune on the piano, titled Lorena. "It's absolutely the rage in Tuscaloosa," Frances said.

"I can understand why, and you sang it so beautifully," Phoebe complimented. She then added, "You absolutely must sing it when everyone is here on Christmas Day."

Will and Henry talked of the war, nearly until bedtime. Will said he looked for President Davis to begin drafting young men into the army after the first of the year.

Little William, Phoebe, and Frances had a good time playing Tic Tac Toe and watching 'Junior' as he drew different things on one of the pamphlets he'd brought from home.

The menfolk eventually tired of talking about the war and joined the other three in conversation. Henry showed his grandson how to draw a hump-back camel, for the Christmas scene the boy was sketching. But all the coaxing in the world couldn't get their grandson to sit in either his or Phoebe's lap.

Frances held her hand to the side of her mouth and whispered, "Don't feel bad, he won't sit in my lap either. He does give really good hugs, though," she added.

"He's growing up," Phoebe said.

Frances nodded her head, then told Phoebe the teacher had told her that he was at the top of his class.

Will interrupted them long enough to say that his son was also good in sports. "His coach said he had the fleetness of a deer and can sling a softball straight as an arrow."

"Wow, not only smart, but an athlete, too!" Henry exclaimed proudly, reaching over and ruffling his grandson's shiny blonde hair.

Will yawned and stretched, saying, "Well, it's been a tiring day. Better put your things away and let's hit the sack, son."

In William and James' old room, an extra bed had been placed for just such occasions. Will and Junior climbed the stairs and went to bed, after the boy hugged everyone's neck and Will gave Frances and his mother a peck on the cheek.

Henry, sensing the girls weren't through talking about 'woman things,' said that he was going to turn in, too.

Of course, both Wanda Kay and Phoebe had written Frances a letter about Wanda Kay's pregnancy, so after Henry left them to it, the two ladies started their conversation about that.

Frances admitted to Phoebe that she herself would love to have another child, saying, "Not that William isn't my heart, but it would be nice to have a little girl."

"I know the feeling! As you know, I was blessed with three, each one of them different, but I loved one just as much as I love the other," Phoebe said. "Allie, when she was small...I'd dress her in the daintiest, frilliest little dresses. As she grew older, she told me she'd rather dress in breeches, and wear boots. James, he was quick to anger, and just overall rougher than William. Thank goodness Wanda Kay and responsibility straightened him out! And as for William, he was quick to learn on the farm and at the little school they attended. Since he was the oldest, I really relied on his cool-headed way of thinking."

"Well, you did a good job with all of them. I can't hardly wait to see them all," Frances remarked.

"Lord, that little Danny, a clumsier child you'll never see! Looks and acts just like his daddy," Phoebe shared.

Clary and Suzy quietly made their way from the dining room to the stairs, saying "Goodnight," as they walked by Phoebe and Frances.

"Goodnight," the other two women responded.

Phoebe knew that usually the girls would already have been in bed by this time of night, so she guessed they must have been cooking more Christmas things.

"Boy, how nice it must be to have servants and cooks!" Frances exclaimed.

"Yes, I'm truly blessed. And their sister, Ramona, does all the washing and ironing, but you know, it took me a while to get accustomed to it," Phoebe told her.

Frances laughed and said, "Lord, did I ever make some flops learning to cook with that oil stove! It's sure convenient now, though, not having to deal with all that wood and smoke. By the way, thanks so much for the anniversary card and the money. The money wasn't necessary, but it was appreciated, nonetheless. Will does very well on his teacher's salary, enough so that we're looking for a home near Moundville. I'm so looking forward to a place where I can grow some flowers and he can have a small garden. We feel like it would be a good location to raise our son, too. Tuscaloosa has become so crowded, especially since the war," Frances explained.

"Of course, I'd like to have y'all home, but I know Will has to make a living," Phoebe said.

"Well, if it ever comes to that, you can bet I'd come here instead of going back to Dad and Mama's place," Frances stated. She then added, "Poor Dorothea. I can hardly wait to see her."

"Of course, I see Tom and Emma in church, and when I ask about Dorothea, your mother always says she's about the same. I've heard that two of their house servants have left. I guess the poor things are trying to make their way north," Phoebe told Frances.

"Little wonder, the way she treats them," her daughter-in-law remarked.

"Well, I have no idea how far 'north' is, but maybe they've made it; they've been gone more than two weeks," Phoebe said.

She then told Frances that Henry had offered everyone on the place a chance to be set free, but only one accepted.

"Poor souls, it's the only life they know, and they're afraid to leave the place they call home," Frances said.

"I sure pray that Tricademus and Precious doesn't go anywhere, they're family," Phoebe remarked.

"They've been with you a long time, I know. The time does fly by, doesn't it? It's hard to believe that Will and I have been married eleven years, and tomorrow is already Christmas Eve," Frances said.

"I know. Do you realize how long it's been since I've had all my family together?" Phoebe asked.

"I imagine it's been since we left town," Frances laughed.

"Yep, and I'm going to enjoy and try to remember every single minute of it while you're all at home," Phoebe promised, as she got up and threw more wood on the fire. "Brr! After that rain stopped, I believe the wind is blowing straight out of the north," she stuttered.

"I hope William has built a fire in our bedroom," Frances said.

"I'm sure he has," Phoebe answered.

"You know, Mom, I really feel bad about not staying with my parents. It's as though I'm shunning my father, and he's such a good daddy," Frances said.

"Well, Tom's an intelligent man; I'm sure he understands the situation. I think it's quite common for a daughter to be closer to her father. I know I was," Phoebe told her.

"Really? So, I'm not in the boat by myself. You know I loved you from the start! You never judge, and I can talk to you about anything," Frances confessed.

"With me, what you see is what you get. I taught all my children to just be themselves, and never to put on airs. The old caste system has ruined so many youngsters. Just because a person might be poor doesn't mean they're worthless, nor their children," Phoebe said.

"You are so right about that! There are so many youngsters near us who struggle financially to get through school. You know that Will and I have fed many of them, and I do believe your son gives them special attention," Frances told her mother-in-law.

"I believe you," Phoebe replied lovingly. "That's just the way he is."

The two women talked about things that interested them for about another hour, then they wished each other a good night, and went to bed.

On Christmas Eve day, everyone awakened to a cold frosty morning. The shallow mud holes, especially the ones in the driveway, were frozen solid.

After a breakfast of grits, eggs, fried ham, biscuits, and an assortment of jellies, they each did their own things.

Frances and Phoebe helped each other wrap Christmas gifts. William, as on the night before, busied himself with his artwork. He even drew a star and colored it bright orange. After cutting out the star with a pair of blunt scissors, he insisted the star be pinned to the top of the Christmas tree. Phoebe bragged what a good job he'd done with it, while Frances brought one of the kitchen chairs into the room and, standing on it, she pinned the star at the top.

Phoebe waited until ten o'clock, then put out a saucer of the cookies and candies she'd made on the kitchen table, along with a glass of milk. After getting permission from Frances, she told her grandson to help himself.

Henry and his son decided to ride over and visit Tricademus and Precious, who were especially thrilled to see Will when the two men arrived at their house. They started in right away, telling things he'd gotten into as a youngster, and they couldn't keep their hands off him.

As usual, the house was filled with children, so Henry whispered to Tric that he and Will would bring their Christmas gifts over after the young'uns were in bed.

Tric nodded his head, and said, "I hates fuh y'all to gits out in de cold. I can send one of de boys ober and save yuh de trip."

"That'll be fine. Now, remember, it's slim pickings this year," Henry told him.

"I knows," Tric answered. He then said, "I believes wese in fuh a cole spell, I'll makes sure de boys keeps y'all plenty of wood to bun."

"Well, Merry Christmas, you two," Henry said, as he patted Tricademus on the back and hugged Precious, which made some of the older children giggle.

215

Will hugged the grizzly white haired Tricademus, and Precious, too.

"Lawd, you's looking good Massuh William, dat's de puttiest outfit you hab on," Precious said.

"Thank you, ma'am," Will said, and he followed his father out of the door as quickly as possible to prevent the cold coming in, and the warmth going out.

Henry, knowing Ivey's store in Belleville would still be open for last minute Christmas sales, turned his horse left at the crossroads, with William following on his own mount.

"I just can't let Christmas come and not have anything to give those children but hard candy, shoes, and material to make clothes with," Henry told his son.

Will was about to freeze, but he smiled and said, "I understand."

After reaching the store, Henry bought seven dozen oranges, a case of raisins that were still on the vine, and seven dozen apples. He paid for his purchases with Confederate money, as the local stores frowned if you used U. S. currency.

After leaving the store, the two of them tied the box of raisins onto the back of Will's saddle, and Henry threw the sack of apples and oranges over his saddle.

"If I'd known we were going shopping, we could have come in the covered carriage I rented in Camden," Will said.

They barely had time to make it in and carry the items inside, before Jasper and Robert knocked on the door.

"You'll need a wagon to carry all the things back," Henry told them.

"Yassuh, Pap, he sent us in one," Jasper said.

After all the gifts were carried out of the house, including their recent purchases, Henry smiled and thought to himself, "That Tricademus, he knows me. Not so slim pickings, after all, I reckon."

Supper that night was mostly reheated leftovers dinner, as Clary and Suzy would be busy into the late night, preparing things for the next day.

Will and Henry resumed their talk about the war, while Phoebe and Frances finished wrapping the gifts.

Phoebe saw to it that Clary and Suzy would have new white jumpers to wear over their clothing, and more colorful hair barrettes.

Everyone turned in early that night, except for Clary and Suzy, who stayed up late working on final preparations for the next day's feast.

As Henry and Phoebe prepared for bed, he turned to his wife and said, "In spite of everything, I have to say it's been a wonderful year."

Chapter Twenty-One

The first visitor to arrive on Christmas Day was Henry's brother James. He arrived early enough to eat breakfast with them. Of course, he came in one of his carriages, in order to bring all the Christmas gifts. Phoebe wondered where all the gifts would go, for they were already stacked on the floor four feet high around the tree. Frances, Clary, and Suzy managed to find room for everything, though.

A smoked ham, a roast goose, cornbread dressing, greens, baked sweet potatoes, an assortment of pies, and several vegetables were already cooked.

James, Will, and Henry visited with each other while Frances and Phoebe helped the girls in the kitchen.

Henry, while visiting Monroeville, had bought several different kinds of fruits, which were usually sold during the Christmas holidays. He'd brought home two coconuts, oranges, apples, lemons and raisins. Phoebe made a big bowl of ambrosia, while Frances beat the icing for a lemon cake. Some of the lemons were squeezed and the juice was mixed with water and sugar for lemonade. Phoebe made two big pitchers of the tart drink. It was covered, then put onto a shelf on the back porch, so that it would stay cold.

After Phoebe was satisfied there was enough food prepared to feed a small army, she and Frances began setting the tables with silverware and her best dishes.

The long table in the dining room would seat eighteen people, while the one in the kitchen would seat ten, at the most. Clary and Suzy said they'd eat after everyone else had dined, saying they'd already sampled enough of the food, and they weren't hungry.

Allie, Daniel and little Danny arrived the same time that James and a very pregnant looking Wanda Kay did. They, too, had brought gifts, and, like James, they were covered to their necks with a heavy woolen quilt, due to the cold weather.

The first thing each one of them did was rush to the wide fireplace for warmth. After James and Danny were sufficiently roasted and they could feel their fingertips again, they went outside to bring in the gifts.

Henry and his brother couldn't help but laugh at the chaotic women when they all gathered in the big parlor. Phoebe would go from one family member to another, putting her arm around their waist and joining in on their conversation.

Danny, Will and his brother James, didn't care how cold it was outside; they went out the back door to supposedly check on their horses. They eventually built a fire in the forge of the blacksmith shop, and they, too, had a good time talking about current events, while waiting for dinner to be served.

Tom Jones, Emma, and Dorothea didn't arrive until 11:30. Frances had already told her mother-in-law that she looked for her mother to come at the last moment, "So she can make a grand entrance."

Will was surprised at how Frances' three relatives had aged. He, along, with Danny and James, ran from the blacksmith shop to help the ladies from their carriage.

All the young men shook hands with Will's father-in-law. Will managed to give Emma a chaste kiss on the cheek before they went into the house, with Emma complaining about the cold weather. Dorothea was so huge, Danny grabbed her by the hands while James and Will pushed from behind, in order for her to make it up the steps.

Without being told, everyone lined up in the parlor to shake hands with Tom and hug the two ladies' necks.

Frances was shocked at how much weight her aunt had gained. Afraid that she'd squash some of the chairs in the parlor, Frances directed her to a stout bench that had been brought in from the porch.

Emma had brought the quilt inside that she had used for warmth in the carriage. Henry threw more wood into the fireplace, so Emma didn't stand in front of the roaring fire for very long.

Tom and Emma saw their grandson for the first time that day. Tom tried to coax little William into his lap. The young boy, not knowing them, balked at the idea, and instead stood at the side of Henry, who was sitting in his favorite chair.

Emma was clothed to the nines, in a long black dress with a diamond stick pin at the collar, *"As though she's going to a funeral,"* Frances thought.

She had to admit that her Aunt Dorothea, despite her size, was dressed nicely in a bright red dress with had a white lace collar. Frances noticed the waist of the dress looked like it had elastic sewn in with the fabric. The white collar of Dorothea's dress had a small twig of greenery pinned to it.

Phoebe went into the kitchen and the girls said that all the food was ready on the big table in the dining room. She asked Allie to follow her outside to retrieve the two pitchers of lemonade. After they'd set a pitcher at each end of the table, Phoebe announced that Christmas dinner was ready.

Surprisingly, there was enough room for everyone to sit in the dining room. Phoebe announced that if anyone needed elbow room, they could prepare their plates and eat in the kitchen.

After Henry blessed the food, Danny, Will, and his brother James prepared their plates and went into the kitchen to eat.

"My goodness, I've never seen so much food!" exclaimed Dorothea, making sure she received a big portion of every dish that was passed around to her.

Phoebe noticed that Emma ate well also, and even boasted about how good the dressing and ambrosia were. Phoebe had found out at church that the two slaves who had escaped from the Jones household were the cooks, so she wasn't surprised at their positive reaction to Clary and Suzy's efforts.

When the desserts were passed around, Dorothea really got big portions of each of them, especially the pies.

Emma even scolded her at one point, but Dorothea just expelled a loud belch and told her to mind her own business.

"There's plenty more desserts in the kitchen, so everyone can eat as much as they want," Phoebe said.

Even after everyone else had eaten and had gone back into the parlor to open gifts, Dorothea was still eating.

"I don't see why she doesn't get sick," Emma snapped, as she resumed her seat back in the parlor. Then, as if momentarily forgetting her manners, she cupped her hands over her mouth and shouted toward the dining room door. "Dorothea, darling, let us know when you're finished eating so someone can help you stand."

Little Danny was sitting in Phoebe's lap, when Frances came over and told Phoebe, "My son says, it's past time to open the gifts."

"I'm all for it. Would you and Wanda Kay please pass out the gifts?" Phoebe asked, for she was enjoying holding her grandson.

The girls decided to put the boys' gifts near the front door, as there were so many of them. Squeals of excitement came from the boys as they opened each of their presents.

Phoebe was sure she had told Emma at church that gifts would be exchanged, but Emma and Tom hadn't brought any.

Phoebe had bought Emma a pretty, covered candy dish, while Frances had bought both her mother and Dorothea a gift. Emma's gift wound up being a beautiful thick black shawl. She felt certain that Dorothea's gift would be a shawl too.

Tom got a nice three-bladed pocketknife.

"I hope everyone remembered that we have to go home on a train," Frances remarked, as she and Will began to open their mound of gifts.

Out of all their presents, both Henry and Phoebe each ended up getting three pairs of bedroom shoes. In addition to the carved ivory cameo brooch that Phoebe wore proudly pinned to her dress, her second gift from Henry was completely unexpected. He'd bought her a beautiful silver turquoise ring and matching necklace.

The girls received mostly household items, except for Frances, for Will had bought her a fur stole. "Well, the weather is colder in Tuscaloosa than it is here," Frances said, as she exaggerated a fashion model's stroll across the room with the stole around her neck.

"It's beautiful. And just look what a beautiful emerald ring my husband gave me!" Allie exclaimed happily, as she displayed the fourth finger on her right hand.

Wanda Kay cleared her throat and said, "Well, I wasn't going to boast, but…" then she held out her own right hand, which sported a gleaming twenty-dollar gold piece attached to a golden ring.

"Well, we girls must be doing something right," Allie crowed, which brought out screams of laughter from the whole family.

Will, Danny, and the two Jameses received gifts of boots, woolen coats, and pocketknives.

Phoebe had left Clary and Suzy's gifts in the kitchen. She saw them as they ran upstairs, probably to slip on their new white jumpers and put the new barrettes in their hair.

Phoebe felt sorry for Henry's brother James. She knew he had to be thinking of Christmases in the past when Mary and the children were home. She had to give him credit, though, he acted as though he was having a good time, and she hoped he had enjoyed his dinner.

After all the gifts were opened, Allie was asked to play Christmas carols on the piano, which she gladly did. Both Wanda Kay and Frances pulled up chairs next to her and sang along with her.

Allie saw Clary and Suzy as they came downstairs wearing their crisp white uniforms. "Come play for us, please," she asked Suzy.

Suzy was hesitant at first, but finally crept shyly toward the piano.

"Eyes aint neber played fuh white folks," Suzy said, as Allie slid to the end of the piano stool and Suzy sat down.

Phoebe had to admit, she, along with everyone else in the room, was stunned how beautifully Suzy played and sang "Silent Night." That was all the girl played, and as soon as she finished, she practically ran from the piano, amid enthusiastic applause from the listeners. She stopped at the dining room door and took a bow.

Phoebe had no idea at the time that it would be the last Christmas they'd all spend together.

Suzy and Clary hadn't been in the dining room long, before everyone in the parlor heard a thunderous crash, and then girls screaming.

Henry shot to the dining room door and found Dorothea lying on the floor. He called out for Tom.

They both felt for a pulse but couldn't find one. Henry then ran to the kitchen for a wet cloth, and wiped her face, but there was still no response.

Henry pried the piece of ham from her stiff fingers and told Tom that she was dead.

The girls screamed again, then Clary said shakily, "Wese thought she wuz sleeping when wese covered de table. Wese aint neber seed no daid purson before!" She and Suzy then went quickly into the kitchen, both sobbing.

Everyone but the two young boys sat in suspense when Henry called Phoebe and Emma to the room. As soon as Phoebe saw the body, she went to the kitchen and asked the girls to go get a bedspread. The body was lying in their path and they both let out a whimper as they jumped over the purple body of Dorothea.

"Poor Dorothea, she finally did it! She ate herself to death. I should have known something was up when the girls played the piano and she didn't make an attempt to come in there and play," Emma said.

"Well, at least she died happy," Phoebe replied, shaking her head at the callous attitude of the dead woman's sister.

Clary soon returned to the dining room door, but didn't enter the room. Instead, she just stuck her hand through the doorway, holding out the bedspread.

"What's going on in there?" Frances asked Clary.

"It bee's Miss Doroty. Massuh Henry, he say she fell ober daid," Clary answered, her face pale.

"Oh, no!" Frances exclaimed as rushed toward the dining room, with Will following right behind her. Henry was covering Dorothea's body with the bedspread when the two of them entered the room.

Frances was surprised that her mother was actually crying. "I just didn't understand her; she was so different," Emma said, as she wiped tears away with one of the cloth napkins.

"Well, she does have a heart after all," thought Frances in surprise, as she eased toward her mother and slid her arm around her waist.

"It looks like rigor mortis has set in; it's going to be hard to get her into a casket. We don't want poor Dorothea to go to eternity in a sitting position," Tom said. He then asked Phoebe if she had a quilt that might be strong enough for them to tote Dorothea's body to the carriage.

Phoebe left the room and soon returned with a thick quilt that Precious had made.

Henry then asked Emma, Frances, and Phoebe to leave the room. "Ask the boys if they'll come here," he told Phoebe.

He spread the thick quilt out beside the still form of the big woman. Once Daniel, Will, and James entered the room, they picked Dorothea's body up and laid her on the

225

quilt. She was still frozen in a sitting position, so Daniel folded the bedspread that had covered her body several times and put it over her knees.

Daniel and James knew what to do; they pressed down on her shoulders while Daniel sat on her knees, until her body was straight.

"Brr, I never thought I'd be doing this today," Danny said.

Henry then unfolded the sheet and spread it back over Dorothea's body.

"Okay, Danny and James, each of you boys grab a corner of the quilt next to her head," he instructed. "Will and I will each grab a corner at her feet. Tom, you go ahead of us and open the back door, please—wide open, then after we're out, open the door to your carriage."

It was a struggle, but finally, they squeezed Dorothea's body into the back of Tom's carriage. Henry was just thankful that it was daylight, and they could see what they were doing.

"Pardon my language, but it's going to be hell getting Emma to sit in front of her sister's body on the way home. Especially with her facial expression being so grotesque," Tom said.

"I feel sure that William will be more than glad to take Emma home," Henry answered.

"It's a little belated," Tom said, but he pulled his purse out of his pocket and gave William three Confederate bills. "One for each of you, my daughter, you, and the grandson," Tom told his son-in-law.

Will looked, and each note was a hundred-dollar bill. "This isn't necessary," he said, as he tried to give the money back to his father-in-law.

"Oh yes, it is. Please accept it as my gift. Frances and little William are all I have," Tom said.

Will couldn't help but notice that his father-in-law never mentioned Emma's name.

Tom told them that he hated to disrupt their Christmas, but he'd better get home while the sun was still shining. "A coffin must be made. I'll set a brief funeral for two o'clock tomorrow at the family cemetery," he told them. He then added, "The weather is so cold, and the sun sets early these days. We shouldn't make it any later than that; it'll give people time to get back home before dark."

"Okay, my friend, but give me time to put on my overcoat and I'll ride with you; I can come back with Will," Henry said, as he patted Tom on his back.

"That would be nice of you," the other man said, as Danny and James led the horses out of the stall to hitch up the two carriages.

Both Henry and Tom went back into the house for their overcoats, and the only sound they heard was the two youngsters playing.

Henry told Phoebe and Emma what Tom and he intended on doing.

"I know this might sound heartless but do your best to try and have a good Christmas the rest of the day. Like Phoebe said, Dorothea died happy," Henry told everyone.

His brother James thanked everyone for a good Christmas dinner and told them he had enjoyed his visit in spite of the sad circumstances. He then announced that he needed to get home while there was still daylight. He then thanked everyone once more, for the gifts.

Phoebe, Allie, Wanda Kay, and Frances all came over to hug James' neck.

"Take some food with you," Phoebe encouraged.

"Well, now that you've brought it up, I did just so happen to bring an empty platter with me," James chuckled agreeably, somewhat lightening the somber mood in the room.

"Good; one thing's for certain. It's so cold out there, you won't have to worry about your food spoiling on the way home," Phoebe said, as James headed out the door to get the dish.

Henry, Tom, Will and Emma donned their overcoats. Henry made sure that he hugged his brother tightly on the back porch before they all loaded into the carriages. Tom stayed in the lead on their way to Belleville.

Tom was able to contact Reverend Travis that night, and the funeral was set for two o'clock the next day, as planned.

Due to Emma's request, Dorothea would be buried in the dress she had been wearing when she died.

She explained to Tom that the dress she had on was the only one that fit her. "That's why she wore robes around the house all the time," Emma expressed.

An oversized coffin was built in the shop that afternoon, and by early night, Dorothea's body was shifted from the carriage to the coffin and the lid was nailed closed. The coffin was then moved to the little house that had been originally built for Dorothea, where Will and Frances had lived. Tom figured that would best, due to her weight. The body wouldn't have to be carried but a short distance, which was only about a hundred feet.

A fire was built for the slaves as they dug the hardened dirt that night, with Tom giving strict orders to not leave signs of where a fire had been once they finished their grim task.

About thirty people showed up for the funeral. After her aunt's coffin was in the ground, Frances tossed in the unopened Christmas gift.

The whole affair was over in about twenty-five minutes, and the mourners went about their separate ways, while the slaves shoveled dirt over the coffin.

Frances and Will had ridden to the funeral with Phoebe and Henry. At the Belleville intersection, Frances said, "Well Aunt Dorothea couldn't have picked a prettier day. Just look at that gorgeous sunset showing out in the western sky. It, too, will soon be gone from view, as it sets."

"You were so brave today, Darling. I know how you loved Dorothea," William said, as he put his arm around Frances, pulling her close. Phoebe nodded her agreement.

"I can understand Wanda Kay not coming, her being pregnant, but James gave me the sweetest sympathy card from her," Frances told them.

"Wanda Kay is a gem; I love her, as I do all my children's spouses," Phoebe said.

Allie and Danny had been chosen to stay at Henry and Phoebe's to babysit the boys. And just like that, Christmas of 1861 was over.

Chapter Twenty-Two

It had finally happened, the event that had worried them all for so long. President Davis began conscripting men ages 18-35 into the Army of the Confederacy in April of 1862, which made James and Danny eligible for the draft. William missed it by one year, so he was not called into service.

After hearing that James was joining after his and Wanda Kay's baby was born, William turned in his resignation from the university, knowing it would just be a matter of time for President Davis to lower the age limit. He wanted to spend as much time with his wife and child as possible before that happened.

He and Frances sold what they could, knowing they wouldn't need anything but their clothes and Little William's toys. There wasn't a doubt about where Frances would be living; she and her son would be staying with Henry and Phoebe for the duration of the war.

Wanda Kay gave birth to a beautiful baby girl on April 21st. They named the baby Shelby Rae.

Phoebe was elated that she finally had a little granddaughter. After making three or four visits, taking Henry away from his busiest season, Phoebe saw that Wanda Kay made a good little mama, so she stopped going as often.

James thought little Shelby Rae was the best thing that had ever happened in his life. She was so fragile and completely dependent on others, especially her mama. He began to have second thoughts about joining the Confederacy.

After William's return from Tuscaloosa, he advised James that if he waited to be conscripted instead of volunteering, he'd surely go into the infantry.

There were many battles fought that spring and summer, which took place mostly in the southeastern states, especially Virginia. The Southern soldiers proved to be tough in battle; even though they were outmanned, they came out the victors. This, of course, just set the young Southerners on fire to join up and personally run the Yankees right back to where they came from.

Word got out that the 3rd Alabama Cavalry would be accepting soldiers in Monroeville on May 12th. William and James were there, along with many other young men.

Jasper was given a pass to accompany them there, and then to make a return trip back. It was a good thing that he had accompanied them, for both William and James were inducted into Company B, 3rd Alabama Cavalry that day, and were sworn in.

"Gentlemen, you are now the property of the Confederate States of America," the Colonel told them.

They never dreamed they'd be leaving that very day. They thought they'd at least have a chance to go home and say goodbye to their loved ones. After discovering that they, along with their horses, would be departing that same afternoon for Sparta to catch a train north, William sent Jasper home to tell him to let his father know. "We'll be coming up Belleville Road. Tell Pa to meet us at the intersection with two of his muzzleloaders and two good pocketknives."

"Yassuh, I sho will," Jasper said, and he left in a hurry.

William had asked the commanding officer, Colonel Hagan, if it would be okay if they brought their own rifles.

231

"We live near Belleville, and Pa will meet us along the road," William told him.

"Well, as you can see, most of the young men already brought their rifles with them, but long as it doesn't slow the column down, I suppose it will be all right," the colonel said. The Colonel then added that they'd all be issued sabers once they reached their destination.

As the men stood by their horses, waiting for the Colonel to give the order to mount, James exclaimed, "My Lord, I thought I'd at least get to kiss my wife and baby goodbye!"

"You heard what the Colonel said. We are now the property of the Confederate States," William told his brother.

They left Monroeville at two o'clock that afternoon, and by three-thirty, the column were nearing the intersection that led to the house.

The road was lined on both sides with people from Magnolia. Jasper's word had echoed throughout the community. Tricademus, Precious, and most of their clan were there. Of course, Henry was there with the muzzleloaders, with Phoebe, Frances, and little William at his side.

Colonel Hagan, who was riding at the rear, motioned that it would be okay for them to drop out of line.

Phoebe, Frances, and Precious dabbed at their eyes with their handkerchiefs. William embraced Frances and kissed her, while James kissed his mother on the forehead, then took the flintlocks from his father. "Get word to Wanda Kay that I love her and little Shelby Rae, and I'll be coming home as soon we run the Yankees out of the Southland."

Phoebe answered that she would pass his messages along, then added, "You boys watch out for each other, and come home safely."

William left his wife's side, then kissed his mother on the cheek, before he hugged his son.

James gave William one of the weapons before they remounted and got their horses back in line. They both then saluted Tricademus and Precious.

The troops left Sparta, Alabama by early night, headed north. As the train left Conecuh County and entered Wilcox County, James wondered if his brother-in-law, Danny, didn't have the right idea. Maybe he should have just waited to be drafted.

Chapter Twenty-Three

Several memorable things took place at Magnolia that year. The first of June, Rum returned from Ohio in a wagon led by two mules. Ramona was absolutely beside herself, with mixed emotions. Rum and Ramona had produced six children, three of which were big girls who, like Ramona, considered Magnolia their home.

Tricademus, who really hadn't expected Rum to return for his daughter and grandchildren, had little to do with him.

Henry did as he had promised, though, and the next day after Rum's arrival, with Rum, Ramona, and their children following him, they made the trip to Sparta.

After they had all signed their "X" on the legal document, they were free.

Once they got outside the courthouse, Ramona told Henry that she couldn't hold up to going back to Magnolia to say goodbye to everyone. "'Sides," she said, "Eyes skeered deese oldest gals might jump outen de wagon and hits de woods."

"Okay, if that's the way you want it, but please get someone to write me a letter when y'all are in Ohio, so I can read it to your folks," Henry said.

"You been a good massuh, Mister Henry," Ramona said.

"I can agree wit dat, and thanks you, Massuh Henry, fuh eberthang," Rum said, as he slapped the two mules with the reins, and the wagon jolted forward.

Henry watched them for a short while and saw that, along with Ramona, the children were crying.

A letter got through to Frances that month from William. Among other things, William wrote they were stationed near Chattanooga, Tennessee. He also informed them that both he and James had been promoted to Sergeant. "We had to buy our own gray uniform, though, from a tailor that lives near the camp. We've been issued plenty of lead balls and black powder, along with our sabers."

Of course, more things were written of a more personal nature that Frances didn't read aloud. William ended the letter by asking Frances to hug their son for him, "And tell Mother and Father I said howdy."

By the end of June, 1862, Danny was inducted into the 4th Alabama Regiment.

Daniel had told Allie to get Red to nail the windows and doors closed. "I'd feel better if you and little Danny moved in with your parents. I've talked to Red, and he knows what to do. The only thing you might have to do is sign a legal document now and then," he'd said. "The place is barely clearing enough to pay for itself. If the slaves run off, they run off; there's nothing I can do about it."

The next day, Daniel's regiment left for Vicksburg, Mississippi from Sparta, with a local drummer and fife playing "Dixie." Allie promised herself that she'd be brave at the depot, for her husband's sake. However, after their last goodbye embrace and Daniel had boarded the train, Allie couldn't hold back the tears any longer. Henry helped his daughter and wife into the carriage for their return to Magnolia, with Phoebe sitting in the back of the carriage with her daughter.

"Well, that makes all three of them," Phoebe said, as she patted her daughter on the back.

"Poor Danny, he's so tall and clumsy, it'll be hard for him to hide from the Yankees," Allie sniffled.

"I know it's tough, daughter, but young men are leaving home from both the North and the South. Ol' Danny is pretty sly; he'll be alright," Henry reassured her.

With an attempt to lighten the dark mood in the carriage, Phoebe told them that little William now wanted to be called just William, not Little William.

Allie managed a grin. "Well, in that case, we'll do the same for Little Danny," she said.

Allie had moved back into her old room at Magnolia, while Frances now occupied into William's old bedroom. The two boys claimed James' room.

With Ramona being gone, Jasper's oldest girl, Ruth, asked for Ramona's former job as the laundress. "It sho beats werking out dare in dem fields," Ruth had said.

Both Allie and Frances helped with the kitchen work, and also with laundering the clothes and bedding. They told Phoebe the extra work helped them keep their minds off their husbands.

It was as if time stood still, with everyone anxiously waiting to hear from their loved ones in battle in faraway places.

Henry kept up with the news through the local newspapers and knew that his sons had been in several skirmishes. It seemed that the whole state of Tennessee was involved in one battle or another.

Mail was scarce, to say the least, but two letters had reached them from William in August, saying that he and James had seen a good bit of fighting. "The 3rd Alabama has proved a tough nut to crack," he boasted. He wrote that they were fine and in good spirits. He told everyone not to worry about them. "The unit looks after each other," he wrote. Of course, most of the letter was for his wife's eyes only and was private from Henry and Phoebe.

At the bottom of the letter, William wrote, "It would be useless to try to write us back, for we stay on the move. We go where we're needed. I pray all is well at Magnolia. Please get word to Wanda Kay that James is fine, in case his letters aren't getting through.

William kept from his family all the horrible things he and James experienced: men all around them blown to pieces, dying of dreadful wounds before their very eyes, the diseases, the hunger…the list of horrors was endless. There was never enough to eat. William had no idea on the day they joined that the Southern army was so poorly equipped. Once in a while, supply wagons would slip through, and they'd eat well for a couple of days.

William also failed to mention that he was nursing a wound in his left hip. It happened at a skirmish in McKnight's Mill, Tennessee. James and he were riding as scouts that day when, from out of nowhere, the Yankee Cavalry rushed toward them from behind some trees and a building that stood beside a rushing stream.

Everything happened so fast! William's eyes quickly scanned the Yankee Cavalry and counted six soldiers. His intention was to turn his horse around, since they were outnumbered, and ride back into the woods. That's when he heard James' musket fire and saw the lead Yankee fall to the ground from his horse. James then slammed his musket into the holder that was attached to his saddle, then grabbed his saber. William leaned to the right of his own saddle, grabbing his saber with his left hand and his musket with his right. The muzzleloader was so heavy, it was difficult to holding it with just one arm, but he knew to fire it fast, so he did. He saw the back of Yankee's head as it was blown away.

At that moment, he felt a sharp, burning pain in his left hip. William couldn't see anything but the arm of a blue uniform unless he straightened up in his saddle, which he knew enough not to do, so he just blindly hacked at the blurry blue shape with his saber, giving it all the strength in his arm.

The Yankee cursed as his own saber fell to the ground. William, knowing the Yankee probably also had a rife, knew he had to finish off the enemy soldier before the man could do the same to him.

He sat upright in the saddle. The Yankee was struggling to get his rifle with his left hand. With all his might, William hacked at the center of his foe's head, and that Yankee, too, fell to the ground.

William looked for his brother. He saw that James was hacking at his own opponent with his saber. He also noticed that James had killed another Yankee, giving him a total of two kills also.

A rush of adrenaline coursed through William's body the instant he saw James in deadly danger, and in his hip suddenly diminished as he rushed to his brother's aid.

William gave the Yankee's horse a swat on its buttocks with the flat of his saber. The horse whinnied, then reared up, causing the Yankee to almost lose his balance. That's when both James and William struck him with the sharp blades of their sabers. His dead body toppled to the ground along with those of his comrades.

"Are you injured?" the brothers asked each other, both breathing harshly from fear and exertion.

James was the first to reply.

"The top of my head—is it intact?" he asked William.

The adrenaline was beginning to simmer down for them, as William carefully examined the top of James' head.

"Other than a few more of the usual head lice, it looks the same to me," he told his brother.

James was about to ask again if William if he was okay, but then he saw that William's trousers were bloodsoaked on the side of his left hip.

"You've been hit. Let's go behind that building; you can drop your drawers there, and we can get a looksee at how bad it is," James said.

They reloaded their muskets and stayed mounted on their horses until they made it behind the building, which they both recognized as being a grist mill.

"You boys made short stuff out of them damn Yankees," a bearded old man said as he stepped from the door of the building. Both William and James had him in the bead of their muskets after his first word.

"Whoa, whoa, I'm on your side," the old fellow blurted out, holding both his hands out in a conciliatory gesture. He then continued, "Would you believe them bastids wuz about to steal all my meal until you fellers showed up?"

"We can talk later. Right now, we need to take a look at my brother's wound," James said, as William unbuckled his saber, then his pants.

After all three of them examined the wound, the old man told them to jump into the creek. "Take some of that sulfur clay along the banks of the creek. Be gentle with the wound but wash the hell out of them heads; both of y'all are ett up with head lice," he instructed.

Once he had gotten a closer look at his injury, William saw that the cut wasn't too deep. He and James did exactly what the old fellow had told them to do, and even with the stab wound, the bath was very invigorating.

After they'd gotten out and dried themselves, the old man reached up to the branch of a tree and pulled down some moss.

"Now, you pack some of this moss into that wound, and change it twice a day. It'll be cured in a week's time," he told them.

They each thanked him and dressed in their uniforms again. They told the helpful old man they were claiming the Yankees' two mules and wagon as property of the Confederacy. "We'll also have to take your corn and meal. There's some mighty hungry boys and horses back at the camp," James said.

"Hell, tell your commander there's a heap of Yankees jist over the ridge. Unless they's a bunch of you boys, I'd skedaddle," the old fellow said.

"We'll sure let him know, and thanks again for everything," William told him, and then asked him his name.

"What difference does it make? I'm jist an 'Merican like you," the man responded, then he added, "Hell, it's the least I can do fer my country." He even helped James load the wagon with the cornmeal and grain.

William mounted his horse, then grabbed the reins to James' horse so it would follow, while his brother drove the mules and wagon back to camp.

When they arrived, William shared with Captain Allen what the old fellow had told him about the large number of Yankees camped nearby. Allen instructed his men to wait in place until that night, and then the small detachment of cavalry slipped back toward their main body of troops.

They were thankful for the small amount of cornmeal and grain for their horses. It wasn't much, but would stave off starvation for a few days, at least.

Chapter Twenty-Four

In September of 1862, word got back to Phoebe that Precious was feeling low, so Phoebe decided to take her on a trip to Belleville. At first, Precious was dead set against it, but Phoebe knew how her old friend loved sweets. When she told her she'd buy her a big box of bonbons all to herself, Precious hesitantly agreed to go.

When Frances found out about the trip, she asked Phoebe if she could accompany them, saying that she'd like to visit her father. Of course, Phoebe said that she'd enjoy her company, so Frances made plans to leave William with Allie.

"Father's heart is going to be broken, because he'll miss William, but my child said he'd rather stay and go fishing with his grandaddy and Tricademus," Frances said.

All but the sugarcane had been harvested, so Jasper had time to drive them to Belleville.

For the first time since their marriage, Henry rationed the money he'd given his wife to fifty dollars, and that was in Confederate money.

They stepped into the carriage and rode down the lane about nine o'clock that morning. Knowing they were looking at the last vestiges of summer, they enjoyed looking at the colorful leaves on the trees.

"Boy, you never really think about ol' Mother Nature being so beautiful until you get out of the house," Frances remarked.

"It is a gorgeous day for an outing," Phoebe agreed.

They both were astounded at how prettily Precious was dressed. As Jasper helped her into the carriage, they smelled the scent of verbena in her clothes. It was clear that the woman had made a real effort that morning to look her best.

"Precious, you look absolutely gorgeous this morning," Phoebe complimented her.

"Thanky, Miss Phoeb," Precious said, and then laughed, as Jasper pulled the carriage out of the yard, with her and Jasper sitting up front.

Phoebe smiled at Precious and asked her what had crossed her mind that was so funny.

"I spose I dasn't say dis wif Jasper next ter me, but dat Tricademus must've thought I lookted good too," she said, with a wicked grin and a wink.

Precious' words got through to the girls in the back. When they caught onto the meaning behind what she said, they laughed loudly along with her, as Jasper turned into the road.

When the ladies finally stopped laughing, Phoebe told Precious that Frances and she had been commenting how pretty the leaves were.

"Yeh, eyes been seeing de leabs falling. It'll be hawg killing time foe we knows it, and syrup making time too," Precious said.

Phoebe didn't believe Precious even realized how funny she was, but from the way she talked and the silly little stories and innuendos she shared along the way, all three of them stayed in stitches. Phoebe knew the little outing was doing them all good. They had all spent far too much time dwelling on the war, and its dangers to their beloved men in the field of battle.

When they reached Belleville, Phoebe told Jasper that Frances had planned to visit her father first, so he drove them through the busy little village. As they neared the little cottage that William and Frances had lived in, they noticed things seemed busy around the small dwelling. Frances could see her father on the front porch, and it looked as though he was instructing some of his people things to do.

"Stop here, please, Jasper," Frances requested. "I'll only be a minute," she said, as she almost jumped from the back of the carriage.

The workers parted and went about their way.

Frances opened the gate, went to her father and they hugged.

"It's so rare that I can catch you by yourself," she told him. Tom grabbed his daughter's hand, and they went inside. She noticed right away that the house looked as though it was lived in, then she clearly heard voices coming from the kitchen.

"Father, is someone living here?" she asked.

"Sit down; I might as well tell you, but please keep it to yourself," Tom told his daughter.

"Of course," Frances answered.

The words poured out of her father's mouth in a rush of feeling. "It's your mother. I'd had enough! She was bad enough before your Aunt Dorothea died, but since then, she has made it impossible for me to live with her any longer.

"It's one tea party after another, or some other kind of women's get-together. She spends as if money grows on trees! I've begged and pleaded for her to watch the spending, telling her there's a war on, and how expensive things are. I don't know if Henry has told you, but there isn't money to be made in farming anymore. It takes all I can do to feed, clothe, and provide shelter for everyone. For the last three years we've been living off what I had saved," he said, and his frustration was clear from the bitter tone of his words.

"So, you've moved up here?" Frances asked.

"Yes. I can concentrate on my books, I don't have to listen to all her putting on airs, and I eat regular foods, not that fancy stuff. Another thing, I sleep like a log up here. And I tell you now, the house servants didn't run off—the truth is, she made it unbearable for them. I freed them, and they left for the North. She'll run off the ones she's got up there now, too; she's impossible to please," he told his daughter.

Frances reached over and squeezed Tom's hand. "I don't blame you. As for myself, I was a happy young woman when William Smith got me out of that house!" she exclaimed. "And it was all because of Mother."

"Well, I'm sorry, daughter. Lord knows, I tried for you to have a good upbringing, but according to her I never did anything right. I think it was because her family didn't have much when they were growing up, and when I started to accomplish a little something, it went to her head," Tom said.

Frances got up and hugged her father's neck. "You'll be seeing more of your grandson and me, but I'm sure you saw that I'm not by myself, so I'd better get moving. Who's in the kitchen?" she asked.

"That's Coot and Frankie, my cook and housekeeper. They sleep in their cabins in the quarters, then come over here in time to cook my breakfast."

Frances hugged him again, then he followed her to the carriage and had a brief conversation with Phoebe.

On the short trip back to Belleville, Phoebe couldn't help but notice the glow in Frances' eyes, and she knew that Tom must have told his daughter some good news.

The first thing they did was check the mail, and lo and behold, Frances had a letter from Will! Phoebe and Henry also had one in their box; it was from Ramona. Of course, Phoebe knew the letter was actually for Tricademus and Precious, but she was excited about it anyway.

The two women were so excited about the letters that they barely took time to shop. Phoebe did buy the bonbons for Precious, however, along with a red silk head scarf. She also bought Jasper a pair of red socks.

Frances bought a box of bonbons too, "For the boys," she told Phoebe.

They hurried out of the store and stepped back into the carriage.

"You have three gifts: two from me, and one from Ramona," Phoebe told Precious, and she handed her the bonbons, the scarf, and the letter.

"From Ramona?" Precious grinned, clasping the envelope to her voluminous bosom. "Lawd have mucy, I spose eyes ougta waits and lets you reads it so Tricademus can hears it too, but eyes too 'cited!"

Phoebe saw Frances carefully open the small letter that she'd received from William. She watched as Frances scanned over the words, then took a deep breath and smiled.

"Is everything alright?" Phoebe asked her.

"I guess it is. William and James are okay, and they also met Danny; they're all in Memphis. I'll read it to you when we get home," Frances replied.

Phoebe exhaled in relief, then handed Jasper the pair of socks she'd bought him.

"Thanky, Miss Phoebe," Jasper said.

"That's a little thank-you for being our escort today," she told him, smiling.

Precious held Ramona's letter next to her heart for another moment, then handed it to Phoebe.

After opening it gently, Phoebe read it out loud:

Dear Maw and Paw,

Someone is writing this for me, but I'm planning on learning to read and write, too. The children are going to school just like white folks do down there.

Things are different here. You have to pay for everything you get, even food and clothes.

Rum rented us a house close to where he works, making wagon wheels.

The white folks treat you good up here. You can go in the stores and buy what you need. Mostly the white folks live in one part of the town and we blacks the other.

There's never enough money, so I started washing and ironing for the white folks. The oldest girls help me when they come home from school.

Rum said to tell everyone hello. We're doing good, just working hard.

The black folks have their own churches up here. They don't preach like the white preacher did, back home. Sometimes he'll preach for two or three hours.

I love you, Maw and Paw, and my brothers and sisters.

Tell Mr. Henry and Miss Phoebe I love them, too.

Love, Ramona

Phoebe carefully folded the letter and gave it back to Precious, who was crying. Precious held the letter for a few minutes, then stuck it into the bosom of her dress.

"Old Tric will be glad to look at dis letter," she said. She then thanked Phoebe for the headscarf and candy.

Precious tore into the box of candy as Jasper left the store and headed back home. She offered the others some of her bonbons, but they refused, saying they were for her to enjoy all to herself.

"Boy, dis is the bestest candy," Precious said as she closed the box after eating four pieces of the sweet confection. She then said, "I don't cares if it aint eben windy, eyes wearing dis red headscarf to chuch Sunday!"

Phoebe was anxious to hear more about William's letter. Allie would be glad that James and William had seen Danny, as she'd gotten but one letter from her husband since the day he left.

Jasper pulled into the lane that led to his mother's house first. He stopped so close to the front of the house that all Precious had to do was step out of the carriage directly onto the porch. After Precious plopped into the first available chair, children seemed to come from behind every bush and tree in the yard, running toward her.

"Well, I really enjoyed my trip. It gots me away from deese bad debils for a lil' while," she laughed, as she opened the bonbon box.

One of the children looked like a miniature version of Tricademus, and Phoebe was a bit ashamed that she didn't know his name or who he belonged to.

When they arrived at Magnolia, Phoebe and Frances stepped out of the carriage, but no children ran to greet them, as had when Precious got home.

"You needs to gib me a pass," Jasper said to Phoebe, before she had time to make it to her front porch.

"A pass?" asked Phoebe, as she turned around to face Jasper.

"Yessum, you know, to Miss Wanda house. I knows I wasn't spose to bees listening when Miss Frances reads dat letter," the man answered.

"Oh, Jasper, you're so right! Give me a minute," she said quickly, as she followed Frances through the back door, and hastily scribbled Jasper a pass to make the trip to Wanda Kay's.

Frances had told Allie about the letter by the time Phoebe had given Jasper the pass and returned to the parlor.

The letter must not have been too personal, for Frances unfolded the letter and told them to gather around, as Henry and William weren't back from fishing to hear all the news.

Frances began to read:

My Darling wife,
Paper is scarce here, so the letter will be short.
We witnessed the first naval battle on June 6th. I hate to write this, but the Northern Army gave us a good licking and sunk a lot of our boats.

James and I were stationed in Memphis for a short while. Danny saw our 3rd Alabama banner and looked us up. He's a head taller than most folks, so I spotted him and called his name. Tell Allie that he looks healthy, but still ugly, haha.

He'd said that he's written her several letters and hoped they were getting through. It's nigh impossible to write James and me, for we don't stay in one place long.

249

Danny said that Allie could write to him by using his name, in care of 4th Alabama Regiment, Vicksburg, Mississippi.

We move around so much until we haven't received one dime from the Confederate Army. I'm praying when winter comes, we'll stay put for a while. Maybe Father can send us a pair of boots apiece. Y'all know the sizes. Don't dare send money, for it'll get stolen.

I reckon little William is getting to be a big boy. I sure miss my family! Tell everyone I said I'm sending love, and I pray everyone's health is good.

> *Your loving husband,*
> *William Smith*

"My goodness, William wrote this in June. It's taken three months to get here!" Allie exclaimed, as she looked over Frances' shoulder

"I wonder why William aways writes with a graphite pencil," Frances remarked, as she folded the letter and kissed it.

"I would imagine, what with them being on the move so much, it would be hard to carry around a bottle of ink," Phoebe surmised.

"Oh, my baby, my baby, I miss you so much!" Frances cried, as her eyes began to fill. She wiped the tears away with the back of her hands.

Both Phoebe and Allie came and embraced her; Allie was crying, too.

Hearing the sobs, Clary and Suzy peeped into the parlor from the dining room door, alarmed. After deciding the women looked pretty much all right, just sad, they returned to the kitchen.

By this time, Phoebe was weeping, too. They only dried their tears when they heard Henry and William's voices outside. Then all three ran to their bedrooms to splash cold water on their faces.

When they came back to the parlor, after looking at each other, they broke out in laughter, and hugged each other.

Phoebe finally stopped laughing enough to say, "I guess we're just being silly women!" But she knew the crying had been a welcome release of all the worried feelings the three of them shared, but seldom talked about.

Before long, Henry and William came through the back door with a pan of cleaned fish.

"I hope we made it in time for Clary and Suzy to cook these for supper," Henry remarked, as he proudly held the big pan of fish in front of Phoebe to see.

"Pew wee! I'll open the doors for you two, and y'all wash your hands before you touch anything in this house," Phoebe ordered the two men, her smile taking the sting from her words.

William laughed as Phoebe went ahead of them to open the doors.

When they came back into the parlor, Henry told his grandson, "Maybe we need to go to our rooms and change clothes!"

Henry soon returned to his chair and sat down. Frances read William's letter again.

Henry let out a breath, and said, "Thank God, they're all okay! As soon as possible I'll get them those boots, and a pair for Danny, too."

He could see the somber mood on everyone's face, so he changed the subject. "I read the letter from Ramona to Tricademus. Poor things! That letter sure didn't make it sound like their freedom has been all that great. And I sure do miss them around the place. We're to start digging sweet potatoes tomorrow; Ramona loved sweet potatoes," he said sadly.

Phoebe knew he meant every word, and that his thoughts, as hers, were with his sons and the danger they faced every single day this godforsaken war dragged on.

Chapter Twenty-Five

William and James' unit was stationed in Chattanooga, Tennessee, long enough for them to receive their new boots. Danny, who was stationed in Vicksburg, Mississippi, also received his. Letters to and from their families were received, until July 4, 1863, when Union General Ulysses S. Grant finally defeated Confederate General Pemberton and his men at Vicksburg.

The Confederates had fought to keep the Mississippi river town under Southern rule since May of that year. A siege of the town had been imposed by Grant and his men, and people were starving. The town was bombed so often, with such devastating results, that the citizens were forced to resort to living in caves they'd dug along the river's embankments.

Surprisingly, after Pemberton surrendered his army of twenty thousand men, he gave them all a thirty-day furlough to go home. He then told them that, after their thirty days were up, they could just join the nearest Confederate unit near them. The men wasted no time leaving Vicksburg. Not only were the citizens of the city starving, but so were the Confederate soldiers and their mounts, if they still had horses at all.

Danny left that very day to come home, leading his skeletal horse by the reins. Surprisingly, he didn't have as much trouble finding food and water for himself and his horse when he got away from Vicksburg as he'd thought he would. The Southern families he encountered on his way home were generous to him and his poor mount, and gladly shared food for both man and animal if they had it to give. Without words, Danny realized that every mouthful they shared with him was as if they could somehow sustain their own son or brother or father and help maintain the hope that their own loved ones would find similar aid on their way back home.

Danny was also surprised to find that the further south he traveled, the more prosperous the people seemed to be. *"Looks like the damned destructive Yankees didn't make it this far,"* he thought.

People went out of their way to be good to him, and when he reached the Tombigbee River the ferryman allowed both Danny and his horse to cross for free. It was a good thing, too, for he didn't have a penny in his pocket.

By the fifth day of walking, Danny came to the Alabama River at Claiborne. He was so excited that he thought about just swimming across the wide muddy stream, but he didn't. Instead, he crossed on the ferry, once again free of charge.

Once he reached the other side of the river, Danny saw a detachment of Confederate soldiers. They were dressed in nice gray or brown uniforms, with shiny brass buttons.

"Hey, soldier, if that's what you are? You wouldn't last long in our outfit wearing that filthy bedraggled uniform and riding that skinny-assed horse," one of the men said.

Danny just wanted to get home, and not confront anyone, but when some of the others laughed at his appearance, that was it. He strode angrily over to the dandy that had made the remark. With one of his big hands, he grabbed the fellow by the lapels of his uniform and pulled him off his feet.

"Pretty boy, if you'd gone through what I have, you'd have more respect for a soldier!" Danny exclaimed, then he dropped the man to the ground.

"Danny? Danny Malone?" a voice from behind him asked.

Danny turned around and recognized that the voice belonged to Red, his overseer.

"What in the world?" he asked, as he hugged Red, then shook his hand.

"I'm in town, sending the last of the peanuts to Montgomery. Here—I might as well give you the receipt and save me a trip to Magnolia," Red told him.

"How are Allie and little Danny?" Danny asked urgently.

"Allie is doing fine, since you've started writing now and then. And your son, he's doing fine, too. Boy, you look as though you've been washed and hung out to dry!" the man told his boss.

"Red, soldiering isn't what it's cut out to be. First, you nearly starve to death. What little pay we get is very infrequent. I've seen so many men and horses killed! They took just enough time to bury the men in shallow graves, but the horses were thrown into the Mississippi River," Danny said.

"Damn, that's rough. Looks like that skinny horse of yours wasn't far from being thrown in the river, then! He looks like he's near about starved to death. I'll tell you what; there's a little fodder left in the wagon. I was saving it for my own horse, but you go on and take that pitiful thing of yours to the wagon and let him eat it, while we have a good meal at Miss Dolly's. My treat," Red told him.

"Man, that sounds too good to be true," Danny quickly agreed, as he led his horse Charlie to the wagon and tied him, leaving plenty of loose rein so the animal could eat. He and Red then went into the eatery where they dined on

255

beef hash with gravy, hot biscuits, to sop the gravy with, and plenty of butterbeans.

"They don't have desserts anymore because the price of sugar has gone through the roof," Red told Danny.

"Is the place making any money?" Danny asked.

"I doubt it, but you'll have to ask your wife to find out for sure, and you can believe she might not live there, but she keeps up with everything," Red laughed.

"Red, I know you have a lot of responsibility on you, and I appreciate you looking after things for me," Danny said.

"Shoot, you gave me a job and a roof over my head; you don't have to thank me," Red answered.

"What about the slaves…are they getting enough to eat?" Danny asked.

"Well, we're practically living off the land. Some of the younger ones have run off. It suits me, though. They've heard about this freedom stuff, and I guess they're trying it out. I've heard there's a lot of runaways that are living in the swamps across the river. There a mess of thieving going on in that area. The older ones and the ones with lots of children are still with us, though," Red explained.

"Well, we have twenty-five days to talk about things, but right now, I'm ready to see my wife!" Danny exclaimed with a grin.

"I understand. Say, why don't we ride double, or one of us can ride in the wagon? That nag of yours needs some rest. You can tie him to the wagon so he can take it easy, then when we get home you can get a better horse, and maybe a bath before you meet Allie," Red told him.

"Sounds like a winning combination," Danny answered.

Outside, they thumped one of Red's coins, to see who would travel in the rough-riding wagon. Danny wound up riding the horse on the way home. Of course, since Allie's Uncle James' house was on the way home, Danny knew he had to stop by for a few minutes.

As soon as James saw him, Danny could actually see his face fall, then, in spite of how shabby he knew he must have looked, James hugged his neck.

"What the hell have they been feeding you, pine needles?" James demanded.

"Oh, just what we could find. You see, I was at Vicksburg for over two months, and the place has been under siege. Nothing in and nothing out," Danny replied.

"Yeah, I've been reading about it in the paper. You need to stop by your house to take a bath and change clothes; I wouldn't let Allie see you like this," James told him.

They were all standing on the front porch along with Red, so James invited them in.

Danny thanked him but said he was in a hurry to get home.

"I can certainly understand. You know, all this rigamarole started from the damn Northern politicians. It hasn't been a gravy train around here, of course, but nothing like you boys have been going through. We don't have much, but at least we are eating," James said.

"Have any of your people run off?" Danny asked.

"Yeah, four or five. They were all insolent young folks, though, and practically worthless. All my old hands are still here, but clearing a profit is a thing of the past," James answered. "If we lose this war, I honestly don't know what the South will do. You can bet we'll be made to pay, and we'll live a life that has been unknown to us."

From the way things were headed, both men knew in their hearts that the Old South was soon to be a thing of the past, forever. But Danny didn't want to say out loud how he thought the war would end, so he just said, "Well, we're fighting to preserve the life that we knew." He then bade his uncle goodbye.

"Goodbye, son, and keep your head low," James replied.

On the ride home, Danny thought that he could have told James plenty more but had chosen not to. For instance, he could have mentioned the fact that the Union Army soldiers were well supplied, and many times in a battle or skirmish they outnumbered the Southern troops. It was true that the Southern soldiers were better horsemen, and better fighters in most cases, especially in hand-to-hand combat. No matter how many "bluebellies" you killed or wounded, there was always a fresh supply of them to take their place. The Southern army didn't have that, and it was hard to fight on empty bellies and with skeletal horses. Danny wondered if the entire Southern army was as ill equipped as his own unit had been. *"If so,"* he thought, *"The South had better throw in the towel and piss on the fire!"*

After making it to his house, however, Danny's spirits lifted. Red ran to the shop for a claw hammer, then pried the nails out of the door so Danny could go inside. Red told him that "Miss Allie" had him to pull the nails out every month.

Once inside, Danny didn't waste time; he went right to his closet for clean clothes, along with a pair of his boots and socks. He then went to their bedroom for a sheet and a cake of soap. Danny was tired of "spit baths." He drew a large quantity of water out of the well, pouring it into a fifty-gallon barrel. He then put the sheet over his head, removed the filthy uniform and took a good bath.

Afterwards, he pulled himself out of the barrel, then dried himself, stepping on a corner of the sheet to prevent his feet from getting dirty. Never taking the sheet down, he put on the clean clothes, socks and boots. He took the belt that had "C. S.: on it out of his filthy, tattered uniform pants. After he was dressed, he went back into the house, which was stifling, for the day proved to be a hot one. He went directly to his stash of money and found it in the same place. He saw that Allie had really been working on it, for all that was in the covered dish was two fifty-dollar Confederate bills and a twenty-dollar gold piece. Still, it was more money than he'd had in his pockets since he'd left home. The trousers were so big on him that they had pleats in the waist when he cinched them in with his belt. Feeling clean and wearing clean clothes lifted his spirits, and Danny was more than ready to reunite with his family.

While Danny had bathed, Red had quickly saddled a slick-looking white stallion. Danny mounted it, enjoying the feeling of riding a healthy horse again for the first time in months, and left the place at a full gallop. He couldn't wait to get home.

Chapter Twenty-Six

For twenty days, it was as though the two Dannys and Allie were on a vacation. The weather was hot, so Allie would pack a picnic lunch and the three would go to Burnt Corn Creek. Daniel would pick a nice, shaded spot along some shallow water, and all three would wade out into the water, sit down and just splash water on each other and play. Some of the time, William would come with them. Frances had taught William to swim, so he was allowed to venture out further into the deeper parts of the stream than young Danny. William could only come on Saturdays, though, for the little school where Allie and her siblings had attended was in full swing again. Like his father, the teacher told Frances that William was very advanced for his age.

Danny Junior missed his playmate tremendously when William started to school, but after the boy's father came home, he was more reconciled to his friend's absence.

One night while they were lying in bed, Daniel asked Allie about their money. Allie told him that they had only about two thousand dollars in Confederate money left. "Red tells me what supplies are needed at our house, and usually Mother or Frances will go with me to Belleville. I buy a little more than half of what Red asks for. The place isn't making money on anything but corn and peanuts. Those are sold to the Confederacy, and you can believe it's barely enough to feed everyone on the place for three months, much less buy them clothes and shoes," she explained.

"Hmph, just about what I expected," Danny said. He then continued to talk. "Honey, I guess I shouldn't tell you this, so keep it to yourself."

"Sure," replied Allie.

He began, "From what I've seen, the South wasn't prepared to get mixed up in this war. We're not supplied like the Yankee army is. Shoot, I haven't drawn but three thirteen-dollar checks since I've been in the Army. Before Vicksburg, if we wanted coffee, pork, meal or anything, we'd have to catch the Yankees off guard and raid their supply wagons. I talked to James and William in Memphis, and they said they were doing the same thing."

Allie interrupted him to ask how her brothers looked.

"Well, they weren't as skinny as I am, but you have to remember, we were under siege at Vicksburg, meaning we didn't get anything to eat. Some soldiers, and citizens, too, actually starved to death. I survived by eating frogs, lizards, grasshoppers and what few fish I could catch. Thank God for poke weed! I ate that, too, when I could find it. I guess what I'm trying to say is, I want you to prepare yourself that we might lose this thing. I say, let all the slaves leave if they're mind to," Danny said.

"Do you truly think we're going to lose this war?" Allie asked, shocked at his words.

"We might survive it if England recognizes the seceded states as a country; we could begin selling them cotton again, and if that happened, we would be better supplied. You can believe the Confederacy would tax the cotton; that way, they'd have money to do something with. But as it's going now, I don't see how we can win," he answered grimly.

"Oh, Danny, please don't go back!" Allie exclaimed, grabbing one of his arms tightly.

"What? And be labeled a coward, and be sent to prison? I'd rather just fight it out. Who knows—things might change," Danny replied, and he was sorry that he had told Allie the harsh things he'd been forced to do to survive. He had planned to also tell her that her brother had been wounded but decided not to; William had healed from the wound, anyway.

"You may already know that, according to Abraham Lincoln, since September last year all the slaves in the rebellious states were freed," he said instead.

"Yeah, Father read it in the paper. Shoot, he offered all his slaves a chance to be free, but at the time, the only one who took him up on it was Rum. Since then, Father freed Rum's wife and children and they're living with him now in Ohio. Ramona wrote Precious and Tric a letter after she got up there. If you ask me, the situation sounded pretty bleak," Allie told him.

"Well, if you ask me, the poor black folks are caught in a quagmire. The North doesn't want them, and since there's so little industry in the South, all they can do is be house servants or work in the fields," Danny remarked.

"What will the black people do if the South loses, and they're forced to be free by the Yankee government?" Allie asked.

"Well, by then, probably all the Southern planters will be penniless and they won't be able to pay for labor, so I look for most of the former slaves to move up north. Folks up there might not welcome them, but they'll get them anyway, especially the young ones," Danny answered.

262

"Poor Tricademus and Precious! I can't imagine them being forced to move away," Allie said.

"I can tell you right now, that ornery old rascal isn't going anywhere," Danny laughed.

He then changed the subject. "I want our son to go to school. Shoot, he's smart! The little school might be primitive, but it's better than no school at all."

"His cousin William has taught him a lot. They get along like two peas in a pod. He'll start the primary grade this fall," Allie told him.

"So," Danny asked, "when this mess is over, are you going to stay on here, or move back in with a poor farmer?"

"I thought I'd answered that earlier—and don't be silly! You know that you and our son will always come first," she replied, hugging him tight. She then suggested, "Tomorrow is Saturday; let's pay a visit to Wanda Kay, and little Shelby. She's such a darling," Allie asked.

"Honey, your wish is my command. I'd like to get back early enough to pay Red a visit, though," Danny agreed.

The last thing he remembered his wife saying before he fell into a deep sleep, was how much she had missed their talks in the bed at night.

The next morning when the whole family was at breakfast, Henry came into the kitchen with a folded newspaper in his hand.

"Good grief!" he exclaimed, waving the paper. "On the first of July, there was a tremendous battle in Gettysburg, Pennsylvania that lasted three days. The paper also states there were *fifty-one thousand* casualties!"

He continued, "What's General Lee doing that far north? My gracious, we need to be in the south so he can run the

Yankees back up north, seems to me. Lord, that's a lot of soldiers," he spouted.

A worried Phoebe asked Danny whether he thought William and James might have been at Gettysburg.

"No, Ma'am, that's the Western theatre. We're in the Eastern campaigns," he stated.

"Whew, thank goodness!" exclaimed Phoebe, relieved to hear it.

No one asked Henry which side won the slaughter, but Danny already knew the Yankees had won, after a hard-fought battle.

Phoebe wasn't aware that Henry kept all the news about the Eastern campaigns from his wife. After reading his newspaper, he'd fold it and hide it in the shop, then send up fervent prayers that his sons were safe.

Later that day, when Danny and Allie visited Wanda Kay, Danny got to see his pretty little niece for the first time. They also learned some things about James and William that the rest of the family didn't know about. Wanda Kay told them that both James and William were suffering from dysentery, along with most of the others in their camp. They were drinking chamomile tea to relieve their symptoms.

James also had written Wanda Kay that he and William had traded haircuts. He wrote that they didn't have a pair of scissors, so they used their pocketknives.

Wanda Kay told them that she had moved back in with her parents for a short while, but all her father talked about was the war. "It only made me worry that much more, so Shelby and I moved back home; it's so much more peaceful here, anyway," she laughed.

Allie remembered that Danny had said he wanted to go visit Red, so they didn't stay long. She could have stayed all day, though, for little Shelby was so sweet. *"Oh, how I wish I had a little girl to primp and make dainty clothes for!"* she thought.

After about an hour's visit, the two headed back to Magnolia. On the way back home, Danny begam whistling several tunes, among which was, "Camptown Ladies." Allie remembered Dorothea when she heard that song and thought of what a miserable life she had led due to her sister Emma. *"Poor Dorothea! She was such a gifted person, and her own sister didn't appreciate her one bit,"* thought Allie.

She looked over at her husband's long, muscular arms, and she thought of how painfully thin he'd been when he got home. Just three weeks of eating regularly had really put the meat back on Danny's bones. She knew he had to report back to the recruiting office in Sparta the on Monday, and they had made every minute together count. She realized he wanted to tell Red what to do around the place while he was gone.

Allie was really surprised when they got back to Magnolia; he invited her and both the boys to go with him on his visit to see Red.

The boys were excited about the trip, and Danny tried to persuade his son to sit in his lap on the ride. He did for a short while, but then began to squirm; he wanted to sit in the back seat with his cousin.

After arriving, some of the older slaves came out to greet them. Allie spoke to them for a short while, then went to the shop for the claw hammer so she could pull the nails from the door.

She knew she had some gray material in the trunk at the foot of her bed, and she intended to work on Danny's tattered uniform after church. Danny and William did some exploring in the house while Allie looked for the material. It was just her luck that the material was at the bottom of the trunk. She unfolded the paper around it, and it was as she remembered it, a coarse thick gray. *"Good for the wintertime,"* she thought.

The boys brought a few of Danny's old toys out with them. Allie put everything into the carriage, then hammered the nails back into the door.

Danny soon joined them, and he left their house at a gallop. Allie felt the plucking of her heart strings as they left the home they had shared. She knew her husband felt the same way, too, for he didn't look back, nor slow down until they reached the main road.

Not all of Tricademus' and Precious' family went to church, but along with the other slaves, the gallery to Belleville Baptist was always full. The bottom pews were full almost every Sunday as well.

Emma would always be there, dressed in her finest clothes and jewels. Tom sat beside his wife, but he sure didn't look happy, whereas Emma always kept a fake smile on her face.

After services the men would gather outside and talk about the war and the price of farm goods. The ladies preferred to stay inside and talk about newly born babies, social events, and the price of staple goods. The women generally gathered in three distinctly different groups: the common folk, the poor people, and the socialites.

Phoebe was never invited to any more of Emma's parties. If she had been, she wouldn't have gone anyway, so she and the rest of her family congregated with the commoners. The women wouldn't gossip long, however, before they'd be telling their husbands it was time to go.

The slaves seemed to stay longer than their masters, for they had a good time of it. There was always someone in the crowd who could pick a banjo or fiddle. They'd gather under the shade of oak trees which were far enough away from the church so it wouldn't be disrespectful. They'd sing, dance and have a good time.

There was one particular dance they'd do, called "The Mammy Hunch, and The Pappy Hunch."

It was reported back to Henry that Tricademus was doing a good job of the Pappy Hunch. Tric wasn't able to show out for very long at all, though, because Precious witnessed the spectacle and whipped him with a pine branch until they reached the wagon and they left for home.

On their way home from church that day, Allie thought of something. She thought that she'd sew a hundred-dollar bill in Confederate money inside the lining of Danny's coat. She wouldn't tell him about it until they reached the depot, and that way, he couldn't refuse It.

When they reached Magnolia, they all ate dinner that Clary and Suzy had prepared that morning before they, too, had gone to church. Danny told Allie he needed to go back to their house and give Red some final instructions. She thought that he was perhaps hinting at her to come with him. When she told him her intention of working on his uniform, he said he understood, and he'd just go on horseback. "That way I can get back faster."

After church, Henry had changed from his Sunday best, and as usual, he was in his easy chair reading Saturday's newspaper again.

Phoebe, knowing how short Magnolia must be on money, was in her room mending old dresses of hers.

Allie had to admit, she now loved Sunday afternoons at Magnolia. Life seemed to float by as if she was on the wings of a fluttering butterfly or something of the nature. The church sermon was still fresh on her mind. She watched her son and nephew from her window as they chased the falling leaves outside.

Ruth had washed Danny's uniform next day after he had arrived. Allie could hear Frances as she played the mournful tune, "Lorena," on the piano. She softly sang the lyrics while she worked the needle in and out of the gray material:

The years creep slowly by, Lorena...
The snow is on the grass again.
The sun is low in the sky, Lorena...
The frost gleams where the flowers have been.

As she sang, a fleeting thought came to Allie that Danny would be leaving the next morning. She fought the thought back into the recesses of her mind. She continued with her sewing, then looked out the window at their tall clumsy son, playing in the leaves with his cousin.

"Identical to his father," she thought, and she smiled to herself.

She was finally through with Danny's coat. The biggest problem had been that the sleeves had needed to be almost completely restored. *"They were so torn and stained!"* she thought. Allie went to her room and got the Confederate note and sewed it on the inside of the coat's yellow lining. She then mended a tear in one of the lapels, then started on his long tattered trousers. About all she could do for them was sew patches in the knees. She sewed the stitches so tiny that they were barely noticeable.

After she'd done all she could do, she hung the uniform on wooden hangers in their bedroom.

Danny soon returned and told the boys, who were almost completely submerged in leaves of all colors, that it was time to come inside. "Brush all the leaves off; you don't want to make your mothers mad," he told them.

Clary and Suzy generally just warmed up what was left from dinner, for their supper, so by early dark they were all gathered around the table to eat.

During each grace at the table, Henry not only blessed the food, but he also always asked the good Lord to look after his sons and Danny.

Once they had all eaten, Frances and Phoebe helped Clary and Suzy clean the kitchen, while Allie made sure the boys took proper baths. After making sure the boys were clean and in the bed, she and Danny bathed and went to bed as well. The downstairs was quiet, so she knew everyone in the family had gone to bed. In about five minutes, she heard Suzy and Clary slip up the stairs. It was time to share the private hours of their last night together.

After their lovemaking, Allie and Danny talked for a while, and then, both knowing they had an early morning, the soon-to-be-parted couple went to sleep.

The next morning, after eating a hasty breakfast, Danny said his goodbyes to his son, and along with Allie, Henry, and Phoebe, he left for Sparta.

It all seemed so rushed! Danny wished he had the power to stop time, or at least slow it down. But much sooner than he wanted it to happen, he and a few other young men were met at the depot by a Lieutenant Knowles. They were told they'd be going to Montgomery to be deployed. Danny stayed at the depot as long as he could. As the train began to pull away, Allie and Danny embraced, then Allie told him about the money she had sewn inside the lining of his coat. Danny turned around and his long legs had to run, before he jumped into an open door of the train. He had no way of knowing how long it would be before he was able to return home…or if he would even outlive this damnable war.

Chapter Twenty-Seven

Two weeks later, Allie received a letter from Danny, saying that he had a very safe position guarding Mobile Bay at Spanish Fort, Alabama. He said the citizens made sure they were well fed, along with the Confederate army. He also wrote things were so much better than Vicksburg, and he had been promoted to Sergeant. "Whoopee," he wrote, "I'll be making fifteen dollars a month."

In spite of the reassuring words to his wife, however, things were heating up for William and James. In September, the Confederate Army surrounded the town of Chattanooga, Tennessee.

They camped in the mountains and set siege to the town. General Joseph Hooker commanded the Union Army, while the Confederates were commanded by General Stevenson.

The Confederates wouldn't allow supplies in or out of Chattanooga.

At the beginning the Union supply line wasn't well guarded, so the Rebels would dash down, kill or run off the Union guards and capture the supplies.

William and James, along with the rest of their regiment, hadn't eaten so well since they'd left home; they even had coffee and sugar.

There were several battles around Chattanooga, but the Union couldn't break the hold the Rebels held in the mountains.

President Lincoln soon tired of the situation and sent General Ulysses S. Grant to the rescue. On November 24th, Grant attacked the Confederate Army, now led by General Braxton Bragg.

It took three days of bloody fighting, but finally the Union Army broke through. The Rebels retreated to Missionary Ridge, where another fierce battle was fought on the 25th. William and James had run on pure adrenalin for four days. William stopped counting at six Yankees killed or wounded by the flintlock his father had given him that day near Belleville.

Overpowered by men and cannons, Bragg and his remaining forces retreated to Dalton, Georgia.

During the melee, William and James were temporarily separated, until they reached Dalton. After discovering that they each were safe, they embraced, then laughed.

"Boy, it's miraculous that we came out of that in one piece, much less unhurt!" James exclaimed.

"It's certainly not something to write home about," William answered.

Grant, knowing that the gateway to the South was open, put William Tecumseh Sherman in charge and decided he'd concentrate on General Lee.

There were several battles in and around northwestern Georgia, but the Confederate Army managed to hold Sherman at bay.

Sherman was a brilliant tactician, though. He held out until May of 1864, until he could build up his army and artillery. He had the manpower now, so he split his forces and marched around the entrenched Confederates.

The Rebel army had to double-time to get back in front of Sherman's troops and entrench their own dwindling army again. This maneuver went on until July, until Sherman reached his objective, the outskirts of Atlanta.

Sherman began to cut the railroads going into Atlanta, and several battles were fought on the outskirts of the city.

The Union Army lobbed shells into the city, killing citizens and destroying homes and businesses with the unrelenting, deadly explosions.

Sherman set siege to the city. President Davis replaced General Joseph Johnston with the more aggressive General John Bell Hood. Hood launched an attack on the center of Sherman's line but was beaten back. On July 22nd, Hood launched an attack on the left of Sherman's lines and was again beaten back with several losses.

William and James were involved in several cavalry charges, and each time they came out victorious and unharmed.

Battles and skirmishes around Georgia continued throughout August. Finally, Sherman, knowing that the Confederate Army was so diminished, launched an all-out attack on Atlanta. On September 3rd, Sherman was notified that the Confederate Army had pulled out. Sherman and his troops entered the almost demolished city that same day.

James had lost three of his mounts in the battles and William had lost two. There were so many unoccupied horses running loose, however, that they didn't have any trouble finding replacements. They always got the Union horses when they could, for the Northern mounts were better fed.

The beleaguered brothers road out of Atlanta together, thanking God they weren't injured, even though they'd witnessed Hell itself.

General Hood had already lost an arm and a leg in previous battles; he wore an artificial leg and had to be strapped to his horse. The men under him wanted General Johnston back.

Hood, knowing that Sherman needed time to rest and recuperate, turned his beaten army to the west, into Alabama and Mississippi. They, too needed to rest, after enduring continuous fighting for months.

As the Confederate Army moved through Alabama, James and William asked their company commander if they could go home for a visit. They explained to him that they hadn't been home since the war started. They, like Danny, were granted thirty-day furloughs. The Colonel gave them official papers to report back to duty on November 10th in Monroeville. They were near Selma, so they and their horses boarded the first steamboat available and arrived in Claiborne late the next day.

The two brothers couldn't believe they were back in their stomping grounds.

"Boy, if I knew how to dance, I'd dance all the way home," James said.

"Now, that would be a sight to see!" William told him.

The brothers had fought elbow to elbow for over three years. They'd built a comradeship that would last them a lifetime. They hugged each other's necks when they came to the crossroads that led to their two different destinations. "Just think, I'll see my daughter," James told William.

"Well, *I'll* see a young fellow that's probably forgotten me," William said, then they both spurred their horses, going in opposite directions.

James' house was closer to Claiborne than where William lived, so he naturally got home first.

Wanda Kay saw the bearded soldier riding up the lane. *"He looks to be a Confederate,"* she thought, as she looked out of the window.

274

As the soldier got nearer, she saw that it was James. Shelby was playing with her doll when Wanda Kay snatched her up and rushed out the door.

James saw his wife running toward him, calling out his name. He dismounted, temporarily forgetting about his horse, and dashed toward his wife and baby. He wanted to grab Wanda Kay in his arms and swing her into the air, like old times. He couldn't, though, due to his daughter, so the couple threw their arms around each other and kissed and embraced.

"Is the war over?" Wanda Kay asked, as she stepped back a little.

"Not that I know of. William and I are home on a furlough for thirty days," James replied, as he lifted his daughter out of her mother's arms.

Of course, Shelby began to squirm and held her hands out for her mother to take her back from the strange man.

"That's your daddy," Wanda Kay told the child as she reached to get her daughter. "Little wonder she doesn't want you, William—you're a mess! Your uniform is filthy, and that beard...it must have been months since you've shaved."

"Well, it's not like I've been on a social picnic. Some of those stains you're looking at are blood. But thank goodness, none of the blood is mine," James said. He grabbed his astonished wife's hand with one of his own, and the reins to the horse with the other, and they walked toward the house.

William's homecoming was very different from his brother's.

Tricademus and Precious were sitting on the front porch, enjoying the last vestiges of the day's sun, when they saw the horse coming up the road.

"Lawd hab mucy, I believes dat's Massuh William," Tric told his wife. After looking closer, he exclaimed, "It *is* Massuh William!" then he yelled for William to come over. Tric sent one of his grandsons to run to Magnolia and tell them that, "Massuh William be home."

William kicked his horse in the ribs and, after reaching Tricademus and Precious' home, he dismounted and tied his Yankee horse to a post on the porch.

Both Precious and Tricademus had trouble getting up from the bench, so William asked them to just sit back down, which they gladly did.

"Lawdy, lawdy," Precious said with tears in her eyes, as she reached out her arms to hug the disheveled young soldier.

William removed his hat, and gladly allowed his second mother's arms to encircle him.

"Lawd, is wese glad ter seed you!" Tricademus told him, as William broke Precious' embrace, then the two men hugged.

"Yo folks show gwine be prouds to seed you. Eyes sent lil' Tom up de lane to tells dem you's home," Tric said.

"Yes, well, I'd better get on home before they start coming down the lane," William replied.

"What dat is, a big knife?" Tric asked as he pointed to William's saber.

"Yep, that's a big knife," William agreed, laughing.

"What you do's wif a long knife lake dat?" Tricademus demanded.

"Oh, most anything. I've hacked vines with it, cut meat with it, and killed Yankees with it," William answered.

"Kills all of dem. Eyes jist don't sees why dey wants us black folks so baid. Wese don't wants dem!"

"Yeah, well there's lots of them," William said. He then asked Tric and Precious how their family was.

"Dey's alright; course, you heard 'bout Ramona. Dat Rum, he done took her and de chillun up Nawth. I don't thanks Ramona and de cheerun lacks it, dough. Dey all be werking fer de white folks up dare."

"I have about four weeks off; I'll be sure and visit y'all again," William told them, as he stepped off the porch and remounted his horse, after untying it from the post.

"Lawd, chile u's skinny as a rail, but Clary and Suzy will fatten you up foe you leabs," Precious promised, as William rode toward home.

He met Tric and Precious' grandson about halfway up the lane. William knew the child was doing his best to get home to safety, before dark.

His guess was right; his entire family was standing on the back porch to greet him. He barely had time to make it to the corral before Frances and his son ran to greet him.

William quickly tied his horse to a rail, and with both arms, he grabbed each one of them with a free arm, picking them up and swinging them around. He hugged his son, then kissed Frances on the lips.

Of course, the others came out into the dim daylight and took turns hugging William and welcoming him home. He allowed his son to unsaddle and unbridle his horse while he tried to answer a hundred questions being asked, as they all made their way into the house.

"You're just in time for supper, so run to our room and get washed up," Frances instructed.

"Well, I'm all for that," William said, as Frances led him upstairs, with Allie grinning. As soon as they were in their room, they embraced and kissed for a good five minutes.

"We'd better stop that, or we'll have folks talking," Frances teased, as she gave her husband a peck on his cheek. "We'll make up for it tonight," she promised, smiling.

William put the flintlock pistol he'd captured, his saber, and the trusty muzzleloader on top of a tall wardrobe, so the boys couldn't get to them.

"So, is the war over, or you're just home on furlough?" Frances asked, as William washed his face and hands at the wash bowl.

"I wish the slaughter was over, but James and I are just here for four weeks. I look for the thing to be over soon, though," he said, while drying his hands with a clean white towel.

"So, James is home too?" Frances asked.

"I imagine he's in the bed with Wanda Kay about now," William laughed.

"Good! I'm glad that both of you are home, where you belong," Frances told him.

"Boy, I didn't realize I was so filthy, until I looked at that towel," William said.

"Then you are both alright, no fingers, toes, or anything else blown off?" Frances asked.

"Well, I *was* stuck with a saber once, but it healed pretty quickly," William said.

Frances wouldn't be satisfied until William dropped his trousers and let her look.

278

"Yes, I see it, poor baby. Boy, that was close!" she said, trying not to laugh, for she knew it had to have been painful.

"Whew, that has to be washed before bedtime," Frances said, as she held her nose.

William pulled his trousers back up, and that cured the scent.

"I'll take a cake of soap and dive into Burnt Corn Creek, if necessary, but we're sleeping together tonight," William said, as he gave Frances a final lingering kiss on the lips.

"Of course we are," she agreed, as they walked down the stairs arm in arm. She made no mention of how shocked she had been at seeing how skinny her husband was.

Everyone was waiting on them when they reached the dining room. Seeing the steaming bowls of food made William's stomach growl. "My goodness, what a feast,…and y'all had no idea I was coming home," he said.

Henry blessed the food, then thanked God his son was home safe from the war. After that, the bowls were passed around the table. Before the meal was over, everyone knew that James was home too, and he was safe.

Like Danny's furlough, the time flew by for William and James. They each spent a lot of time with their families, their wives daring them to do any kind of work. The weather was getting cooler, but William did manage to take the two boys, along with Allie and Frances, to the creek. William and the boys actually jumped into the creek and swam around a little, but the girls refused, saying it was too cold.

James, Wanda Kay and Shelby visited one day.

Henry and Phoebe felt bad they weren't getting to see James as much as they'd like, so on another day they took

James and his family to Claiborne. They ate a good meal, and other than that, with money being as it was, they didn't spend much. They did buy William and James each a good pair of boots, and little Shelby a baby doll and two pretty dresses.

James tried his knee-high boots on in the store. After standing up and walking around a bit, he said they were a perfect fit. "Look, up top is a little pouch where you can put your pocketknife," he said.

Phoebe hated to let go of her son and granddaughter when it came time to leave, but she knew they had to get back to Magnolia before dark.

"My, don't we have a pretty granddaughter, and some handsome grandsons! I feel sorry for your brother James; he never gets to see his grandbabies," Phoebe said to her husband.

"Yep, we're very fortunate, in both aspects," Henry replied. Phoebe knew her husband and could tell that something was bothering him, and it was. He did his best to keep bad things away from Phoebe. He didn't tell her that Yankees were already in Alabama, and he feared they'd soon be headed south.

Clary and Suzy did their best to put meat back on William's skinny bones while he was home, and he took them up on it.

It was a sad day when the entire family gathered at the recruiting station on November 10th.

Instead of leaving on a train like Danny, William and James left Monroeville with the other soldiers on their horses.

"Our boys look good, wearing their new boots," Phoebe said, as she choked back tears.

After consoling his wife, Henry pulled Frances and Wanda Kay to him, and all he could think to say was, "They'll be back; this thing will be over before you know it."

Allie managed Wanda Kay's carriage back to Bermuda, staying for only a short while. After all of them hugged her neck, Allie stepped into the back of Henry's carriage, and they made their way back to Magnolia to await the inevitable.

Chapter Twenty-Eight

William and James had orders to return to their regiment
in Georgia. They left Monroeville and arrived in Camden
late that same afternoon. From Camden, they and their
horses rode by rail to southern Georgia. Making a detour
around Atlanta, they arrived at their unit on November
14th. They should have reached their destination sooner,
but the Yankees had torn up the train tracks in many areas.

The two worn-out soldiers didn't know if it was bad
timing or not, but they were so near Atlanta that they
witnessed Sherman's final destruction of the city.

Sherman knew the Confederate army was whipped, but
they somehow continued to hang on.

Sherman marched out of Atlanta on November 15th with
sixty-two thousand troops. He made a brave move by
splitting his forces in two, making his army a full sixty miles
wide. He gave his soldiers orders to destroy, loot and burn
everything within sight; he was determined to bring the
South to its knees.

William and James were attached to General Joseph
Wheeler's cavalry, even though General Hood was still over
the entire organization. There wasn't much the Southern
army could do, though, but maneuverer behind the
Northern aggressors and harass them, because they were so
outnumbered by the Union Army.

A herd of beeves trailed behind Sherman's army, and
occasionally the Rebels would find a stray and eat it. Since
they didn't have food supplies, the Confederate soldiers
would catch the Yankees off guard, especially at night, and
raid their supply wagons.

It was a pitiful sight to see. William and James witnessed homeless women and children. Their houses had all been burned to the ground, and every one of their smokehouses and corn cribs were stripped, along with all the farm animals and fowl. They met whole families walking aimlessly, praying to find a place to eat and get out of the weather.

There were several skirmishes between the two armies, especially the cavalry units. Before long, however, Yankee reinforcements would rush to their aid and the Rebels would have to flee or be killed or captured. The Confederacy would usually get their objective, though, which was sleek Yankee horses that were stuffed with stolen grain and fodder.

The Confederate soldiers got to keep everything the saddlebags contained, too. Sometimes, it would be quite a bit of stolen money. Mostly Confederate money, though, and sometimes stolen jewelry.

All the harassing they did, failed to slow down Sherman's march to the sea. The Union Army reached the outskirts of Savannah, Georgia on December 21st, 1864.

A fellow Mason rode out and confronted Sherman and begged him to not destroy the city. Sherman, belonging to the same organization, said the city was too beautiful to destroy. As long as his army didn't meet resistance, he added, he would allow the city to stand.

It was said that Sherman went to the telegraph office on Christmas Eve, and wired President Lincoln that he wished to present to him the city of Savannah as a Christmas gift.

There wasn't much the Confederate army could do but stay outside of Savannah and try to survive.

General Hood hoped to get reinforcements from General Lee, so they could squash Sherman when he left Savannah. Hood didn't know that General Grant was guarding every movement that General Lee made.

Sherman rested his troops until the first of the year, then he pulled out, headed north toward Charleston. The Union troops burned and pillaged their way through the state, and Sherman's army reached Columbia, South Carolina on February 17th of 1865. They ransacked the city, leaving only charred remains in their wake.

Chapter Twenty-Nine

On the same day that Sherman was burning Columbia, South Carolina, Dr. Smith verified the fact that Frances was pregnant.

She had gotten one letter from William, and he wrote that James and he had rejoined their old outfit and were following Sherman's army. The letter was very short, written on a small piece of scrap paper.

Frances was thrilled beyond belief. It was hard for her to believe that she had a son going through puberty, and now, she was pregnant again. She so prayed that it would be a little girl. *"If it is a little girl, I'm going to name her Violet, since Violet was Dorothea's middle name,"* she thought.

Of course, the entire family was thrilled, to say the least, and Frances was pampered beyond belief by everyone in the household.

Frances being pregnant made her take a closer look at her son, who now preferred to be called Will. He was already taller than she was, and like his father, he was an excellent horseman. Will was a gifted student in school, too.

Frances thanked her lucky stars that Will had his grandaddy to go to for manly things. She knew that William had missed out on several things concerning the raising of his son. Henry, along with Jasper and his sons, had taught Will so many things. Henry had taught him to prime, load and shoot a rifle. He also taught the boy how to ride a horse. Jasper and his boys taught Will to love the sport of hunting, and how to hook up a carriage, and so many things concerning the farm. Will, who was unlike his father, loved the farm life. He had read a book concerning the grafting and budding of different fruit and nut trees. By the time he was twelve he had four different type peaches growing off one tree. He looked like his father, but Frances thought if he kept growing, he was going to be taller than William.

Will had become Henry's shadow, and Henry loved it. That wasn't to say that Henry shunned Danny in any way, for he took a lot of time with him as well. After Henry stopped growing cash crops, except peanuts, he had more time to spend with his grandsons than he had been able to do with his sons.

The boys knew better than to interfere with their grandad when he was reading his newspaper, though. They never followed him into the shop after dark, either, for they knew he'd gone out there to pray.

Henry was reading the paper late one afternoon, waiting to be called to supper. It was hard for him to believe that man could be so cruel to his fellow creatures. He was reading about Sherman's march to the sea, and how he was leaving nothing behind him but scorched earth.

"Lord, have mercy on those poor souls in Sherman's path, and, God, please protect my sons!" Henry closed his eyes and prayed briefly.

It was March 25th, 1865. Jasper had all the seed and grain ready to be planted. He had the seed hanging in onion sacks, so they'd get air and prevent rot.

The morning was bright and sunny; Phoebe's yellow and white daffodils were in full bloom between the magnolia trees.

Jasper liked to have beat the front door down, shouting, *"De Yankees is heah, De Yankees is heah!"*

Henry barely had time to make it to the front door, and when he opened it, a Yankee soldier had the butt of his

286

rifle drawn back to break the door in. Instead, he hit Henry in the face with it, knocking him down. In just a matter of seconds, while Henry was still addled in the floor, the room was full of Yankee soldiers.

He could hear his family's screams, and the breaking of glass, as Phoebe came running with a wet cloth and began to wipe his face, checking his injuries.

Henry was soon able to sit up, and, using the wet cloth, he found that he had a big knot on his forehead and a bleeding cut.

After the Yankees plundered the rooms, taking everything of value they could find, including the lady's jewelry, they ordered everyone to come downstairs.

A big Yankee grabbed Henry by his shoulders and picked him up to a standing position.

"Leave my husband alone! Haven't you done enough?" Phoebe shouted.

"Shut up, bitch, or you'll get the same thing!" one of the Yankee's yelled in her face.

"Where's the gold? Not that Confederate crap, either," the big Yankee hollered as he shook Henry hard enough to snap his neck.

"There isn't any gold left! I spent what little I had on my family and my people," Henry said, while still holding the wet cloth tight against his head.

"Lying rebel, no account," the fellow hissed, as he flung Henry against the front door. "I know how to make you talk. Just you look out that front door!"

When Henry looked outside, he was still dazed, so he squinted one eye, thinking he could see better out of the other. The first thing he saw was a cannon at the road, pointed straight at his house. He also saw hordes of

Yankees as they ran by the house holding squawking chickens, turkeys, and ducks. He could hear the squealing hogs down the road, as they were being slaughtered.

"Say where you're hiding the money, or your house will be blown to smithereens," the Yankee said, slapped Henry on the back of his head.

"What gold we had, we exchanged it for Confederate money; we had to. Gold wasn't accepted in local places of business," Henry replied.

"Alright, you asked for it, so you're going to get it," the Yankee said.

"Please, give the women and children time to get to the road," Henry told him.

"No dice. No one is to leave this house. You all stay right where you are," the soldier snarled, as he followed his men out of the house, who were all ladened with different loot.

Henry saw two of his wagons go by the house, loaded with corn and fodder.

Giving the Yankees time to make it about halfway to the road, he told everyone in the house to run out the back door. "Run to the woods, then turn left," he said. The last thing Henry saw before he closed the door was Tricademus, as he waddled across his yard toward the Yankees with the cannon.

"I'm not going anywhere without you; they'll just have to blow me up, too!" Phoebe exclaimed.

"No, please go! I'd go with you, but I'm too weak," Henry told her.

"Hurry, do as he said, go quickly," Phoebe told everyone else.

"Wese skeered, deys mo dan likely Yankees out dare, too!" Clary cried.

"Come on, follow me," Will urged, and they all ran out the back door, headed toward the woods.

Phoebe wouldn't budge; she insisted on staying with her husband.

"Please, help me to the cellar," Henry said in a faint voice, as he grabbed for Phoebe's hand.

About the time that Phoebe was leading Henry into the cellar, Tricademus made it to the cannon.

"Is you gwine blows up Massuh's house?" Tricademus asked, as he stepped in front of the barrel.

"Just soon as you move your dumb black ass out of the way," the hateful Yankee replied.

"Den, you's will hab to shoots through me. Eyes a big togget, so you's wants hab no troubles," Tric said calmly.

"And just who the hell are you?" asked the Yankee.

"Eye's be Tricademus, and thangs go round heah as I say goes, and eye's say you don't shoots de massuh's house," Tric said in a firm voice. He then did something that stunned the Yankees. With his enormous hands, Tricademus grabbed the barrel of the cannon. With the strength of Samson, he lifted the thing up and turned it over, just as the cannon fired. The cannon ball sailed off down the road leading toward Belleville before it exploded, killing two of the retreating Yankees.

The big Yankee backed away before he spoke.

"You fool, don't you know that everyone is free and can leave this place?"

"Yassuh, we'se been free. Massuh, he don't makes us stays heah," Tric replied. He then shoved the Yankees to the side, and with labored steps he walked back toward his cabin, and the awaiting Precious.

With a lot of cursing, the Yankees used two of Henry's mules to pull the cannon upright. With their stolen booty, the disappointed Northerners made their way back down the road. Some of the chickens got loose and flew up on two of the stolen mules' backs, frightening them. The mules kicked their way free and ran back toward the safety of their corral.

"Let them go," the Yankee sergeant said wearily. "They're not worth the trouble."

"Damn Yankees, dey thanks dey owns eberthang," Tricademus said with labored breaths, as he sat back down on the front porch.

His and Precious' offspring came running from everywhere.

"You showed dem debils who runs dis place!" several of them said, as they begin to crowd around him and Precious.

"Go away, lets me catch my breaf," Tricademus said. Then he asked Jasper to go to the big house and check on everyone.

"Boy, you showed dem," Jasper said once more, as he hurried toward the still standing Magnolia. "Yassuh, you sho' did!"

Chapter Thirty

William and James always tried to stay close to each other, unless they had orders to go in different ways. One day toward the middle of April, the two of them came upon a couple of stragglers from Sherman's army. They quickly noticed that the two soldiers were from a cavalry unit, for they were wearing sabers.

The brothers drew their sabers and rushed the men, giving them time to draw their own sabers, for a fair fight as professional soldiers should. As it turned out, the stragglers must have been amateurs, for James and William had the bleeding Yankees on the ground in a matter of seconds.

As usual, they grabbed the reins of the Yankees' horses and, still on their own mounts, they pulled the dying Yankees' horses into a thicket.

The brothers were hoping to find something to eat in the saddlebags of the captured mounts, for they were both nigh starved to death. They did find some parched corn and bacon, but their biggest surprise was money! Each saddle bag contained a large amount of gold and silver coins.

"All this money had to have come from a bank," William said.

"Yeah, but what bank?" James asked.

"We'll never know, but it's little wonder they were lagging behind," William said.

The brothers knew the war couldn't last much longer. One of the biggest problems was desertion; there simply wasn't anything for the starving Confederates to eat. Sherman had seen to that.

James and William came to a decision. There was a big iron rock in the thicket. They were so emaciated that it took both of them to move the huge boulder. The dirt where the stone had lain was moist, so they easily dug a hole big enough to hold a full saddlebag.

Pouring all the money into a single saddlebag, James pulled the pocketknife from the top of his boot and cut the leather bag away from the saddle. William dropped the bulging saddlebag into the hole, then he and James covered it with dirt, then rolled the huge stone back where it had been. They then swapped saddles and horses for the better fed Yankee animals, slapping their former mounts on the rumps and causing them to run out of the thicket.

After pouring some of the water from the dead Yankees' canteens, they washed their hands and savored their scant meal of parched corn and bacon.

Later, they rejoined their unit that trailed Sherman's army.

They continued following Sherman's army for three more days until they neared Durham, North Carolina, then the army stopped.

Word passed around that General Johnston was talking to Sherman about surrendering. They also heard that General Robert E. Lee had surrendered to Grant on April the 8th.

Several of the soldiers had heard that they'd be required to surrender their weapons also, so both William and James climbed a tree and hid their flintlocks.

Sure enough, on April 26th, Johnston surrendered to Sherman at Bennett's Farmhouse, which was near Durham Station.

The rumors were right; they were told to stack their rifles in piles, take the oath of allegiance, and sign a paper which stated they'd never take up arms against the nation again.

They were all issued food rations, and right before daylight, the brothers rode back to the tree where the flintlocks were hidden and retrieved their weapons.

The two brothers took a good look at each other, and James said, "Let's go get the money; no telling what we'll find at home."

"Whew!" William exclaimed, "The war is over. We'll divvy up the money when we get there." He then added, "Let's go around where Sherman marched; I'd sure enjoy a good meal."

"Now, you're talking," James agreed, and the two brothers spurred their horses toward the gold, then onward to Alabama.

Epilogue—1875

After the war, with only a small amount of money, Henry wasn't capable of hiring many workers to farm his fields. He continued to farm, though, until his death in 1878. Phoebe had developed a cough in 1866, and died of pneumonia.

To Henry, Magnolia wasn't the same after Phoebe died. He, Precious, and Tricademus spent a lot of time on their front porch talking of years gone by. Henry signed a legal document giving Tric and Precious the use of their house until their deaths. He also willed Tricademus and his heirs twenty acres of land at the very end of his property. Tricademus passed away in 1872, and Precious followed him to their Heavenly home in 1874. After more than a hundred and fifty years, some of their descendants still live in the immediate area.

Clary and Suzy remained with the family at Magnolia until their own deaths.

Wanda Kay and James wound up moving to Walnut Hill, Florida.

With the Yankee gold, William saw to it that his two children received a good education, plus they lived comfortably for the rest of their lives.

Allie and her family remained with Henry, William, Frances, and their family at Magnolia. William never went back to teach in Tuscaloosa; instead, he taught Greek and Latin at Belleville Academy.

Danny Malone sold his house and land, preferring to stay at Magnolia with all the others. He used some of the money to build two more rooms onto Magnolia.

Jasper and Robert continued to farm the land at Magnolia, and Jasper also built a blacksmith shop, making decent money with it. Robert farmed and continued to run the grist mill on Burnt Corn Creek.

William died one cold January morning in 1900. When word reached James the next day about the death of his brother, he keeled over and died with a heart attack from the shock of the news.

Magnolia continued to stand until 1988, when it caught fire and burned to the ground.

James' mansion in Snow Hill still stands until this day, and it's as beautiful as ever.

William's great-grandson owns the portrait on the front of this book. His great-great-grandson, Caleb Gulley, now owns the old flintlock rifle, and he keeps it in mint condition.

Gone are the pioneers of yesteryear, but their blood still pulses in the veins of their descendants today.

Made in the USA
Middletown, DE
25 January 2023